The Sunshi

John Niven was bo... author of the novella ...... Big Fink and the novels *Kill Your Friends*, *The Amateurs*, *The Second Coming*, *Cold Hands* and *Straight White Male*. *Kill Your Friends* was made into a major motion picture in 2015 starring Nicholas Hoult.

'A rollicking road caper … Hugely enjoyable.'

'[I was] hooked by this tale of rampaging women growing old disgracefully … An enjoyable romp spiced up by the author's sharp and perceptive eye.'

'Featuring the greatest female duo since Thelma and Louise, John Niven's novel is a total gem.'

'A bawdy, gaudy, rock 'n' roll spree of a book … It's as filthy as a weekend in Clacton-on-Sea, with the requisite pain and loss hidden just beneath the bedsheets … By the end, you're cheering the ladies on, wishing them well, hoping they find their escape route.'

'An entertaining read.'

ALSO BY JOHN NIVEN

Music from Big Pink
Kill Your Friends
The Amateurs
The Second Coming
Cold Hands
Straight White Male

The Sunshine Cruise Company

JOHN NIVEN

✦ WINDMILL BOOKS

1 3 5 7 9 10 8 6 4 2

Windmill Books
20 Vauxhall Bridge Road
London SW1V 2SA

Windmill Books is part of the Penguin Random House
group of companies whose addresses can be found at
global.penguinrandomhouse.com.

Penguin
Random House
UK

First published by William Heinemann in 2015
First published in paperback by Windmill Books in 2016

www.windmill-books.co.uk

A CIP catalogue record for this book is available from the British Library.

ISBN 9780099592341

Typeset by Palimpsest Book Production Ltd, Falkirk, Stirlingshire
Printed and bound in Great Britain by Clays Ltd, St Ives Plc

MIX
Paper from
responsible sources
FSC
www.fsc.org   FSC® C018179

Penguin Random House is committed to a
sustainable future for our business, our readers
and our planet. This book is made from Forest
Stewardship Council® certified paper.

To Sheila Sheerin

ONE

So much blood, Susan Frobisher thought. *So much blood.*

She was at the kitchen counter, absolutely covered in the stuff. It was spattered all over the worktops, her apron and her face. A huge bowlful of it stood in front of her. The horror-show aspect of the scene was hugely magnified by her kitchen's whiteness. Traditional Shaker. They'd only had it done last year. All the gadgets: sliding chiller drawer at knee height, waste-disposal unit, one of those bendy taps like you saw on the cooking shows and even a built-in wine cooler. Not that she and Barry drank very much these days, but still, it looked nice, all those frosted bottles lined up like missiles in the bomb bay. (Emperor Kitchens on the Havering Road had done it. Barry had negotiated a very good deal, as always. He loved doing it. Negotiating.) Susan checked her reflection in the smoked-glass door of the cooler and, blood aside, was pleased with what she found as she approached her sixtieth year: her complexion was still youthful, her eyes clear and her figure trim. Her hair had been grey for nearly a decade now, however, and Julie was always on at her to have it done, although the days when it would have been Julie's 'treat' were now long past . . .

Outside, through the double glazing, the dew was already lifting from the half of the garden the sun was hitting. The first week of May and, finally, spring had properly arrived down here in Dorset. Susan stuck her pinkie into the bowl of blood and put it in her mouth. Mmmm. Not quite sure about the texture. It had to be just right.

If you get it just right, as her great hero the special-effects wizard Tom Savini said, 'You can create illusions of reality – make people think they've seen things they really haven't seen.' Horror movies were Susan's private little vice. (Barry couldn't stand them, couldn't stand movies of any kind in fact. 'Load of rubbish,' he'd sneer. 'Somebody just made it all up!' He liked documentaries. War stuff.) She'd seen everything Savini had ever done – *Friday the 13th*, *The Burning*, *Dawn of the Dead*. She'd watch them curled up with her tea when Barry was working late.

As if on cue Barry Frobisher walked into the kitchen, knotting his tie. He surveyed the scene and said: 'What the bloody hell . . .'

'Not quite the right consistency,' Susan said. 'Too thin.'

'Look at the mess!'

'I've got to get it done now. I've the shopping to do and then Julie's birthday lunch this afternoon, then dress rehearsals tonight.'

'Christ. Can't you just . . . buy this bloody stuff, Susan?'

'No budget, darling.'

Barry sighed as he moved towards the coffee pot, his

partially tied tie still loose around his neck, picking up a cup from the kitchen table as he went. (They always laid the kitchen table for breakfast the night before, before they went to bed.) 'I don't know what you get out of this, Susan, I really don't.'

He took a slice of cold toast from the rack and started buttering it thickly. He'd have been better off with some cereal, Susan thought, that waistline of his, really starting to crawl over the band of his trousers. A 42-inch waist she'd had to buy him, the last time they went clothes shopping in M&S. Not to mention what it was probably doing to his arteries. Susan heard him wheezing a bit in the mornings these days, just with the effort of levering himself out of bed. (*His* bed. They'd finally gone down that road a few years back: his and hers single beds on either side of the room. They both liked different mattresses anyway. Better to get a good night's sleep. And, as Barry pointed out, his back was bad and it's not like they were newly-weds. That side of things happened only very occasionally these days. In fact, when was the last time? Susan strained to remember. Around Christmas? Maybe before.)

'It's fun,' Susan said, answering his question.

Barry snorted.

Wroxham Players – Susan's 'creative outlet'.

She was no actor. (Not that many of them were.) She'd started out helping with wardrobe and had now been in charge of Costumes and Props for the past three years. Jesus, Barry thought, the first nights he'd been obliged to attend. Bunch of pensioners and starry-eyed teenagers stepping into the scenery and over each other's lines. Still, it was harmless enough, he supposed. Kept her off the streets and all that. He poured himself some coffee while, in the background, Susan added more corn syrup to the fake-blood mixture. 'What is it this year?' Barry asked over his shoulder.

'*King Lear*.'

He thought for a moment. 'That's . . . Shakespeare?'

'Yes,' Susan said. Not a reader, her Barry. A good provider. An accountant. A *chartered* accountant, Susan used to hear herself saying proudly.

'What's it about then? That one,' he asked, sipping his black coffee.

'Oh, the indignity of old age you could say,' Susan said, stirring the mixture, wondering if there would be enough of it. She feared Frank, the director, was intending to go a little Peckinpah in the eye-gouging scene. She wondered if the sensibilities of the average Wroxham audience could take it.

'Sounds cheery,' Barry said, opening the *Daily Mail* over at the table, already only half listening. *Look at this – bloody East Europeans. All over the place.*

Old age.

They'd both be sixty this year. Their thirty-fifth wedding anniversary. What was that? Susan wondered. Jade? Topaz or something? And was it really ten years since their silver wedding? Such a lovely little party Tom and Clare had thrown for them, in the function suite down at the Watermill. Not that they saw much of Tom and Clare. Both caught up with their careers. At that age now, early 30s. Still, Susan did find it odd that their son and his wife had been together over a decade now and still hadn't produced a grandchild. It seemed to be the way these days. She'd been nearly thirty when she had Tom, back in 1983. They'd classified her as an 'old mum'. Special attention. Nowadays thirty seemed young to be having children. What was Clare now? Thirty-two? Thirty-three? Anyway – they wanted to be getting a move on in Susan's view.

She gave the water/corn syrup/ketchup mixture a final stir, pleased with the consistency now, and started looking in the drawer beneath the sink for the plastic ziplock freezer bags.

How best to ask him? Susan was wondering.

Tricky ground. Julie and Barry had never enjoyed good terms. Julie, Susan suspected, thought Barry was boring. Barry, she very much knew, thought Julie was completely mental. A bad influence. True, Julie had always been wilder than Susan, *way* wilder back in the day, but she wasn't crazy. Still, she'd had a hell of a life, Julie. Maybe play to Barry's sense of superiority. 'Oh, darling?'

'Mmm?' *Eight hundred quid a week in benefits? Shiftless bastards.*

'Could you put an extra three hundred into my account please?'

'Eh? What for?'

'Well, I spent a little more than I meant to on Julie's birthday present.'

'For Christ's sake, Susan –'

'It's her sixtieth, Barry! And she's had a terrible time of it these last few years. Losing her business. That bugger running off with all her money. That flat she's in. That awful job. I wanted to get her something nice.'

'Well, you know what I think.'

'I know, but –'

'One thing after another. That stupid hamburger van. That "boutique". Woman couldn't organise a piss-up in a brewery.'

'She's been unlucky.'

'You have to learn to budget, Susan.'

'I do!'

'Every other month it's a couple of hundred for this, a hundred for that.' He was getting up now. Placing his coffee cup in the sink, finishing the knot in his pink tie, a neat full Windsor.

'Please, Barry. Don't be mean.'

'I'll transfer the money, OK? But that's it till next month.' *Another bank transfer to do today too, Barry boy, rather bigger, from the shell account in Holland . . .*

'Thank you, darling.'

'I don't bloody know . . .'

It had always worked this way, their finances. Barry took care of everything. (Susan had worked, briefly, back in the mid-1970s, in the art gallery in Poole, in the brief window between finishing her fine art degree and marrying Barry. When had she left the gallery? Yes, 1977. Julie had turned up unexpectedly, back from her travels, all her hair shorn off and rows of safety pins running up her lapels. The gallery owner had nearly thrown a fit – Barry too when he met them later that night. Later still they'd gone back to her and Barry's flat where Julie had made fun of them for listening to Fleetwood Mac on Barry's reel-to-reel tape machine. State of the art that was at the time. Whatever happened to it? The stuff you have over the years, where does it all go?) Susan only noticed money when her 'allowance' account ran low. Barry loved money. Moving it about.

Doing this and that. 'Restructuring' their finances. Always on the lookout for a sweeter credit card deal, a better interest rate for their savings.

'Right, I'm off,' Barry was saying, pushing himself up from the kitchen table with a reluctant grunt.

'OK, darling. There's cottage pie in the fridge for your dinner. You can do yourself some peas, can't you?'

'I guess I'll have to. I might work late though . . .' He moved to kiss her cheek, then surveyed the mess and thought better of it. He blew one across the counter and Susan smacked her lips back.

'Good luck, Susan,' Susan said as he walked towards the door.

'Eh?' Barry said, turning back.

'Good luck with your dress rehearsal tonight, Susan.'

'Oh, right. Yes, yes, good luck.'

Well, thank you, Susan thought as he left.

Barry, in his turn, thinking, *What a load of old bloody bollocks.*

TWO

While Susan wrestled with the problems of blood, her oldest friend was dealing with bodily fluids of a different stripe. The thing about piss, Julie Wickham was increasingly coming to believe, was that it was like snowflakes or finger-prints; no two examples were exactly the same.

Take Mrs Meecham at the end of the hall. Hers was always extremely acrid. Sharp. Old Mr Bledlow, Alf here, not so much. Mild, almost scentless. Why? They both had much the same diet, the same three meals a day doled out by the home, tipped out of huge, ultra-cheap plastic catering bags and then boiled or baked or fried. Maybe it had some-thing to do with the kidneys, with their varying degrees of decrepitude. Yet Mr Bledlow was nearly ninety, sitting quietly in the corner over there in the clean pyjamas the nurse had helped him into while Julie worked her mop all around and under his stripped bed, where the overspill had gone. By God it had been a fair old load. Julie dunked the mop into the bleach/water mixture, rinsed it out by pressing it into the colander bit of the metal bucket, and started swabbing again. She caught her face reflected in the shining linoleum, still pretty in the right light, her black hair hanging down, very little grey for her age, and thought to herself, as she had nearly every day in here for the past three months, *'Forty hours thirty-six dollars a week — But it's a paycheck, Jack.'*

'Piss Factory' by Patti Smith. She'd been, what, twenty-one or twenty-two when she first heard that? Living up in London, in that tiny bedsit in Finsbury Park. Handy for the Rainbow it had been. She'd been going out with Terry who did the door at the Roxy at the time. He worked at the Vortex later.

Yep — a paycheck, Jack. She'd done things for money over the years, Julie. She'd stolen. She'd . . . well, anyway. But if you'd told her back then that she'd end up turning sixty and working in an old folks' home mopp—

She became aware of a sound, a steady choking noise. She turned — Mr Bledlow, sobbing, his head in his hands, shoulders shaking. She propped the mop against the bed and went over, leaning down by the vinyl-covered armchair. 'Hey, hey, what's this now?'

'I'm sorry,' the old fellow said, hands still covering his face. 'I'm so, so sorry.'

'Come on, no need for all this, Alf. Just a little accident.'

'It ain't right you having to do this.'

'Don't be silly. It's my job.' She slid an arm around his shoulder. His hair was like powder, frizzy and silver. You felt like if you breathed on it too hard it'd blow off his head, exploding into the pale, antiseptic air like the stems from a dandelion. 'Shhh, come on now. Everything's OK.'

She soothed the old boy, waiting for him to calm down, and looked around the room. The framed photographs of the children and grandchildren who visited once in a blue moon. The jug of weak orange squash. The tobacco tin he kept his loose change in. The grim view of the facing Victorian brickwork from the window. Julie was almost thankful she had no children. There'd be no one to not come and visit her when the time came. No one to not remember her birthday. No one to not spend the requisite minimum time on Christmas Day. No one to . . . no. Stop it. Best not to think about all that again. She'd been thinking about it too much lately, back at the flat, at night, with the off-brand vodka and her music playing.

. She felt him regain his natural breathing tempo as the sobs subsided. 'That's better,' Julie said.

He looked up at her through watery rheumy eyes – eyes that had seen nine decades come and go – and said, with simple, perfect clarity, 'I don't like it here.'

Julie felt a spasm in her throat as she stared into the force field of his sorrow: ending your days in a decrepit shithouse run by the lowest bidder, surrounded by strangers. She wanted to say, 'None of us do, Alf. None of us do.' But she swallowed her tears, her fear, and said the only thing she could: 'Cheer up, love. They'll be along with the tea in a minute.'

The English way – milk and two sugars into the abyss.

Alf managed a smile at that as, behind her, Julie heard an electrical whirr, the bang of the door being shunted open and then the bellowed greeting: 'HAPPY BIRTHDAY, YOU FUCKING OLD SHAGGER!'

She turned round. 'Morning, Ethel.'

Ethel Merriman, eighty-seven, sat beaming in her electric wheelchair, her 'grabbing stick' – a telescopic device with a mechanical claw on the end that enabled Ethel to get hold of things that were out of her reach – tucked in behind her the way a coachman's musket would once have been carried. Pushing twenty stone now, her hair a mad shock of reddish blonde framing a face that was somehow still pretty, a face that was right now set in its default expression, one best characterised as a merciless leer. Julie noticed Ethel had lipstick on her teeth. On the front of her wheelchair was a 'WHERE'S THE BEEF?' bumper sticker. On the back another proclaimed 'I BRAKE FOR NO ONE'. Ethel took in Mr Bledlow, the bucket, the mop and soiled sheets wrapped in a ball. 'Oh aye,' she said. 'Shat the bed, is it?'

'Ethel!' Julie snapped.

'Hey, no bother,' Ethel said. 'Like my Oscar used to say – you've not been properly drunk till you've shat yourself. Here, Alf.' Ethel reached under herself and tossed a bag of barley sugars into Alf's lap. 'Get stuck into that lot. Nicked them from that old cow Allenby down in 4C.'

'Ethel!' Julie said again.

'You, birthday girl, shut it. Come on – fag break.' Ethel pulled up the top of her leisure suit – a spectacular powder-blue velour number today – to reveal the pewter hip flask stuck in her waistband. 'I'm holding.'

'Jesus Christ . . .' Julie sighed as two nurses came back into the room carrying fresh bedding for Alf, pushing their way around Ethel, ignoring her. They had previous. *Everyone* had previous with Ethel

'Morning, Nurse Bull, Nurse Diesel,' Ethel said cheerfully to no response.

'Right, five minutes,' Julie said. 'You be OK, Alf?'

Alf nodded, gratefully crunching a barley sugar.

THREE

'Sixty. You old bastard. You fucking *ruin.*'

They were out in the sunshine of the fire escape. 'I know, Ethel. Christ, how did that happen, eh?' Julie dragged deeply and passed the cigarette back to Ethel, glancing towards the door.

With a grunt Ethel levered herself up out of the wheelchair, trotted the few steps over, and pushed the fire door securely shut. Julie knew that the degree of Ethel's immobility, like the degree of her deafness, was selective. She could get out of that wheelchair and move a few steps when it suited her all right, like when another resident had left a bag of boiled sweets temptingly unguarded and just out of arm's reach.

'Oh, shut up,' Ethel said, taking the fag with one hand, the other clamped around her hip flask, glittering in the morning sun out here. 'I'm just taking the piss. Sixty's nothing. Fuck, when I was your age I was ruling. I had it all, bitch, let me tell you. So much cock   ' She took a pull on whatever was in the flask and let out a long, satisfied 'ahhhh' before adding, almost as an afterthought, 'Fanny too.' Julie laughed as Ethel offered her the flask. She shook her head. 'Man up,' Ethel said, still proffering the booze.

'It's just after nine, Ethel!'

'Did I ask you the time? *Did I ask you the fucking time?*'

'And I've got lunch with Susan later.'

'Oof. Let the party begin.'

'Oh, stop it. Susan's all right once you get to know her.'

'*Boring,*' Ethel trilled.

'And then we've got this party thing tonight after her rehearsal. You're still coming?'

'A few hours out of here? Even the Wroxham Players are sufferable for that. But to return to the matter in hand.' Ethel looked at the hip flask, as though it contained the key to all mythologies. 'You seem to have misunderstood me. I did not ask for the time. Nor did I enquire as to your bastard schedule for the next twenty-four hours. I simply requested that you join me in *a drink on your birthday.*'

'Oh God,' Julie groaned, reaching for the thing. She glanced again towards the fire-escape door and took a quick swallow. She felt neat gin scorching her innards, torching through her like a house fire seeking oxygen. '*Shiiitttt.*'

Ethel laughed. 'Martini. My own recipe. Well, I say my own. I nicked it from an RAF boy, just after the war. What was the bugger's name? Cecil? Cedric? Celly? Something wet. Flew Mosquitoes out of Duxford. Not much up top but fit as a Dobermann in the employ of a retailer of meats, if you catch my meaning.'

'Yes, Ethel. It's not that obscure, your meaning.'

'Gin had to be near freezing, viscous, was his rule. And you just rubbed the Vermouth bottle against it.'

She passed the fag back. Julie took it and they looked over the rooftops of the home together: chimney pots, puddles on the flat asphalt, TV aerials, decaying brickwork. The sun was already warm though. It looked like it would be a fine day. Ethel watched Julie smoke, her cheeks flushed slightly from the gin and a faraway look in her eyes. 'Right, out with it,' Ethel said.

'What?'

'Don't fucking what me.'

'It's just . . . sixty, Ethel. This isn't where I thought I'd be.'

'Where did you think you'd be?'

'I dunno. Somewhere nicer than this. Not living in a rented flat. Mopping up piss.'

'You think you've got problems? Here, give us a last drag on that. Look at me – star of stage and screen reduced to mixing my own cocktails in a locked bathroom and stealing barley sugars from sleeping pensioners.'

'Were you really famous, Ethel?'

'From Piccadilly to the Amalfi Coast, darling – if it had a bar and a stage chances are I've sung and danced in it.'

They both turned at the sound of someone trying to force the fire-escape door. It was only a second or two before the door scraped open, but that was enough time for Ethel to deftly peg the smouldering butt over the ledge with one hand while, with the other, she reholstered the hip flask like a gunslinger who'd just blown someone away. They found themselves facing the hulking form of Miss Kendal. Kendal was in her mid-thirties, florid of complexion, her hair hanging in a loose greasy fringe. She was crammed into a business suit slightly too small for her and carried her ever-present clipboard. She looked to Ethel like someone who consumed her meal-for-one alone every night and who masturbated joylessly twice a year. She looked like someone who crapped out in the early rounds of *The Apprentice*.

'What's going on out here?' Kendal asked, already – always – suspicious.

'Papers please!' Ethel said in a heavily Germanic accent. Kendal ignored her.

'Just took Ethel out for some fresh air, Miss Kendal.'

Kendal sniffed nicotine-tainted air, eyes narrowing.

'Miss Wickham, as you're leaving us early today, I'm sure there must be some duties you can be attending to?'

'Yes, Miss Kendal.'

'Right. Well then.'

The door banged behind her. Instantly Ethel had both sets of V-signs aloft and was blowing the world's biggest raspberry.

'Oh, grow up, Ethel,' Julie said.

FOUR

Susan sat alone at the table in La Taverna, the best Italian restaurant in Wroxham, and sipped her mineral water. She glanced at her watch again. Julie was a *little* late. (Susan Frobisher and Julie Wickham — with the names they had Susan sometimes thought that the only place they could ever have existed was in some dreary soap opera about Middle England.) The gift-wrapped box nestled beside her and Susan felt the warm, anticipatory tingle of someone who knows they have bought the perfect gift. She'd lied to Barry that morning — she'd spent a *lot* more on Julie than she'd meant to.

And it did cross Susan's mind — was there vanity involved in the gift giving, the lunching, with Julie? Was there pride? *I can do this, see?* Was there even *cruelty*? Because there had been a time, and it wasn't even so long ago, when it looked like Julie's life was going to outstrip her own. She'd travelled a lot, Julie, in her twenties and thirties. London, Europe, America, Australia even. Then she'd come back

17

home at the end of the eighties and there had been the salon, then the boutique, then the second boutique over in Axminster. Running about town in her little SLK. The string of boyfriends, some from London, some of them impossibly glamorous, older than her, younger than her, Julie didn't care what people thought.

She'd finally settled on Thomas, a debonair colt ten years her junior, and it seemed, for a moment, caught there at the apex of her flight, that Julie 'had it all': her own business, handsome young lover, flash car. And there was Susan – still married to boring Barry whom she'd known since school. Pottering about with her roses and her bread-making and her am-dram.

And then it all came crashing down: the tax problem, the business slump, and, finally, young Thomas disappearing one night with the company chequebook, never to be seen again.

It would be unfair to say that Susan had taken comfort in Julie's fall because it allowed her to be alpha female on deck. Grossly unfair. She *did* love Julie. But lifelong friendships are curious things – the yardsticks by which we often measure ourselves. They were deep pools where there were tensions, currents and strange eddies that it was best to steer clear of. But, at the end of the day and all that, here they were, both turning sixty this year. It looked like the results were in and Susan was the one with her nose across the finishing line.

And here was her yardstick coming through the door now, already mouthing 'Sorry!' Susan's face broke into a smile as she rose to greet her.

'Happy birthday, darling!'

The two women embraced, Julie hoping the last blast of Chanel she'd given herself had masked the lingering reek of ammonia and institution. (It had been almost the last of the Chanel too, the small bottle she'd nursed carefully since Susan gave it to her two Christmases ago.)

'Sorry I'm late. I couldn't get parked anywhere. Where did you park?'

'The little one, across from Debenhams?'

'Oh, right.' *Good. Across from Debenhams. That'd be a left out of the restaurant then. Julie needed to know this.*

Susan was signalling to the waitress now who, as arranged, was coming into view with an ice bucket containing a bottle of Moët & Chandon. She placed it on the table with a flourish.

'Oh God, champagne! Susan!'

'My treat.'

'It'll have to be, love.'

'I mustn't have more than two glasses though. I'll be plastered. You're still coming to the party tonight, aren't you?'

'Yeah, of course. Ethel too.'

'Oh God. Will she behave?'

'You know Ethel . . .'

Susan *did* know Ethel.

Julie had brought her to their Christmas drinks party last year. She'd drunk six snowballs, lit a cigarette *in the kitchen*, then propositioned one of the boys working for the catering company in the downstairs bathroom before turning the music off and singing an – admittedly very tuneful – a cappella version of some rugby song, something called 'Barnacle Bill the Sailor' (Susan remembered a couplet that went '*You*

can sleep upon the mat. Oh, bugger the mat you can't f*** that.'
She'd thought Jill Worth was going to faint) before Julie
wheeled her into the conservatory where she passed out.

As the waitress cracked the cork and Julie settled herself,
fussing with napkin, cutlery and menu, Susan decided she
couldn't wait any longer, certainly not until the end of
the meal. 'Oh bugger, look, here, darling. Happy birthday!'
She placed the box on the table.

'Christ,' Julie said.

'Openitopenitopenit . . .'

'God! OK! Hang on . . .'

Julie started fiddling with the bow as the waitress finished
pouring the champagne. 'I'll give you ladies a few moments
with the menus. And happy birthday by the way!'

'Thank you!' Julie said.

'Come on!' Susan squeaked, clapping her hands together.

With a riiiip Julie tore the paper off. She saw the hallowed
words immediately, inscribed right there on the glossy box:
CHRISTIAN LOUBOUTIN.

'Oh, Susan.'

Another squeak from Susan.

Julie removed the top from the shoebox as carefully as
an archaeologist might remove the lid from a sarcophagus.
There they were – classic black, open-toed, the famous red
soles seeming to almost glow.

'Oh fuck,' Julie said.

'I know it's a bit OTT but it *is* your sixtieth and they
were on sale and you are the only woman our age I know
who still has the legs to carry them off and –'

Susan stopped jabbering. Because she saw that, across
the table from her, Julie's eyes were beginning to brim.

And these did not look like the expected joyous tears of gratitude either. They looked like something else entirely. And Julie was *not* a crier. 'Julie, are you –'

'No. Please. Just give me a minute. I don't want my mascara to run.' Julie fanned at her face with one hand while taking fast, shallow breaths, her eyes craning upwards, as though trying not to look at the tears forming in the ducts below.

Susan glanced nervously around the restaurant. This wasn't going at all as she'd imagined it would. After a moment it looked like Julie had it under control. She took a long draught of champagne and gazed at the shoes sadly.

'What's the matter? I thought you'd love –'

'I *do* love them, Susan. They're gorgeous. It's just . . . where am I going to wear these? Now. At my age. Mopping up at the home?'

'Come on, love. It's only temporary. It was all you could get.'

'Or running for the bus? Sitting in that bloody flat on a Friday night?' Julie sighed. The shoes said impossible glamour. Infinite promise. All the things Julie was flat out of.

Susan said, 'Bus?'

Julie sighed. 'I wasn't going to tell you. That's why I asked where you'd parked. I was going to pretend I had to go the other way. I wasn't late because of parking. I was late because the bloody bus was late. The car broke down three weeks ago. Some bloody manifold arse or other. Five hundred-odd quid they want to fix it.' *About exactly what the shoes cost*, Susan had time to reflect while she tried to picture Julie on a bus. That SLK didn't seem so long ago. 'It might as well be a million.'

'Julie.' Susan leaned across the table, taking her friend's hand. 'I've told you before, if you want to borrow –'

'No.' Julie shook her head. 'We're not starting down that road.'

'But you *need* your car.'

'I can barely afford to run it anyway. Have you seen the price of petrol now?'

'I know.' Susan couldn't have told you the price of a litre of petrol with a gun at her head. It just went on the card. Barry dealt with it all. They sat in silence for a moment. The shoes and champagne unregarded on the table between them. The waitress approached the table, notepad at the ready. Susan smiled softly and shook her head and the girl retreated. 'Well,' Susan said, 'some birthday celebration this turned out to be. Nice going, Susan.'

'I'm sorry. It's not your fault. It's all lovely of you, it's just . . . *sixty*. I mean, you can't go on fooling yourself at this age, can you? I'm not going through some kind of slump or whatever. This is it. This is how my life turned out, Susan. On my own in a rented flat, working in a care home.'

'You're a bit down. Birthdays can be hard.'

'I just . . .'

Julie looked out across the restaurant, through the windows, down towards the pub-encrusted town centre where the two of them had run gleefully in their late teens and early twenties, their lives a blur of fun and possibility stretching ahead of them. Julie seemed to see everything that had happened between then and now, all the wrong turns and bad decisions and half-baked schemes appearing to her as a mad parade. 'I got a gas bill the other day for January to April. Two hundred and fifty quid. For a one-bedroom flat. I just . . . we're old, Susan, aren't we? I can remember bloody *Wilson* getting elected and I can't remember life ever being as hard as this. It's just so fucking *hard.*'

'You know what we're going to?' Susan said. 'We're going to eat something and drink this champagne and then we're going to go and return these stupid bloody shoes and we'll use the money to get your car fixed and pay your gas bill. That's what we're going to do.'

Julie smiled for the first time in a while and said, 'Never speak ill of the shoes, Susan.'

FIVE

Despite her excitement Jill Worth took the time to fully engage the handbrake before she got out of her ageing Polo and hurried round to the boot. Using all her strength she lifted the big jar out. It was the kind of jar used to store boiled sweets in old confectionery shops. A hole had been cut in the metal lid and the jar had been filled nearly to the brim with money: silver and bronze coins mainly, but there were a good few crumpled five-pound notes threaded through there as well. 'Nearly six hundred quid I reckon, Mrs Worth,' the barman at the Black Swan had told her, proudly slapping the lid. And that was just since Christmas! Less than five months!

She walked carefully up the short path, carrying the jar sideways, like a newborn, and rang the doorbell. She waited a few moments then rang again. Nothing. 'Linda?' she called through the door. Muffled noises from up the stairs. Then shouting. *'Come in, Mum.'* Jill opened the door and walked into the hall grinning with her prize in her arms. When she saw her daughter sat halfway down the stairs, slumped against the wall, her grin crumbled. Linda was a mess – panda eyes, mascara blotched down her cheeks, a sheen of sweat on her forehead. 'Darling,' Jill began, 'what hap—'

'Oh, Mum, we've had a hell of a night.'

Jill set the jar down and came up the stairs towards her. 'What happened?'

'Shhh. He's sleeping now. I just finished getting him down.'

'Come on,' Jill said, threading an arm around Linda, helping her up. 'Let's go in the kitchen and I'll put the kettle on.'

In the kitchen, as the kettle began to rumble while Jill busied herself with the cups, tea bags and milk, Linda sat at the small table and talked. 'He wouldn't eat, we've had to put him back on the drip, he just didn't want to take his medicine, the new stuff, said his throat hurt, kept spitting it out, getting himself into a right state, till finally Ken and I were both holding him down and it got to a point where he couldn't breathe, he just . . . couldn't catch a breath. It was, Christ, it was horrible. Sorry.' Her mum didn't like swears.

'That's OK, darling. You're upset.'

'Then he couldn't settle so we were both up and down half the night. God knows what Ken must be like at work today.'

'Isn't there some other way to give him the medicine? Tablets? Could you put it in his food?'

'Apparently not. It's a suspension. Something to do with the way it works on the lungs.'

Jill brought the tea over and sat down. Her poor daughter

Linda was thirty-five and looked fifty. These past three years, since Jamie was diagnosed, had been brutal. Jill, meanwhile, was wearing quite well at sixty-seven. Still drove herself everywhere. 'The day you drive a car is the day they carry me out of here in a pine box,' her Derek used to say. He was right in the end – Jill had started taking driving lessons right after he died. Twelve years ago now.

'What's that, Mum?' Linda asked, nodding down the hall towards the jar sitting by the front door.

'Oh! One of the collecting jars, from the Black Swan on the high street. Nearly six hundred pounds they think! Since Christmas! How about that?'

'Oh, bless them,' Linda said. Then she burst into tears.

'Shhh, come on, darling.' Jill pulled her daughter to her. 'Inch by inch. We'll get there.'

'Oh, Mum, I don't think we're ever going to get there.'

'Of course we will. Rome wasn't built in a day.'

'If you'd seen him last night . . . he . . . he . . .' the words coming between sobs, her face buried in Jill's neck, 'he looked like he was drowning, Mum. The fear in his eyes. He was *terrified*.'

'Oh, darling.'

'All this bloody *Rome wasn't built in a day* and *we'll get there*. Chicago, the whole thing, I sometimes think it'd be kinder if he just, if he just –'

Jill grabbed her daughter's face and twisted it up to hers. 'That's enough, Linda. You hear me? Enough now. I won't have that kind of talk. I simply will not have it. God has a plan for that boy and he is going to live.' Linda collapsed sobbing in her mother's arms. 'There, dear. There, there,'

Jill said. 'You're just exhausted. You're not thinking properly. We are going to fix this.'

'Oh, Mum . . .'

Jill held her while she cried. After a while she said, 'Go on now. I'll go up and sit with him for a bit. You go through and lie down on the sofa and have a lovely nap. You'll feel much better. I can stay tonight if you want.'

'Haven't you got your am-dram stuff?'

'Oh, I'm sure they'll manage without me.'

'No, please, Mum, you go. Ken's back at five. If I can just get forty winks . . .'

'OK. Come on, let's get you settled. I'll come down in a bit and make us some lunch.'

After she'd laid a blanket over her daughter Jill crept quietly up the stairs and into her grandson's room. The curtains were drawn, giving it the authentically sleepy tang of the sick ward. Jill sat down in the armchair next to the bed and looked at Jamie, sleeping. It was incredible, you'd never have thought it to look at him. Other than the canula going into the back of his left hand, leading to the bag of glucose on a stand, there was nothing to tell you how sick he was. A bit pale, yes, but basically a perfectly beautiful five-year-old boy. Nothing to suggest that, in the words of one of the doctors, he had the lungs 'of a seventy-year-old miner'.

De Havilland's syndrome – which was about as rare as it came. Basically the tissue of his lungs was corroding unusually fast. Breathing difficulties obviously. He struggled to clear his airways. Eating and drinking were difficult. In many ways it was like Linda and Ken had been dealing with the stress of a newborn for five years now. There was one specialist unit in the world performing an operation that had proved successful in stopping, even reversing, the disease. At St Michael's in Chicago.

Jill looked up from the bed, towards the wall above it. On it was a big poster, a poster Jill had helped to make. It was a thermometer. Below the thermometer were the words 'JAMIE'S OPERATION'; above it the target figure: £60,000. The level of the thermometer had been coloured in red up to just below the £30,000 mark. It had taken all of the tiny bit of savings Jill had, all of Linda and Ken's, donations from friends and family and three years of writing letters and putting jars and tins in local pubs and shops to get here, to get to just below halfway.

Jamie coughed and stirred a little in his sleep.

Jill swept a strand of the boy's fine blond hair out of his face and soothed his brow. He murmured and turned onto his side. She held his hand and leaned back a little in the chair, gazing up at that home-made thermometer on the wall still hopelessly, infuriatingly short of the magic figure. Jill allowed herself to think something that she never, ever thought.

Would another three years be too late?

SIX

'BLOW, WINDS, AND CRACK YOUR CHEEKS!'

Susan watched, only mildly astonished, as Lear, played by that frightful old ham Bill Murdoch, roared and threw his hands out wide, catching the Fool, played by sweet little Freddy Watson, square in the face with the left, sending him careering sideways into a piece of heathland scenery, sending it crashing onto the floor, making Jill Worth jump up in her seat, causing her to scream as she plunged the needle she was using to sew Regan's torn costume into the soft pad of her thumb. 'Bother!' she yelped. (Jill was about the only person Susan could think of who actually would say 'Bother!' or 'SUGAR!' when hitting her thumb with a hammer.) Frank the director put his head in his hands and emitted a low whine as onstage the rehearsal – the final dress rehearsal – ground to a halt amid the bickering familiar to anyone who had attended their fair share of Wroxham Players rehearsals.

'Bloody hell, Bill!'

'You were too close! You know I do that then!'

'Oh, this bush is cracked now.'

'Yes, gentlemen, can we –'

'I need to stand there so –'

'Can't you –'

'Where's props? Props!'

'The audience won't *care* where you are, Freddy! It's –'

'EVERYONE!' Frank roared. Silence. 'Can we, let's just take a moment.' He got up from his seat in the row in front of Susan and headed for the stage, a muttered 'Jesus' escaping him.

'Are you OK, Jill?' Susan asked. Jill was furiously sucking her thumb.

'Mmmm. Just . . . didn't want to get blood on the costume. We don't have a spare.'

'Shall I get you a plaster?'

'No, thank you, Susan. It'll be fine.' She shook her hand like she was holding an invisible thermometer.

'Bloody Bill Murdoch,' Agnes Coren said, looking up from her magazine. 'You take your life in your hands every scene you're in with him.' Agnes was playing Regan and took great relish in every sadism the play allowed her to visit on her co-star. 'Did you see earlier? In his whole "reason not the need" bit? Grabbed my bloody hand. I thought he was going to break my wrist!'

'Yes,' Susan said. 'He does rather like to go for it.'

Agnes looked at her watch. 'Roll on six o'clock. I'm dying for a drink.' Over on the side of the hall glasses, a case of red wine and a few bowls of nibbles sat on a trestle table. Next to the table was a black plastic bin filled with ice containing white wine and beers. It was tradition, after final rehearsal, before opening night: a small gathering for friends and family, all of whom had undoubtedly helped with learning lines, contributing clothing for costumes and buying more tickets than was strictly reasonable.

'Mmmm,' Susan said, sipping her coffee. Her head was still fuzzy from the champagne earlier with Julie. She shouldn't drink at lunchtime, she really shouldn't. 'Mind you, I can't help feeling this party might be a bit premature.' She nodded towards the stage where Frank was negotiating between Bill and Freddy. Johnny Grainger was hurriedly repainting the damaged bit of scenery.

'Be all right on the night, love,' Agnes said. 'It's like this every time.'

'True.'

'I'm making some tea. Anyone want one?'

'No thank you,' Jill and Susan chorused as Agnes went off across the hall.

'OK!' Frank was saying, coming back down the steps, clapping his hands together. 'From the top of the scene, let's go again.'

'BLOW, WINDS, AND CRACK YOUR CHEEKS!'

Susan sipped her coffee and turned the page of her magazine. She became aware that, in the seat in front of her, Jill's shoulders were shaking.

'Jill . . . are you . . .?'

'Oh dear, I'm sorry, Susan.'

Jill turned round and Susan saw in the half-light that her face was glistening. Surely she couldn't have hurt herself that badly?

'What is it?'

'Oh, just . . ,' Jill blew her nose on the hanky ever present in her cardigan sleeve. 'Sorry, just . . . our Jamie. The poor lamb.'

Susan stroked Jill's shoulder. Her grandson – some rare disease. His lungs, Susan remembered. 'Not getting any better?'

'No.' Jill sighed. 'It's not going to either. Unless he gets this operation.'

'Oh, love,' Susan said. 'How's your –' Susan had to search quickly for Jill's daughter's name – 'your Linda holding up?'

'She's just exhausted all the time, Susan.'

'Poor thing.'

The two women sat there for a moment before Susan added, reflexively, 'Is there anything I can do?'

Jill sniffed and smiled. 'You don't have a spare thirty thousand pounds I could borrow, do you?'

Susan smiled too.

SEVEN

'You want it all this time, don't you? You dirty bastard,' she said. 'You greedy, dirty fucking bastard.'

'Mmmf! Unnnnggg!' came his muffled reply.

She was circling him slowly, pointing at him with it, the only sound in the room the creaking of her patent leather boots. The boots had savagely spiked heels and stopped three-quarters of the way up her thighs, just revealing her stocking tops. She was naked from the waist up, huge breasts dangling free, the nipples an incredibly bright red from all the lipstick slathered on them, the way he liked it. And 'room' was an inadequate description. 'Dungeon' was more accurate. He had spent considerable time and money getting this place just right. The walls were completely plastered with pornography – S&M stuff, group sex, some strong bestiality images – and the only light came from a blue neon sign he'd had made at a specialist place. It said 'RAPIST'. The shelves were covered with sex toys – restraints, costumes, vibrators, dildos, eggs, Ben-Wa balls, nipple clamps, anal beads, strap-ons and the like – and jars of lubricants. Countless DVDs. Behind the circling domi-natrix the black eye of the video camera stared unblinklingly at them from its tripod.

Yes, much time and money had gone into getting this place exactly as he liked it.

'Unnff, urrrgh!' He was straining forward, trying to get to her. But it was hopeless – his arms were tethered to the ceiling by leather straps. He was kneeling on the table, a kind of massage table, naked save for the leather mask that completely encased his head. Her knickers were stuffed in his mouth forming a makeshift gag. Only his eyes had free reign – mad white globes staring through the eyeholes in the mask, following her around the room, never leaving the tip of the dildo she was pointing at him.

The dildo was a specialist custom-made job. He called it 'The Rectifier'. It was matt black, close to two feet long with a girth of just over six inches: basically four coke cans stacked on top of each other. The sides were ridged, with additional spiked knobbles close to the base.

'You can't take all of this, can you? Can you – you fucking loser?'

'Hnngggg! Uhnnnnn!' He was nodding frantically, denying this vicious slur as she moved around behind him, out of his sight. He tried to crane his head to follow her but couldn't. The top of the mask had a D-ring that was also tethered to the low ceiling. He could hear a wet, thick dripping sound. *Oh God, what was she doing back there?* The delicious agony of not knowing, of being uttterly defenceless.

What she was doing was slathering KY jelly onto the Rectifier. His buttocks were already well greased with the stuff. (He bought it by the case from CostCo – got a good deal.) He was shaking his arse frantically now, trying to lean backwards as far as the harness would allow, proffering his glistening cheeks towards her. She smiled as she noticed this. Nearly laughed. *Begging* for it, he was. She had a few weirdo clients – you were in this racket long enough you'd get a few nutters – but this guy really was out there. Loved it up him. *Loved it.*

She came up behind him and whispered close to his ear. 'I'm not going to do it this time. You've had enough. You filthy piece of shit. I'm going. I'm just leaving you here.'

'UNNGHHHHH! ARRRRRR! ARRRRRR!' He was going absolutely bananas now. Trying to talk. Shaking his head from side to side, trying to spit the gag out.

'Do you really want it?' she purred into his ear. *'How much do you want it?'* She slipped the tip between his cheeks, very gently probing his anus with the monster.

'MMMMMFFFFNNNGGG!'

She tore the gag out and he screamed:

'PLEASE! PLEASE PUT IT IN MEEEEEEEEEE!'

She began to work it in, cautiously at first. It was like trying to force a truncheon into a closed sea anemone.

Unseen by her, working away back there at the coalface, his eyeballs flipped upwards in their sockets and he began to emit a long, grateful, musical sigh.

EIGHT

The clinking of glasses, the squeak and pop of corks and the happy chatter of the Wroxham Players and friends unwinding. There were about fifty people — cast, crew, close friends and family — packed into the set of three interconnecting dressing rooms, where a makeshift bar had been set up in the corner of the largest one.

'Not much talent,' Ethel said sadly, scanning the room. 'He's not bad though . . .'

'*Ethel*,' Julie said warningly, as she followed Ethel's gaze through the crush, to see that it had settled on the unlikely lust figure of 72-year-old props man Johnny Grainger.

'Oh, keep your knickers on and get me a top-up,' Ethel said, proffering her empty wine glass. 'I'm just window-shopping.' Julie thought that, even by her own standards, Ethel had outdone herself tonight on the outfit front. She was wearing some kind of ball gown, its taffeta ruffles bubbling up and all around her like foam, like there was a wave breaking beneath her and spilling out all over the wheelchair. The dress revealed more cleavage than most would think appropriate for a woman approaching her tenth decade. It looked like a bricklayer had fallen down into her chest, leaving just his bum crack visible.

'How many have you had?' Julie asked, taking her glass as she turned to see Susan pushing her way through the crush towards them, trailing Jill Worth behind her.

'Hello, Ethel,' Susan said, bending down to kiss her cheek. 'Thanks for coming. You look . . . wow! Julie, you know Jill, don't you? She helps with costumes.'

'Of course. Hi, Jill.'

'Hello, Julie.'

'Jill, you remember Ethel.' Jill looked down to see Ethel grinning up at her.

'Aye-aye, Jill,' Ethel said. 'How's your arse for love bites then?'

'My . . .'

'Just ignore her, Jill,' Julie said. 'She's senile.'

'Yeah, senile like a fox,' Ethel said.

'Look, I'll get you one more drink if you promise to behave,' Julie said. 'Susan, gimme a hand at the bar. Can I get you anything, Jill?'

'Oh, just an orange juice please.' This request caused Ethel to look suspiciously at Jill.

'Right, back in a mo.' Julie led Susan off towards the makeshift bar.

'So, Jill,' Ethel said, 'speaking of foxes – who's that fine silver piece over there?' She pointed with her grabbing stick.

'The silver . . .' Jill looked across the room. 'Oh, Johnny? He does props and scenery. Lovely man.'

'Yeah, yeah. Married?'

'I'm sorry?'

'Is he married? Hitched?' Ethel spoke as though Jill were senile. 'Taken?'

'Johnny? I, well, yes.'

'Ach, well. There's many a family cat keeping a few stray bitches happy on the side, eh?' Ethel dug an elbow into Jill's ribs.

'Cat?' Jill said, really confused now.

Over at the bar, Julie and Susan waited their turn. 'All set then?' Julie asked.

'As set as we're going to be. I think opening night might be a bit hairy.'

'Look, Susan, about this afternoon, I'm sorry for being so down. Not fair after you'd gone to all that trouble, with my present, with lunch and everything.'

'Darling, honestly, it's me who should be apologising. I'd no idea things had got so tough for you. I wish you'd let me help me you out.'

'You already have.'

'More I mean. I'm sure if I asked Barry to move some money around —'

'No, no. Something'll turn up. The solicitors think there's still a chance I'll get some money back off Thomas.'

'Oh, that bloody bastard,' Susan said reflexively, while doubting the validity of Julie's hopes here. Her Barry, who knew a thing or two about this stuff, reckoned there was more chance 'of her winning the lottery than seeing a penny of that back'. Barry had looked at the case. Thomas had been a co-signatory on the business accounts — perfectly entitled to take money out. If Julie hadn't been keeping an eye on what he was up to then that was her lookout. 'Three white wines and an orange juice please, Kevin,' Susan said.

Julie sighed. 'You never get smart about it, do you? Love. Men.'

Behind them, unseen by either woman, two uniformed policemen – a sergeant in his forties and a constable of what looked to be primary-school age – had entered the party and were talking to Frank the director. Frank was pointing over towards Susan and Julie.

'Well, you've picked a few in your time, Jules. No two ways about that.'

'They weren't *all* bad . . .'

As Susan took the first two glasses of lukewarm Chardonnay she noticed that Kevin the barman (and sometime lighting technician) was looking past her, just behind her, a concerned expression on his face. She turned round – straight into the uniformed bulk of the police sergeant.

'Mrs Susan Frobisher?' he asked, the whole party looking on now.

'Yes.' A clammy spasm of fear hit her. Their Tom: a road traffic accident. A mugging. London.

'I'm Sergeant Black. I'm afraid I need to talk to you in private.'

'Is . . . is it bad news?'

The sergeant just looked at her. 'Is there somewhere private we can talk?'

Susan felt her legs going. She clutched at Julie's arm.

'Can . . . can I come with her?' Julie asked.

'That's up to Mrs Frobisher.'

Susan nodded, biting her cheek, fighting to keep the tears out of her eyes.

How long does it take to change a life entirely?

A little over three seconds was the answer. The amount of time it took Sergeant Black to say the words, 'I'm afraid we think your husband is dead.'

Susan burst into tears.

They were in the theatre manager's office, windowless. Two desks, two chairs. The walls covered with posters for past productions by the Wroxham Players. Susan was sitting on one of the chairs, a black faux-leather swivel job, with Julie standing beside her, holding her hand, Sergeant Black towering over them. The young constable, Julie noticed, hovered in the background, going extremely red in the face. Was this the first time he'd done something like this? 'Oh God . . . oh no . . .' Susan sobbed. Then, catching herself, finding something to cling onto, she said, 'You *think*?'

'You're married to Mr Barry Frobisher?'

'Yes.'

'Of 1B Wellington Street, Wroxham?'

'No!' Oh thank God. Thank God. They had the wrong man. 'We live in a house. 23 Beecham Crescent.'

The two policemen exchanged a look. Susan and Julie stared at them. 'Excuse me a moment please, ladies,' the sergeant said. He left the room, taking out his radio as he went. As the door closed behind him they heard the squawk and hiss and Black saying, 'Control?'

'So . . . what . . . what's happening?' Susan asked, wiping tears. 'Is it my husband?' They looked at the young constable, who, in turn, was looking like his head might explode.

'I . . . think . . . we'd best wait for the sergeant . . .'

Silence. Susan looked at Julie. Julie looked at the constable. The constable scanned the posters on the walls. 'Oh look,' he said after a moment. '*The Pirates of Penzance.* My auntie was in that.'

Before Julie could ask what the fuck that had to do with anything the door was opening again and Sergeant Black was coming back in. 'I'm very sorry, Mrs Frobisher, but there does seem to be some confusion. I've been told to ask you to accompany me to the scene, to provide a positive ID. Or otherwise.'

'The scene?' Susan repeated.

'The crime scene.'

'Right,' Julie said. 'What on earth is going on?'

'I really think it'd be best if you just came with us, ladies . . .'

NINE

Susan had never been in a police car before. (Julie had. A long story – one unknown to Susan.) She was surprised by how much stuff seemed to be crammed into the front of it. How much technology: computers and radios and equipment and whatnot. And the constant chatter of the radio – could all this really be going on in Wroxham? Sleepy Wroxham with its Victorian marketplace and its corn exchange and its carpet factory? She was aware of Julie holding her hand as she looked at the orange street lights passing without saying a word, her other trembling hand clamped over her brow. What had happened? Nothing? Was it the wrong man? Or an accident? Or an attack? And 'attack' was starting to loom larger in her mind now, as they came off the dual carriageway and started heading into the Mansfield Estate, one of the rougher parts of town. But, at the same time, some cause for optimism: what the hell would Barry have been doing around here? He had a few rough clients, down at the accountancy firm. A few local characters who Susan suspected skirted the fringes of the HMRC's approved practices, but no real *criminals* surely? God, she felt sick.

Julie watched her friend out of the corner of her eye and tried to stay calm and practical, tried to play the next few moves out in her head.

Suppose they're right and Barry's dead? What would happen then? Susan would go into shock. She'd be a wreck. I'd have to take her home and spend the night with her. Maybe even the next few nights. When would Tom get here? Who would tell Tom? Would Susan be capable of calling her son and telling him that his father was dead? Would the police take care of that if she couldn't? Would I have to do it? And then the funeral arrangements. Who would —

Julie stopped herself, ashamed. Her best friend's husband of nearly forty years was very possibly dead. Barry Frobisher. They'd all known each other since they were kids. True, Julie and Boring Barry had never been one another's favourite people but she'd have to be there for Susan.

The car was stopping. The policemen were getting out and opening the rear doors for them. There was a police van and another car parked in front of them. Two constables stood on the street in front of the house. Neighbours were leaning from casement windows and standing staring on doorsteps.

Julie was on the pavement side. She got out and looked up: a crumbling Edwardian town house loomed above them in the street light. Once grand, the place had long since been subdivided into flats and bedsits. Julie had lived in a fair few places like this herself over the years. Her current place wasn't much grander. And for a moment she allowed herself to think what Susan had thought when they headed into the estate: this is a mistake. A stupid mistake. What on earth would Barry Frobisher, Chartered Accountant, be doing around here?

'This way please,' Sergeant Black was saying, opening the gate that led down some steps to a basement entrance. He turned and blocked their path momentarily. 'Now, I have to warn you. This is going to be very difficult for you. It's not a pretty scene . . .'

Susan clutched at Julie's arm again as they went down the few steps, towards an open basement door and into a hallway, an eerie soft blue light seeming to glow at the end of it.

They followed the huge, black back of the sergeant down towards that blue light, the blue being displaced suddenly by a phosphorescent sheet of white and the raaap and whine of a camera. Someone was taking photographs. Susan glanced to her left into what was presumably the living room: old furniture and every available surface covered in boxes and crates with files spilling out of them, stacks of papers everywhere.

Sergeant Black stopped in the doorway in front of them and, yes, just like in the movies, lifted up the yellow-and-black tape stamped with 'POLICE, CRIME SCENE, DO NOT CROSS'. He lowered his gaze as first Julie, then Susan went under the tape and into the room.

Julie's first reaction was: *Is this all the pornography in the world?* Because the walls were just *covered* in the stuff. And the ceiling. All five available flat surfaces. She caught a few random images, you couldn't help it, there was nowhere else to look. And this was strong stuff. This was not petrol-station issue. A man dressed as a Nazi taking what looked like a nun from behind. A . . . was that an Alsatian? Yes.

An Alsatian with a woman dressed as a cheerleader. Another woman strung in a harness beneath a horse. And what were all those things on the shelves? Around the walls? Were those . . .? Christ. She'd never seen so many dildos. A forest of dildos.

Susan straightened up and stuffed a knuckle into her mouth to stifle a scream.

There he was, kind of kneeling on a table, partially suspended from the ceiling.

Barry.

Naked.

Dead.

Behind him was the source of that eerie blue lighting, the word 'RAPIST' in three-foot-high neon tubing, like it was the name of a bar, or a nightclub.

Someone, a man in plain clothes, was coming towards them out of the blue-tinted semi-darkness. He was saying, 'Mrs Frobisher, is this your husband.?'

Susan was nodding, her mouth hanging open. There seemed to be something . . . behind Barry. Sticking out of him. His head was dangling down and to the side but you could clearly see his face – the eyes bulging, staring, the teeth bared in a mad snarl, his hair matted to his forehead with sweat. His arms still lashed to the ceiling. *Someone must have tortured and killed him*, Julie was thinking. She kept staring, horribly transfixed, but she was aware that someone was shouting *'MRS FROBISHER!'* and she turned just in time to see Susan disappearing out of her line of sight, clattering backwards, into the wall as she fainted, her flailing left hand tearing a roll of pornography off the wall, exposing the bare brick behind it.

Julie looked down, her own legs weak beneath her, and saw her friend unconscious on the floor, Sergeant Black and the plain-clothes detective both bending over now. Susan's wedding ring glittered on her hand, a hand that clutched a scrap of paper showing a semi-erect penis dangling inches from a greedy mouth.

TEN

Detective Sergeant Hugh Boscombe tapped the chewed blue biro against his teeth as he flipped through the manila folder on his desk. He let out a low whistle. Twenty-four years on the force, you think you've seen it all, and then a doozy like this comes up. The sheer amount of evidence at the scene too – boxes and boxes of it. The uniformed boys were still bringing it in downstairs. Videotapes, DVDs, Polaroids, magazines, sex toys. And a lot of paperwork like the stuff he was looking at now, financial records and so forth. He took the last chunk of pork pie from its waxy paper and munched on it as he kept reading.

'*Macros Holdings, Incorporated Netherlands, agrees to loan Mr B. Frobisher the sum of £14,000 sterling at the rate of 0.05% interest against security of his shares in the same to the value of . . .*'

He yawned. What time was it? Nearly midnight. He'd spent the last couple of hours going through this stuff. Some of the videotapes and photos – Jesus H. Over his head most of this financial stuff though. Make interesting reading for the lads over in fraud no doubt. Exciting though – bona fide murder. Crack this and . . .

Christ, he shouldn't have finished that bastard pie. Boscombe patted his gut. The wife was right. Getting out of control. Comfort eating mostly. Hadn't been a great couple of years, with that bugger Hannah making detective inspector before him in the last round of promotions. And Davy Bryant the round before that. Bloody Wilson. The chief inspector had it in for him. That was the fact of the matter. Had to stop all this snacking – easing his grievances late at night with the fruit slices or the coffee cake, or the toasted sandwich before bed. You just didn't burn it off like you used to once you got into your forties. Was wreaking havoc with his bloody bowels too. He glanced into the open bottom drawer of his desk – at the mountain of empty cartons of Rennies, Ex-Lax, the dead Gaviscon bottles.

'Aye-aye, Sarge.'

Boscombe looked up. 'Wesley.' His underling, Detective Constable Alan Wesley, fourteen years his junior. Not a bad lad. College boy, like most of them these days. Just over a year out of uniform though, and still as green as they came sometimes.

'Quite a night, I gather,' Wesley was saying, pouring himself coffee over at the machine. 'Some goings-on down at Wellington Street from the looks of the stuff getting brought in downstairs.'

'It is that, son. Double-headed joy boys and all sorts.'

'Yeah, I just had a quick look through some of it. More on heaven and earth than is dreamt of in our philosophy Horatio and all that, eh?'

'You what?' Boscombe said, not looking up.

'Never mind. Is that the fella's wife down in interview C?'

'It is that.' Boscome highlighted something on one of the documents he was reading with a yellow pen and moved it to the top of the stack in the manila folder. He stacked the manila one on top of a red folder: some choice pickings from the physical evidence – just enough to make the point. 'He's over in the morgue. Should have a COD soon.'

'Nice-looking lady.'

Boscombe sighed. The kid was young. In any case of spousal murder where did you start? You started with *the surviving spouse*. 'Remember, Wesley,' Boscombe said, getting up, slipping his jacket on and picking up the folders, 'still waters run deep. Come on then.'

ELEVEN

'Oh, for God's sake!' Susan said out loud to the empty room, looking at the clock up there in its little cage. Nearly two hours she'd been in here. She'd come to in the back of the police car, Julie stroking her hair and a police doctor taking her pulse. The same police doctor who'd pronounced her fit to answer some questions. As the first hour here in this drab room — metal table bolted to the floor, some kind of recording equipment set in the wall, caged clock and light bulb, a slab of what she presumed was two-way glass, four institutional plastic chairs — bled into the second hour she found that her emotions were, well, not see-sawing, as that implied a shift back and forward from one emotion to another, but rather pinballing around: from horror, to rage, to weeping sorrow, to boredom, to numb incomprehension. Barry was dead. Someone must have taken him there and tied him up and killed him and why were they holding her? Why weren't they out trying to find whoever murdered her husband? As Barry often said, hunched over his *Telegraph* or *Daily Mail*, you pay your taxes and . . . she pinballed back up the table and onto the flipper marked 'anger'.

Just as she felt this, felt her blood rising, she looked up at the sound of the door opening: two men, plain-clothes police officers, coming into the room, one middle-aged, stout, the other one still in his twenties by the looks of it.

'Good evening, Mrs Frobisher,' Boscombe said, sitting down opposite her, putting his file on the table. 'I'm Detective Sergeant Boscombe and this is Detective Constable Wesley.' Wesley smiled pleasantly as he took his chair.

'Sorry?' Susan said, crossing her arms.

'Sorry?' Boscombe said.

'"I'm sorry" would be a good start here, Sergeant.'

'I'm not following you,' Boscombe said.

'I've been kept here for two hours without explanation. I mean, I'm a law-abiding, taxpaying citizen who –'

This fucking woman, who did . . . Boscombe held up a hand. 'Excuse me, Mrs Frobisher, this is a *murder* inquiry. I had to familiarise myself with certain aspects of the case before I was ready to interview you. I'm sure you can understand that.'

'Yes, well.'

'Let me start by asking you where you were tonight.'

'Oh, for goodness' sake! I already told the uniformed officers. I was at a rehearsal for a play I'm involved in and then a party afterwards. With about fifty witnesses!'

'Mrs Frobisher –' Boscombe leaned across the table, elbows resting on it, almost smiling – 'there's no point in being hostile with me. I'm just trying to help you.'

'I . . . I'm sorry. It's just, if I'm to be asked the same

question over and over again . . . Shouldn't you be trying to find whoever killed my husband?'

'Why do you say killed?'

A silence. Both men looking at her.

'What do you mean?'

'Well, we don't know the exact cause of death yet, but you seem to be assuming that someone did this to your husband rather than —'

'What? He tied himself up and —? Look, I don't know what you're getting at but . . . I, I mean I have questions of my own, Sergeant! How did you find him? What d—'

'Ah, now that is a good question. If you'll just hold on a moment.'

Boscombe got up and crossed to the recording equipment set into the wall, taking a cassette tape from his pocket. The police — about the only people who still used these things. He slipped it into the machine and pressed 'PLAY'. A hiss of static, then a digitised 'beep' and then a man's voice saying, *'Emergency. Which service do you require?'*

A woman's voice, common, frantic, panicked: *'Ambulance. There's a man 'ere who's . . . ee's not breav-in. Ee . . . I fink ee's had a heart attack.'*

'Are you able to check for a pulse?'

'I . . . ee's not. Look, I need to —'

'What's the address there?'

'Flat 1B Wellington Street, the basement. It's on the Mansfield Estate.'

'OK, help is on its way. If you —'

'You'll need to hurry. Ee . . . we was playing a game and . . . I TOLD HIM EE COULDN'T TAKE IT ALL!'

'What's your name, Miss?'

CLICK. Static.

Boscombe pressed 'STOP' and leaned against the wall, arms folded, watching Susan.

'Who was that?' Susan asked.

'Going on what I've looked at so far I'd say a local prostitute.'

'A *what*?'

'Call girl. Hooker. Escort.'

'With my Barry?'

'Mrs Frobisher,' Boscombe said, coming back over, pulling his chair out, 'judging from the mountain of material we've recovered from 1B Wellington Street so far your husband has been indulging in deviant sexual activities for a very long time. Since the early 1980s at least.'

Susan just looked at them, her jaw beginning to dangle. 'Since the early . . . what . . . what on earth makes you say this?'

'Some of the older videotapes are on Betamax,' Wesley added helpfully.

'This is ridiculous. I don't believe you.'

Boscombe shrugged and reached for his red file. He flipped through, took out a short stack of Polaroid photographs and handed them to her. Wesley looked at him, thinking *Steady on, Sarge*.

Susan's hand went to her mouth. There was Barry – naked, on all fours, with a bridle in his mouth. An obese black woman was sitting on his back riding him. Another one – Barry's huge flabby backside pointing towards the camera, red raw from some kind of whipping. There were more, lots more. Barry with other women. Different women. Many women. Two women at a time. She started to cry

Wesley reached into his pocket for some tissues and went to hand them to her, but Boscombe leaned forward quickly, cutting him off. 'Sick, deviant acts going on for decades,' Boscombe sighed. 'And you're trying to say you knew nothing about all this?' He reached into the manila folder now.

Susan looked up. 'I . . . what?'

'You're telling me you didn't know about this place? That you weren't involved too?'

'ME? Involved how?'

'You tell me, Mrs Frobisher. Swingers, were you, you and Barry? Down there in this bloody . . . "sex dungeon" of yours?'

Fucking hell, Sarge, Wesley found he had time to wonder.

'WHAT ON EARTH ARE YOU –'

Boscombe slapped a sheet of A4 down in front of Susan, cutting her off.

She squinted at it. It was a mortgage deed. Part of it was highlighted in yellow marker.

Barry's name.

Her name.

Joint owners.

FLAT 1B WELLINGTON STREET, WROXHAM.

'I . . . I've never seen this before in my life,' Susan said finally. 'I'd never set foot in that place until tonight. I DIDN'T EVEN KNOW IT EXISTED!' She banged the table.

A knock at the door. 'Come in,' Boscombe said. The door opened and a uniformed officer came in holding a sheet of paper. 'Sorry, thought you might want to see this, Sarge.'

Boscombe took the sheet and scanned it. He whistled and held it towards Wesley. *Oof*, Wesley thought.

54

'What?' Susan said. 'What is it?'

'Cause of Death,' Boscombe said.

In a voice not quite her own, a voice that sounded like it had come out of a film or something, Susan heard herself saying: 'I want to speak to my solicitor.'

TWELVE

'Are you sure you don't want another splash of this in there, love? You've had a hell of a shock.'

Susan shook her head. Never was much of a drinker. Julie tipped a slug from the brandy bottle into her own coffee and sat back down. They were in Susan's living room, formerly Susan and Barry's living room. Susan was just staring into the empty fireplace, fingering the rim of her mug. It was nearly three o'clock in the morning.

'A "sex addict",' Susan said. 'No – a "*prolific* sex addict", that was the phrase he used.'

'Oh God,' Julie said. In many ways she felt she was struggling to come to terms with this as much as Susan was. Barry Frobisher? A '*prolific sex addict*'? It was like finding out John Major had played bass in the Sex Pistols for a while. Barry. Barry who she'd always imagined had sex twice a year: once on his birthday and once on Susan's. You never knew. You just never knew. 'Mind you,' Julie said, 'I had a similar experience. Remember? With Doug from the golf club? It turned out –'

'Doug?'

'Ginger hair. Sweater vests. He —'

'Julie,' Susan cut in, remembering now, 'it's not similar.'

'No, but he was —'

'It's really not.'

'Remember? It turned out he was seeing me *and* that girl who worked behind the bar *and* the one who —'

'JULIE!' It had been building all night. Finally Susan exploded. 'YOUR SHORT-TERM BOYFRIEND FUCKING A COUPLE OF BARMAIDS BEHIND YOUR BACK IS NOT — *DEFINITELY NOT* — THE SAME THING AS YOUR HUSBAND OF OVER THIRTY YEARS DYING FROM A HEART ATTACK CAUSED BY RUPTURING HIS ANUS WITH A TWO-AND-A-HALF-FOOT DILDO DURING A SEX GAME WITH A PROSTITUTE!'

Silence.

Fair point, Julie thought. 'Sorry, love. I was only trying to . . .'

'I know. Sorry.'

They sipped their coffees for a moment.

'Look,' Julie said gently, 'you need to tell your Tom. Do you want me to call h—'

'No, no. I'll do it. Christ.'

Julie patted her shoulder. 'Susan, for now, I'd just tell Tom the minimum you have to until he gets here. I'd leave out, you know, leave out the stuff about the, you know, about . . . the rupturing with the two-foot thingy.'

'Jesus Christ,' Clare Frobisher muttered, squinting through sleep at the red numbers on the digital alarm clock by the bed. 3.48 in the morning — who the hell was . . . at this

time? And on the landline? Only sales companies rang the landline these days. Well, sales companies and . . . a brief flash of fear. Your parents. She propped herself up and listened to the phone ringing from the living room, down the hall, at the other end of the flat. It stopped and Clare sank gratefully back down into the pillow, already feeling the deep tug of sleep in her bones. *Probably a wrong number.* A few seconds passed and then a soft chirruping began from a corner of the bedroom, from under a pile of clothes. Not hers. Definitely not hers. Hers was in the kitchen. *And* she'd turned it off. She elbowed her husband in the ribs. 'Tom!'

A groan of protest.

'Tom!'

'Mmmm.'

'Your bloody phone's ringing!'

'Jesus Christ . . .'

She heard him stumble out of bed and towards the noise, then the rooting, cursing and muttering as he searched for it, the ringing growing briefly louder for a second between him fishing it out from under a pile of clothes and hitting the 'answer' button.

Clare pulled the duvet over her head and groaned. She could only faintly hear Tom saying, 'Mum? Mum . . . slow down.' Then, '*WHAT?*'

She sat up. She could hear Tom padding slowly back towards her through the darkness, then she could see the pale outline of his pyjamas in the doorway.

'What is it?' Clare said, conscious of her heart clenching and unclenching in her chest.

'My dad. He had a heart attack. He's dead.'

THIRTEEN

'Right, OK,' Roger said again, running a hand through his hair. Roger Draper — partner, Draper, Walker & Ferns, Solicitors and Notaries — was sitting across the dining-room table from Susan. There were three box files at his left elbow. In front of him was a sheet of A4 paper, covered in scribbles. He was clicking his pen on and off with his right thumb. Roger was something Susan had never seen him in the eighteen years he'd been their solicitor. He was *nervous*.

The last twenty-four hours had been hectic for Roger. He'd been liaising with the police, trying to get access to whatever documents they'd recovered from the sordid flat that might cast any light on the financial picture Barry had left behind. He'd also been to Barry's office and gone through all his files. It had made for . . . disquieting reading. 'Oh, Barry,' he'd found himself saying over and over again as yet another innocent-looking lever arch file yielded a fair approximation of hell. He was nowhere close to getting to the bottom of it all but, even this far from the bottom, it was not a pretty picture.

He ran a hand through his hair again, or, rather, what was left of his hair. At fifty-five Roger wasn't quite into comb-over territory, but his gingerish thatch was getting very thin on top.

'Roger, please,' Susan said. 'You're scaring me.'

'Right. The thing is, Susan, I . . . I've not nearly figured this all out yet. Not even close, it's bloody complicated, but, from what I've seen so far –' he placed his left hand on top of the three box files, the files all containing paperwork retrieved from that terrible basement flat – 'I have to say, it really doesn't look good.'

'What doesn't look good?'

'It looks like Barry was, ah, playing a bit fast and loose with the old finances.'

'What the hell does that mean?'

'First off, there's the flat itself. You bought it back in 1981, for seven thousand pounds.'

'Sorry, *we* bought it?'

'Well, I suppose Barry bought it. In the last few years it seems like he's remortgaged it several times.'

'Why?'

'It looks like he's been using that money to pay off the credit cards and –'

'What credit cards?'

'Nine different cards, all with balances varying between five and fifteen thousand pounds.'

'But . . . we don't have nine credit cards! We've got the Visa and the –'

'Susan, I think a lot of this is going to be news to you.

Just bear with me. On top of that there's the fact that he . . . he doesn't seem to have paid income tax or VAT for the past two years, the revenue are due over a hundred grand, and there are indications here, in the paperwork, that he's been making unauthorised payments to himself from the business account. Offshore trusts and things. There are a few loans, secured, unsecured . . .'

'Jesus Christ.' Susan slid her elbows forward across the polished wood and let her head sink into her hands. 'How . . .'

'It seems he's been doing this for some time, funding quite a, um . . . lavish private life. But it's definitely got more out of hand in the last few years. With the . . . the . . .' Roger tugged at his collar, looked at the table. 'The call girls and whatnot.'

It's not like we're newly-weds . . .

Susan felt a sob escaping her but she fought it back and took a deep breath. 'So what does this all mean?'

'Well, as you're a director of the company –'

'Oh, just in name! For the tax reasons.' Barry had explained to her that if she was a director of the company and received a nominal salary it was all money that didn't have to go to the taxman. It seemed to make sense. Back when things used to make sense. 'I never actually did anything! You know that, Roger!'

'I know, I know, it just means, technically, technically, you're jointly responsible for the company debts as well as all this other stuff –'

'But I didn't know about any of this!'

'Exactly. So we've got a very good chance of proving here that you're simply a victim. That Barry was forging your signature on all these remortgages and loan and credit agreements and –'

'Ah,' Susan said.

'What?' Roger said.

'When you say "forging" . . . there's a chance I did sign some of them. A few of them. Maybe.'

Roger looked at her. He reached into the top file and took out a sheaf of papers. 'Susan, are you telling me that this really is your signature?' He pointed at the dotted line at the bottom of a document. 'That you actually signed all this stuff willingly?'

'Well, I didn't know! Barry dealt with all the money! He was a bloody accountant for Christ's sake! He was always "restructuring" our finances! He'd put things in front of me to sign now and then and I'd just –'

'Oh shit . . .' Roger moaned.

'I didn't know about any of this stuff!'

'Oh God . . .' Roger whispered, beads of perspiration visible on his forehead now.

'"Oh God"? What does "Oh God" mean?'

He looked at her. 'It means, Susan, from what I've worked out so far, that you're personally liable for around half a million pounds' worth of debt.'

Susan felt her blood turning to antifreeze, sludging up in her veins.

Just then there was the sound of a key in the lock, the front door opening and bags being dumped down in the hall. A second later Tom stood in the doorway to the dining room, Clare behind him. He took in his mother, Roger, the paperwork on the table. 'Oh, Mum,' he said, his lip already quivering, 'I can't believe he's gone.'

Susan smashed her fists down onto the table as she stood up to face her son and daughter-in-law and screamed, 'HE'S A LYING, SWINDLING BASTARD SEX PERVERT!'

Then she ran out of the room crying.

Tom looked at Roger.

'It's been a difficult morning,' Roger said.

FOURTEEN

Boscombe knocked on the door, just below the brass plate bearing the name 'CHIEF INSPECTOR D. WILSON'. A second passed and he heard the muffled 'Come!' from inside.

He entered. There was CI Wilson, behind his desk, in full uniform, all that scrambled egg on his epaulettes. The desk itself – not so much as a stray paper clip on it. Boscombe thought of his own demented haystack two floors down. 'Ah, Boscombe, good morning.'

'Sir.'

'Please, take a pew.' Boscombe lowered himself into the chair feeling, as ever in here, the chill of someone being called to the headmaster's study. 'How is everything?'

'Fine, sir, fine. Busy.'

'I'm sure.' Wilson wasn't looking at him. He had his half-moon specs on and was already leafing through a few stapled pages of paper. What was the old bastard after this time? 'Now, Boscombe, do you know what I wanted to see you about?' He'd taken the glasses off now and was chewing thoughtfully on one of the stems.

'Er, can't say I do, sir, no.'

'Mmm. That rather alarms me.'

Oh fuck. 'Really, sir?'

'I've just been going through your report on that rather unfortunate, what would you call it, auto-erotic death we had the other day?' Wilson held up the stapled pages.

'Yes, sir.'

'Including the transcript of your interview with the late man's widow, a Mrs Susan Frobisher.'

'Yes, sir.'

'The interview that seems to climax with you calling Mrs Frobisher – who, bear in mind, had only been widowed in fairly horrific circumstances hours earlier – a "swinger". Quote, unquote.'

'Well, it was more of an implication really, sir.'

Wilson sighed and held up the transcript gingerly, as though it were something sordid and unclean, and turned a couple of pages. He slipped his glasses back on, cleared his throat and read aloud. 'DS Boscombe: "Swingers, were you, you and Barry?"' He took his glasses off again and faced Boscombe. 'Seems a fairly strong "implication" to me, Sergeant.'

'Well, I just felt . . . In an interview situation, sometimes you have to . . .'

Wilson leaned forward across the desk. He picked up a letter opener, a vicious-looking blade, and started testing the edge of it against his thumb. 'Why, Boscombe?'

'Like I say, sir, I just had a . . . a . . .'

'Be warned, Boscombe, if the words "a hunch" are

thundering towards this conversation I shall force this letter opener through your testicles to form a crude sort of kebab.'

Boscombe swallowed. 'Well, sir, with all due respect, her signature was on a lot of documents found at the scene. Documents pointing towards substantial fraud. I felt, feel, that's it's unlikely he could have led this kind of double life without her knowing, and I believed that by exerting a little press—'

Wilson waved a hand, cutting him off. 'Yes, Boscombe. And do you feel – just *feel*, mind you – that it's also entirely possible that she knew nothing about the whole thing?'

'Well,' Boscombe said, shifting in his seat, 'I suppose it's *possible.*'

'Yes. In which case it might have been better to think a little more carefully before accusing the poor, bereaved woman of being some kind of crazed sexual deviant. No?'

'Sir, I was just trying to –'

'Here's what you *are* going to do, Boscombe. When forensics are finished with the late Mr Frobisher's personal effects you're going to return them to Mrs Frobisher and you're going to be very, very nice to her so that when she comes out of mourning she doesn't immediately set about suing us for harassment. With me?'

'Well, I –' Wilson stared straight into Boscombe, forcing him to rethink. 'Yes, sir,' he said quietly.

'Excellent. Thank you. You may go, Boscombe.' Chief Inspector Wilson took a fresh document from his in-tray and began reading.

Boscombe had taken three steps towards the door when a frown crossed his face and he turned back. 'Sir?'

'Mmmm?'

'By "personal effects", do you mean all the videotapes and photos and whatnot too?'

Wilson spoke without looking up from his reading. 'Do you think Mrs Frobisher will have much use for a mountain of pornographic material featuring her late husband and a succession of prostitutes, Boscombe?'

'Umm. No. I expect not, sir.'

A knock at the door.

'There you are then. Run along now, Boscombe. COME!'

Fucking pompous old wanker, Boscombe thought as the door opened and Sergeant Tarrant entered with a sheaf of paperwork under his arm.

'Hugh,' Tarrant said.

'Bob,' Boscombe replied, nodding as he left, closing the door behind him.

'These all need your signature, sir,' Tarrant said, placing the paperwork in front of Wilson, who began to sign. 'He's a piece of work, old Hugh Boscombe, eh, sir?' Tarrant added, nodding towards the door.

'That's one way of putting it, Tarrant,' Wilson said, signing one form then turning to the next. 'Another way would be to say he's a crapulent buffoon with the IQ of a tampon.'

FIFTEEN

The sad notes of the organist drifted across the cremato-
rium, masking the soft chatter of the mourners. In the
front pew Tom and Clare gazed sadly at the polished
pine coffin, at the thick purple drapes behind it, which
would soon be parting to swallow it up, to commit the
remains of Barry J. Frobisher (CA, BSC Hons) to fiery
memory. Tom sat doing an unlikely thing for a man at
his father's funeral – struggling to square the image of
his safe, dull, *Daily Mail*-reading father with the crazed
sex monster he'd been learning about for the past week.
A two-foot . . . Jesus. There was an empty space next
to Tom, for his mother who was standing off to the side,
greeting faces she had not seen in a long time. Susan
smiled as she saw Jill coming towards her. 'Jill, thanks
for coming.'

They embraced. Susan was grateful for Jill being there
– she could think of no one less likely to engage with the
topic of *how* Barry had died than Jill Worth. Jill, who

couldn't even say 'shit'. Susan felt . . . she felt lovely actually. Lovely and warm and kind of floaty.

'Oh, Susan, I'm so sorry for . . . goodness. Just everything you're going through right now.'

'Thank you.'

'It's all just . . . horrible.' She blew her nose. Susan noticed Jill's eyes were already red from crying.

In truth, being here was costing Jill a great deal more than anyone knew. As she looked around the sad room, her ears full of the music of death, it was such a tiny hop for her imagination to place her here again, in the very near future, in far, far worse circumstances: *the tiny coffin. 'Jamie was with us for such a short time, and yet he filled our hearts with such love.' Her daughter, breaking. Broken.*

'Excuse me, sorry.' Jill headed for the toilets to get it out of her system. Susan looked across the room and saw Julie and Ethel in a pew towards the back – back-of-the-bus kind of girls, both of them. She smiled and Julie broke off from whispering something to Ethel to give her a tiny thumbs up. Susan nodded. The Valium Julie had given her to get through the day was working very well indeed. She'd never taken Valium before. *Floaty.*

Over in the pew Julie went back to whispering. 'It's a nightmare. I mean, Barry and I never got on but still, I –'

'Yeah,' Ethel said. 'Not how you'd choose to go, is it? A vibrator the size of a fire hydrant exploding up your bum?'

'Ethel!' Julie hissed. 'Not that. I mean I never thought he'd leave her in this mess. Barry. Mr Money Manager. Roger, their solicitor, thinks there's a chance she'll lose the house!'

Was Julie experiencing a vague kind of thrill at the

thought of her friend falling this far, as far as she had? No. *No, definitely not.*

'Poor cow,' Ethel said, scanning the room, her eyes settling on a new arrival, a tall, tanned lean man in his early sixties, with a head of thick silver hair and a matching moustache. He was wearing a well-cut dark suit as he wove through the throng purposefully, craning his neck, clearly looking for someone. 'Hold the phone,' Ethel said, licking her lips, 'who's the sex machine?' An elderly woman in the pew in front shifted uncomfortably, turning a little to glare in Ethel's direction. Ethel returned her gaze evenly with her patented 'Can I help you?' expression.

'*Ethel!*' Julie squinted across the room. *Bloody hell*, she thought. 'Terry bloody Russell,' she whispered.

'Who hell he?' Ethel said.

'We were at school together. Haven't seen him in years. He was a handsome bugger.'

'I wouldn't kick it out of bed now,' Ethel whispered.

'Well, yeah,' Julie said. He'd aged well, Terry, no doubt about it. 'He lived abroad for years. Did something fairly dubious in import/export. Made lots of money too, I heard. A real shagger in his day. What's *he* doing here?'

'Ooh, handsome, rich and mysterious?' Ethel said. 'You reckon he'd let me sit on his face for an hour or so?'

Across the room Susan was gazing at the light coming softly through a high stained-glass window, thinking how pretty it looked. Yes, Valium and plenty of it – that might be the way to go. She wasn't even thinking about the second meeting she'd had with Roger last night, the meeting where Roger had told her they'd have to go into the bank for another meeting. All these 'meetings'. Susan had gone through most of her adult life not really doing that much of anything and now all she seemed to do was have meetings all day. Roger. The undertaker. The caterers. The bank. Roger thought there was 'a chance' she could keep the house. It was the only asset she had, and in itself not worth quite enough to pay off the bank, the credit card companies, the loans, the revenue, the VAT man and the client accounts Barry had 'borrowed' from, but if she could borrow against the house, get some capital to allow her to . . . what had Barry always called it? Restructure her finances. Besides – it wouldn't look very good from a PR point of view, Roger thought, for the Lanchester Bank to kick a poor widow (*almost* a pensioner) out of her home for something she knew nothing about. Of course the onus would be on Roger and Susan to prove she knew nothing about all Barry's dealings. They'd just have to count on her good character. (But hadn't Barry had a 'good character' too? Susan heard a tiny voice saying this, somewhere at the back of her head, trying to break through the warm candyfloss mist of the Valium.)

Suddenly she heard another voice – real, much closer – saying, 'Susan? Susan, I'm so sorry for your loss.'

She turned to see a handsome, tanned face. A moustache. It took her a moment. 'Terry? Terry Russell? It's been . . .'

'Don't even say it,' he said, leaning in to kiss her lightly on the cheek. His aftershave was subtle, just there. Expensive.

'How have you been?' Susan asked.

'Oh, fine, fine.'

'You've heard the whole sorry tale, I assume?'

'Well,' Terry said, 'the old jungle drums have been

pounding, yes. I subtracted about 70 per cent of what I heard, but it still sounds pretty bad. How are you bearing up?'

'I . . . I don't really know. I know it sounds like the worst cliché but . . . I keep thinking I'm going to wake up.'

The vicar was walking towards the front now, the last of the mourners taking their seats. 'Look,' Terry was saying, pressing something into her palm, 'I'll probably shoot off straight after, I'm not much good at these things. But if you ever fancy taking your mind off things, I've got a yacht down at Sands these days. The sea can be very . . . calming. Come over and I'll take you out sometime.'

Susan looked down at the card – *'Terry Russell, CEO, Russell Shipping'* – and then back up at Terry. He smiled, almost apologetically. 'Terry Russell,' Susan said. 'If I didn't know better I'd say you were hitting on someone at their husband's funeral.'

'Just trying to offer a little comfort.' He grinned. Great teeth.

'Ever the good Samaritan, eh?'

'That's me. Look, I'll see you later. OK?'

Susan watched him go – scandalised and amused in equal measure. She tucked the business card into the folds of her purse. And then the vicar was placing his Prayer Book on the pulpit and it was time for it all to begin.

Or end, rather.

She wondered if Julie would let her have another Valium.

Later that night, after everyone had gone home, Susan walked through the house, turning off lights, picking up empty glasses, straightening cushions. She hadn't had very many people back after the service. Julie and Ethel, the

Robertsons, Roger, Tom and Clare obviously, who were now upstairs in the spare bedroom. She paused in the downstairs hallway, next to what used to be the 'telephone table', way back when, before cordless, before mobiles. There was a framed photograph – her and Barry and Tom, on the beach in . . . St Ives was it? Tom was about five or six, so, the late eighties. They were all smiling but Barry's smile, it seemed to Susan now, was more of a sneer, a sly, mocking grin.

Since the 1980s.

Betamax.

Bought for seven thousand pounds.

A lifetime of lies. Everything built on nothing.

She checked the front door was locked, turned the hall light off, slipped out of her shoes, picked them up and padded silently upstairs. The habits of a lifetime.

Coming along the hallway she noticed the light was still on in the spare bedroom down at the end – just a crack through the slightly open door. She could hear voices, voices that had the unmistakable tone of an argument being conducted at whispering level. She edged closer down the hall towards her own bedroom, then past it, closer to that crack of light.

Eavesdroppers never hear good of themselves, Susan . . .

Tom's voice first, strained, an edge to it. 'For God's sake, Clare, I'm just saying, if the worst comes to the worst, if she has to sell the house and she's got nowhere else to go . . .'

'And all I said was surely she'd be eligible for some kind of council housing?'

'I'm not packing my mum off to some grotty council estate!'

'Jesus – don't be such a bloody snob!'

'That bastard. That dirty fucking bastard. I can't believe he did this to her!'

'All I'm saying is that I don't know many women who'd be thrilled at the thought of living with their mother-in-law.'

'It might not even come to that. Look, can we talk about this in the morning please?'

Susan tiptoed away, her shoes clutched to her chest. She closed her bedroom door very, very quietly.

SIXTEEN

The Wroxham High Street branch of the Lanchester Bank, on a suitably rainy Tuesday afternoon in late May. It was a warm day, twenty-one degrees (or the low seventies in the old money Susan tended to think in), and the rain was almost tropical – great fat drops.

Susan and Roger were sitting facing the manager, a Mr Alan Glass. The 'Mr' felt faintly ridiculous to Susan – he was just a freckled boy in a suit and tie – and she'd felt relieved when he said, 'Please, call me Alan.' He looked to be about Tom's age and it occurred to her that he probably hadn't even been born when she and Barry opened their account here. He had a stack of paperwork in front of him, as did Roger. Susan had her hands clasped in her lap as she listened.

'I'm afraid, on that front,' Alan was saying, 'our hands are tied. HMRC have already frozen the account pending their investigation. It looks likely, if the figures you've given me are correct, that pretty much all of the money in there will go to them anyway.'

'What about the flat?' Roger asked. *The flat*, Susan thought. *The Sex Dungeon*.

'Already remortgaged to the hilt, I'm afraid. Twice in the last five years. There's no equity.'

There was a knock at the door and a girl's face appeared. 'Alan? Sorry to interrupt, but Securicor are here. We need you to open the strongroom.'

Alan looked up. 'Oh – is it, is this the last Tuesday of the month already?' He looked at the clock on the wall: 2 p.m. exactly. 'Sorry, will you excuse me for a moment?' he said, turning back to Roger and Susan. He went out into the hallway. Susan overheard another girl saying, 'Is that the supermarket takings? I'll get Gerry to come and help.' 'Thanks, Katie.'

Susan and Roger sat there in silence for a moment. The framed photograph of Alan's wife on the desk. The calendar. The clock ticking. Roger gave her a weak smile then the door was opening and he was coming back in, saying, 'Sorry, where were we?'

'If not the flat the main house then,' Roger said, fishing through his pile, 'the primary residence. There's no mortgage on that. It must be worth six or seven hundred thousand easily. If we could remortgage for even half of that amount –'

'Yes, well,' Alan said. 'How do you propose to meet the repayments?'

'From the savings account.'

'Which, as I explained, is frozen. And likely to all be due to creditors.'

Susan cleared her throat. They both turned to look at her. 'I could get a job. I have some, um, secretarial experience.'

The two men stared at her like she was a child calling a telethon to offer the contents of her piggy bank to try and end African famine.

'I'm afraid –' Alan tapped at a calculator – 'on a remortgage of, what, three hundred thousand? we'd need to have proof of an income of at least seventy thousand pounds a year. And, even then, at your a . . .' He thought how best to phrase it. 'At your time of . . . with the usual term being twenty-five years . . .'

Susan looked up. There was a poster on the wall behind the desk. It featured a happy, smiling, black version of Alan with his arm around a beaming young couple. The girl was holding the keys to a house, the pretty house in the background of the photograph. She was pregnant. In bright red type across the top was the slogan 'YOUR FUTURE MATTERS . . . TO US'.

'Anyway, I'm afraid all of this is something of a moot point.' Alan Glass patted another stack of papers. 'With all the other debts we're looking at here, the loans, the credit cards, the allegations of fraud, we're almost certainly looking at a bankruptcy situation. In which case any kind of remortgage would be impossible. We'd love to help, we really would, but –'

Susan laughed, a short, bleak bark, and said, 'I've been a customer here for over thirty years.'

'I understand how difficult the situation is, Susan,' Alan said.

'Actually I'd much prefer it if you called me Mrs Frobisher if it's all the same to you. You sit here, getting rich off people like me, and the minute we come to you for help, it's –'

'Susan,' Roger said, touching her arm gently. She pulled it away angrily.

'Look,' Alan said, shooting his cuffs, sitting upright and suddenly becoming Mr Glass in the process, 'Mrs Frobisher . . .'

Julie hurried towards the ringing doorbell, thinking *Keep your bloody hair on*. She'd been slicing a tomato for her late lunch of a tomato on toast. (Julie had to shop and budget very, very carefully these days.) When she made these humble meals she often found her interior monologue talking to her in the manner of a TV chef – Ramsay or Jamie Oliver – explaining what they were doing to the camera. *'We're going to make sure the toast is really hot, straight off the grill, and then some lovely thick slices of tomato, plenty of salt and pepper, and . . .'* It made it seem more glamorous somehow.

She had to travel the entire length of her flat towards the front door, from the kitchenette, through the living room and down the hall. It took her just twelve paces and ten seconds to accomplish this. She opened the door to see Susan standing there in the pouring, pouring rain. She was trying to speak. 'I . . . uh . . . uh . . .' Christ, Julie thought. Has she been hit by a car or something? Susan was soaked through and her mascara had streaked all down her face. Panda eyes? Her eyes were those of a panda in August with very bad hay fever who has run out of antihistamines about an hour after they've been told their whole family has been killed. 'Uh . . . they . . . I . . .'

'Easy, easy, darling. What's happened?' She pulled her friend into the hallway, out of the rain. Susan was like a five-year-old in the middle of one of the biggest crying jags known to man: struggling to get the words out between racking sobs, almost like she was permanently riding the crest of a huge sneeze.

'Th . . . they . . . *THEY'RE GOING TO TAKE MY HOUSE!*'

She fell forward, collapsing weeping in Julie's arms.

SEVENTEEN

Much later, the windows were open to the humid night, the coffee table littered with dishes, glasses, bottles and an overflowing ashtray, Julie having broken her own rule about smoking in the flat. Even Susan had taken one! When had she last seen Susan with a cigarette in her mouth? Before decimalisation probably. They were slouched on the floor, out of the Smirnoff now and on to the Popol vodka: a cheeky little number Julie had picked up at a petrol station. A tenner for a litre. Mixed with orange juice it was fine, just about killed the tang of formaldehyde, Julie thought, and Julie knew a thing or two about cocktails. Also, Julie thought, I don't know that I've ever seen Susan Frobisher drink quite this much. She was *knocking* it back. 'Tango in the Night' by Fleetwood Mac played softly in the background on Julie's little CD boom box. The CD. Another relic.

'Little shit looked about fourteen,' Susan said, hiccuping as she topped herself up. 'Your future matters TO US!'

'Bastards,' Julie said. 'They wreck the world, get bailed

out by the taxpayer, and as soon as you're in trouble it's "Fuck you. Fuck you very much."'

'I'm not kidding. He was younger than my Tom.'

'I've got one of them at work. Kendal. Administrator. Horrible cow. Straight out of college and given their own little fiefdoms to run.'

There was a pause as they both sipped their drinks. Susan sighed. 'Homeless and penniless. I didn't see this one coming, Jules.'

'Join the club. It wasn't exactly my master plan to wind up here . . .' Julie gestured around her, at the tiny flat, four small rooms: bedroom, living room, kitchen and bathroom. (At least, she'd thought, the Coalition's new bedroom tax wouldn't hit her.) 'You work all your life and . . .'

'Come on,' Susan said. 'Let's be honest, I never really did a day's work in my life.'

'Well, there is that, yes.'

'At least you did things, Julie. Got out there. Saw the world. Australia, America, London . . .'

'Yeah, well, you can't eat good times and all that. You had nearly forty decent years though.' Julie shook a fresh cigarette from her pack of Ambassador: the cheapest brand available at the local shop. She'd have killed for a lovely Marlboro Light.

'But it was all a lie. I was married to . . . to a sex addict.'

A pause. The two women looked at each and then, at exactly the same moment, both of them *buckled* with laughter. Very quickly they were rolling on the carpet, tears running down their faces. 'Oh, oh, have you met my husband?' Susan said, flattening a hand on her chest, feigning cocktail-party introduction. 'He's a sex addict!'

'Shurrup,' Julie gasped. 'Stop it, please, I can't breathe.' She wiped a tear away and reached for the bottle. 'Here.' She poured them both another. 'Shit, we're out of OJ.'

'Oh sod it,' Susan said. She picked up her glass and pounded it back neat, grimacing, shuddering, shaking from side to side, falling over and kicking her feet in the air.

'SUSAN!' Julie said, amazed.

'Ooh – that'll put hairs on your chest,' Susan said, sitting back up, blinking.

'Christ, Barry,' Julie said, lighting her Ambassador, leaning back against the sofa. 'And here was me thinking I had the monopoly on all the worst men.'

'Oh but you've had some *shockers*, haven't you? Who was the alcoholic? Remember – the Scottish guy?'

'Andy?'

'That's it! And the manic-depressive, wassisname? Tried to light himself on fire at New Year that time?'

Julie let out a squeal of laughter, remembering. 'Michael!'

'Michael. Christ. Oh no no. Wait. My favourite. The hard man. The gangster type you met when you were working in that club in Mayfair.'

'Gangster?'

'You know! He was older than us. Handsome. Looked a bit like thingummy . . . ooh, that actor. Terence Stamp.'

'Terence Stamp?' Julie saw that, fairly incredibly, Susan was pouring herself another vodka.

'Come on, you know who I mean. Had a mad nickname and everything. Screws, or Rivets, or something.'

'Oh – NAILS?'

'NAILS!'

They both collapsed laughing.

'You know what – I got a Christmas card from him a few years back. It's in the sideboard somewhere, I think. He lives over in Tillington.'

'He's still alive? Christ, he must be getting on a bit now surely?'

'God, yeah. He was in his forties back then.'

'He was a gangster, wasn't he?'

'Kind of. You don't remember what he did?'

'No.' Susan sipped her drink carefully this time.

'He was a bank robber!'

Susan sprayed vodka across the room as they both collapsed in hysterics again. 'A bank robber!' she screamed.

'I think . . . I think he wound up doing twenty years!' Julie said, laughing so hard now her ribs were aching.

'A bank robber,' Susan repeated, flat on her back on the floor.

'God, I could pick them, couldn't I?'

'A bank robber,' Susan said again, in a very different tone of voice this time.

'What?'

Susan sat up. She was breathing hard, but she wasn't laughing any more. There was a strange look in her eyes, a faraway, thinking expression, something Julie had never seen before. Or hadn't seen in a long time at any rate, not since way, way before Barry, back when Susan Frobisher was Susan Connors, the girl who put tacks on the teacher's chair, who flashed her knickers at passing buses.

'What is it?' Julie asked.

'A bank robber,' Susan said for the fourth time, looking directly at Julie now.

EIGHTEEN

'You're out of your mind,' Julie said.

'Seriously, how hard can it be?'

'Grief. That's it. Delayed shock. You're out of your teeny tiny mind with grief and shock.'

'You get a gun from . . . wherever, and you walk in and you say, "Give me the bloody money." It's not rocket science.' Susan was pacing the floor now. She was clearly insanely drunk, but she was speaking with conviction, with something passing for seriousness.

'You've never been much of a drinker, have you? I'll put some coffee on.' Julie went to get up but Susan put her hands on her shoulders and forced her back down, kneeling to face her, the two of them eye to eye.

'I mean it, Julie. Why not? *Why fucking not?* I . . . I mean, "You are overdrawn by five pounds. Oh, by the way, the letter we've sent to tell you this will cost you *thirty* pounds!" Or . . . or, "Oh, we're sorry, that cheque you paid in weeks ago still hasn't cleared so we can't let you have your money yet because we need it to help us make another 500 billion pounds in profits." Or – "Oh dear, we seem to have screwed up and lost everyone's money, but that's OK, because you guys can all just bail us all out, thanks. And, and, you know what? We understand your *husband just died* but unfortunately we will still be taking your home off you because, you know, your future matters to us!'" Susan stopped and made a grinning thumbs up, like the poster. '"Your future matters"? Your *money* matters and you can go to hell! I mean it! I've had it! I've never done a single thing wrong or bad in my whole life and here I am – out on the bloody streets at sixty? FUCK THEM! FUCK THE FUCKING BANK, JULIE!'

Julie didn't quite flinch but she definitely blinked. You rarely heard Susan drop the F-bomb. 'Susan, listen to yourself. You're seriously talking about robbing a bank?'

'What's the worst that could happen?' Susan sat back down opposite her on the floor and took another cigarette. She lit it, coughing.

'Er, you go to jail?'

'Oh, come on. You said it – I'm out of my mind with grief. Diminished responsibility and all that. Half-decent lawyer, no previous criminal record, you'd probably only get a few years. You do half the sentence and then come out and sell your story. Might get a fortune. Anyway, from everything you read, prisons are all TV and Wi-Fi these days.' She picked up her glass and drained it, as if to cement this stunning piece of logic.

'I really don't think,' Julie said slowly, 'I've ever seen you quite this drunk. Maybe at Rose Trask's wedding.'

'And besides, you're wrong,' Susan said, taking a deep

draw on her cigarette. 'That's not the worst thing that could happen. Jail? Definitely not. You know what the worst thing that could happen is? I go off to be a barely tolerated house guest at Tom and Clare's while you spend the next ten years up to your elbows in filth at that old people's home before we both move in there together to wait to die. Eh? How about that, me old mucker? How do you like them apples?'

Julie thought about this for a moment. *Christ*. She looked at Susan. Another strange expression had come over her face; she was looking up at the ceiling, as though she'd stopped herself midway through a train of thought.

'Oh dear,' Susan said.

'What is it?'

'Just need to be sick!'

Susan leapt up and ran careering out of the room. Julie listened in amazement as she heard the honking, retching symphony come echoing out of the bathroom.

NINETEEN

The day room held four old ladies. Three of them were dozing in armchairs upholstered in that cheap, easy-to-clean vinyl. The fourth – Ms Ethel Merriman – was in her wheelchair over by the windows, munching boiled sweets and leafing through some photographs. Julie was mopping – old Mr Grant, too much tea this morning, quite a flood it had been – certainly hung-over, but nowhere near where Susan had been on the Richter scale that morning. She was thinking as she was mopping. *'Ten years.'* *'How do you like them apples?'*

'Ethel?' Julie said, laying her mop against the wall and coming across to her. 'If you could go back twenty years or so and you had the chance to do something really crazy, something that might wreck your life completely, but also might change it brilliantly, would you do it?'

Ethel stopped flipping through the photographs and looked at her. 'What's all this?'

'Just – hypothetically.'

'Ah, define "wreck your life".'

'Well, say, just supposing, something like you went to prison.'

'Oh, prison's fine,' Ethel said, going back to flipping through her pictures.

'You've been in prison, Ethel?'

'The first time – Oh, hang on, here it is.' She fished a photograph out of the pile and handed it to Julie. 'Was in '56. Me and a few of the girls were prosecuted for indecency.' Julie looked at the photograph. It was faded and cracked, black and white on stiff card, and showed a line of chorus girls in what were *very* revealing outfits even by today's standards. 'Show we'd been doing in France came to London, Café de Paris, on Leicester Square. We'd been told we'd be arrested if we went on in those costumes. This was back when the Lord Chamberlain had to approve all shows that went on in London, you know. Anyway, fuck them. On we went. Show gets stopped, straight into the paddy wagon, hello Holloway. I'm third from the end on the left,' Ethel said, unwrapping another sweet, passing one to Julie. Julie scanned across the picture and . . . *Jesus Christ.*

'Ethel, you, I mean . . . you were *gorgeous.*' It was impossible to reconcile the girl in the photograph with the bloated old lady sitting before her now. Chestnut curls down to her shoulders, gleaming teeth, legs up to her chin and traffic-stopping cleavage.

'Oh yeah, I was something.'

'I didn't know you were a dancer!'

'I was a singer really, darling, but you took what jobs you could get. There was always work in the chorus line. Cock too. Yards of cock. Miles of it. What were we talking about? Oh, yeah. Prison. Second time was in '61 or '62. I punched a copper in the face on a CND march near Aldermaston. Broke his bloody nose. Bastard fascist beak gave me six months.'

'Jesus,' Julie said, still transfixed by the 28-year-old Ethel in the photograph. 'What . . .'

'Ha! What happened? Age, sweetheart. That and living right. Never trust anyone over fifty who hasn't piled on a few pounds. Look at you – too bloody skinny by half. Wouldn't trust you as far as I could throw you. But, to go back to your question: remember, Jules, it's better to regret something you did do than something you didn't.'

Julie perched on the edge of Ethel's wheelchair and they were both looking at the photo, taken over half a century ago in Paris, and sucking their sweets when suddenly a shrill *'Excuse me?'* cut across their reverie. They looked up to see Miss Kendal in the doorway. 'Miss Kendal,' Julie began. 'I was just—'

'Yes, Julie, you were just chinwagging with Ethel – again – when I'm sure there's plenty to be getting on with.'

Ethel went to say something – Julie could hear the 'F' fricative forming on her lips – but she put her arm on Ethel's shoulder, silencing her, and stepped forward, towards Kendal.

'You know, Miss Kendal, I don't think it's such a bad thing to spend some time chatting with the residents. Some of them enjoy a little human contact. Some of them don't –' She stopped, not wanting to point out that Ethel didn't receive many – indeed any – visitors.

Kendal had no such reservations. She came over and stood in front of Ethel, her arms folded across her chest, clamping the ever-present clipboard to her bosom. 'Yes, well, you have to wonder why *some* of our residents don't get much in the way of visitors, don't you?' She leaned down, coming close to Ethel's face. 'In fact, I can't remember the last time you had a visitor, Ethel, can you?' Kendal smiled savagely.

Ethel held her gaze.

From somewhere behind Kendal came a scrape and clatter, the sound of a mop falling, of something being picked up. Ethel's eyes widened as she saw what was happening over the administrator's shoulder. 'Miss Kendal?' Julie said. Kendal turned just in time to shriek as something unspeakable cascaded over her and her world turned a translucent yellow glow, the colour seen by someone who has their head inside an upended yellow plastic bucket of piss, detergent and floor water. Kendal started gagging and coughing through the stench of Mr Grant's urine. She was dimly aware of Ethel clapping delightedly and Julie saying, 'I won't be working out my notice.'

She called Susan from her mobile as she walked down the pothole-filled driveway, the grim outline of the home disappearing behind her for the last time. 'Susan? It's me. I'm in. Fuck it. Let's . . . let's do it, OK?'

And, in the end, for both of them, perhaps this was it. It was something to *do*. Something they could control. Something that didn't involve just sitting there clapped in the stocks of life while all manner of shit got thrown at them. Because sixty was the new forty and all that rubbish. Anyway, like Susan had said, half-decent lawyer to prove they were crazy and they'd probably only get a couple of years in a minimum security. Be like a bit of a holiday.

TWENTY

Susan pulled the handbrake on and they sat looking across the street at the tidy little bungalow. It was a pleasant cul-de-sac of 1960s houses. All the gardens well kept, sensible nondescript cars in all the driveways – the land of gnomes, pampas grass and the Rover. 'Mmmm,' Susan said. 'It doesn't look like where an ex-bank robber would live. Are you sure this is the right address?'

Julie looked again at the three-year-old Christmas card she was holding. 'Yep. Number 14. That's it. I mean, he might have moved away. He might be dead.'

'Only one way to find out, I suppose,' Susan said.

'Oh God. This is mental, isn't it? We're completely deranged.'

'We're just doing a bit of research,' Susan said. 'We'll talk it through, get a professional opinion, and then take a view on what to do next. If anything. We can walk away any time.' Nestling in Susan's handbag were a bunch of photos they'd taken of the Lanchester Bank, plus some notes she'd made on various comings and goings. Fortunately there was a Costa Coffee right opposite.

'A professional opinion?' Julie said. 'Susan, you're not having some painting done. Or a bunion taken off. We're talking about robbing a bloody bank.'

'OK. Come on then.'

They'd rung the bell for a fourth time and were about to walk away when a shape appeared through the frosted-glass door – a very slowly moving shape. 'Oh God,' Susan said. 'Someone's home.' It seemed to take an eternity for the shape to cover the last few yards to the door and then there was an interminable fumbling at the lock, the sound of a chain going back and, finally, a face appeared. A face, but not the face Julie and Susan had been expecting to see. The only resemblance between Terence Stamp and this fellow was that they were both bipeds. Well, almost, for he seemed to be clutching onto some kind of Zimmer frame. He was also completely bald and a half-masticated, unlit cigar dangled from his mouth. Yes, fair to say he was to Terence Stamp what Hans Moleman from *The Simpsons* was to George Clooney. The man removed the cigar in order to speak in a gruff, east London accent,

'If you're Christians the pair of you can piss off.'

'I'm sorry,' Susan said. 'We were looking for a Mr Savage?'

'Who the fack are you then?'

Julie stepped forward. 'Steve? Ah, Nails? It's Julie. Julie Wickham? Remember me?'

The man looked at her through clouded, rheumy eyes. It took a moment but some light appeared to come into them and his mouth spread into a grin, revealing, oddly, that his teeth were still perfect and for the first time Julie saw a glimpse of the man she had known (a man she had loved in a series of inventive and demanding positions) nearly forty years ago.

'Jules?' he said. 'Jules from Parkers in Mayfair?'

'Yes!'

'Fack me. You'd best come in then.'

'Nails,' Nails said some time later. 'No one's called me by that name in gawd knows how long.' He smiled. 'This one 'ere . . .' he said, indicating Julie to Susan, 'she had 'em eating out of the palm of her hand so she did. I swear. You'd have used her toilet paper as a hanky and been proud.' Susan smiled. The girls were on the sofa. Their host had taken an armchair opposite, which facilitated his access to a tank of oxygen with a clear plastic face mask attached to it. He alternated deep draughts of oxygen with ferocious sucks on the cigar. A pot of tea and three mugs were on the table. It'd taken him a while to get all of this together. 'Look at you, girl,' he continued, beaming at Julie. 'You ain't changed one bit.'

'Neither have you,' Julie said with a completely straight face.

'Shut your lying hole, you slag,' Nails said pleasantly. 'I'm a facking fossil.' He turned to Susan. 'You wouldn't think it to look at me, love, but Nails here was a prince of the West End once upon a time. Flat in Knightsbridge, Savile Row suits, tables in the best restaurants, champagne all the way, Jag parked up out front and a string of pretty girls on me arm. Girls like this one here.' He pronounced 'girls' to just about rhyme with the breathing apparatus of a fish. 'Nowadays? It's meals on wheels, Lucozade and I've been wearing these facking pyjamas since Hitler was a corporal. I'd give a million quid to be able to have a shit that didn't make me burst into facking tears. But we had some laughs, eh, Jules?'

'We did, Nails. We really did.'

There was a pause, filled with a definite sadness. Susan took it as her cue to ease into the main topic of discussion. 'There was actually something we wanted to talk to you about, Nails.'

'You fire away, love. Nails is all ears.'

Susan took a breath, reached into her handbag and placed the stack of photographs next to the teapot on the coffee table: photographs of the Wroxham High Street branch of the Lanchester Bank.

Nails took a deep draw on his cigar and leaned forward to peer at them, smoke wreathing out of his mouth. He brought his head up, looked from Susan to Julie and back again, and said, with great sombreness, 'Are you two talking about a piece of business?'

TWENTY-ONE

Nails exhaled while he unwrapped a fresh cigar from its cellophane slip. This exhalation took about half a minute and was punctuated with many a cough, whoop and splutter. Water streamed freely from his eyes and Susan and Julie glanced at each other, both wondering if he might be about to expire right in front of them. Finally it subsided and he lit the cigar.

The coughing fit this entrained lasted a further minute and a half. Finally he sat back, his face bathed in sweat now, and said, 'Oh dear, oh dear, I gotta give these things up.' He looked at the ceiling and breathed deeply and thought for a long time. 'You know what I learned in thirty years of doing jobs?' he said finally. Susan and Julie waited. 'Doing the job ain't the hard part. Any mug can stick a tool in someone's face and get handed a bag of money. You know what the hard part is?' They waited again. '*Getting away with it.*' Nails paused to let them take this in before continuing. 'See, the filth, they always got a list of the usual suspects.

And the armed robbery fraternity is small. They get to someone who knows someone who knows someone whose cousin's mate's brother's mate was spouting off down the drinker – down the Dog & Ferret, down the King's Tits or whatever – and next thing you know they got one of you and then they get another and then they get the lot of you. I saw it time and time again. Geezers pulling the job off, it's all double Scotches and "we're the facking lads" and we'll lie low for a bit before we move to Spain and, bosh, three weeks later they're all bent over in a cell with some facking great spear-chucker banging away at their coal-hole.' Susan wasn't really following him here, but it didn't sound good, this coal-hole business. 'Which brings me to you girls. You got one thing going for you – you know what it is?'

Susan and Julie looked at each other. Susan said, 'We'll be really well prepared?'

Nails sighed and shook his head. 'Nah. It's this – you pair are most definitely *not* the usual suspects. Ain't no one even gonna be thinking about putting the feelers out for a couple of nice old ladies – no offence, girls. Yeah, I'd say a mob like you could get away clean.'

'So you think wc could do it?' Susan asked.

'I didn't say that now, did I?' Nails said, leaning forward again to re-examine the photographs. 'Look at what you got here. Small-town bank, low security, fewer customers – that's all sweet. On the other hand, high street, pedestrianised, weak escape routes. Plus, these days, you got CCTV up the bloody Ronson, faster response times from the cop shops and all that . . .' Nails rubbed his silvery stubble, thinking. 'At the same time, one thing ain't changed from my day.'

'What's that?' Susan asked.

'If you're sticking a facking great shooter in some tit's face, you're getting the dough. Pardon my French, love. There's one other thing. You gotta know when to hit it. I remember we did the old Barclays on Kingsland Road, in Dalston, back in '72 or '73. We only went in on the day after they had their takings collected. Got about three hundred quid between us. I'll tell you – that wasn't worth two and a half years. Not by a long chalk. Not even in 1972. You gotta know when –'

'I know,' Susan said. They both looked at her. 'The last Tuesday of every month. Just after two o'clock in the afternoon. They get all the takings from the big supermarket in. That's got to be a lot.'

Nails looked at her. 'How do you know that, love?'

'The manager told me,' Susan said. 'Just before he told me they were taking my house.'

'Impressive, love. Very fucking impressive.' Nails took a quick snort of oxygen. 'OK. So there's that. Now then, who's on your team?'

'What do you mean?' Julie said.

'Your team,' Nails said. 'Your firm. Your crew.'

'Well.' Susan looked at Julie, then back to Nails. 'Just us.'

'Two of you? Are you out your facking trees?'

'Well, how many were you thinking?'

'Job like this it's five man minimum. Two for crowd control, two to deal with the staff and get the dough, one driving.'

'But we haven't got five people,' Julie said. 'There's only two of us.'

'Three of us, you mean,' Nails said.

Julie and Susan both took him in. The liver spots. The egg-stained pyjamas. The Zimmer frame. The oxygen tank. They looked at each other, nervously. Julie spoke first. 'Ah, Nails, the thing is, are you sure you –'

Nails's eyes narrowed. 'Are you two trying to cut Nails out?'

'No!' Susan said. 'Of course not.'

'Cos you're gonna need a few tools of the trade. And I don't know where you're gonna track them down without old Nails. I know what you're thinking – if he tries to squeeze a fart out he's gonna have a brain haemorrhage. Listen, he may be eighty-nine, but old Nails can still drive a fucking car, don't you worry about that. But trust me, we're still gonna need a couple more bodies, or doing that place is a one-way ticket to the bum-palace.'

'The what?' Susan said.

'Prison, Susan,' Julie said.

'Oh.'

'All that said, done right, it's the perfect sunshine cruise, innit?'

'How do you mean?' Susan asked.

'A sunshine cruise, love. One last job before retirement.'

'Right,' Nails said, getting to his feet with some difficulty. 'Nails is gonna go strap on the collar and tie and we can discuss this further over the old prawn cocktail and steak and chips. How about that?'

'That . . . well, that'd be lovely,' Susan said.

Nails toddled off across the room on his walking frame.

'When do Tom and Clare leave?' Julie asked.

'Tomorrow morning. Two more people? Where on earth will we find two more . . .? I mean, I've got one idea.'

'Who?' Julie said.

Just as Susan was about to answer they were interrupted by a loud mechanical noise. A buzzing, a grinding of gears. Both women turned to see Nails – he was sitting expressionless in an electric stairlift that was, very slowly, spiriting him upstairs.

As soon as he was out of sight Susan turned to Julie and whispered, 'Yes. It's not exactly the A-Team so far, is it?'

TWENTY-TWO

'You must be out of your mind,' Jill said. 'I know you've been through a lot lately, Susan. That's it. Grief. I think grief has quite simply bent your mind.'

'It hasn't. Honestly, love. I . . . I've just had enough.'

They were sitting in Jill's car, at the end of Susan's drive. Susan had allowed Jill to give her a run home from rehearsals, which was ordeal enough: Jill made even a tame driver like Susan look like Ayrton Senna on crack cocaine. And all for nothing – Susan had gone over everything twice now. There was nothing else for it; she only had one route left to try. 'Look,' Susan said, 'I hate to say this, but with your Jamie, this might be –'

'Don't you dare, Susan Frobisher! Don't you dare bring that boy into this! To use his innocence to try and justify your . . . your *crimes.*'

'OK, OK. I'm sorry.

'You'll all end up in prison of course. Or worse.'

'OK, Jill, you've made your point. The whole thing's

nuts and it probably won't work. But please, can I beg you not to tell anyone?'

Jill looked at her. 'I should tell someone, you know. Get you locked up before you do something really stupid. But anyway, it's not even worth talking about, is it? Because you're going to go inside and have a good night's sleep and wake up tomorrow morning and forget about the whole thing. Aren't you?'

'Probably, yes. But if, if I don't . . .'

Jill stared straight ahead through the windscreen. 'No. I won't tell anyone.'

'Thanks, Jill.'

'Please, don't go through with this, love. Have a think, eh? It's just . . . it's just crazy.'

'Well,' Ethel said. 'Well, well, well.' They were at the top of the hill in Wroxham Park, where Julie took her for their weekly afternoon walk, before Ethel insisted on 'just looking in' at the Brewer's Arms on the way back for a couple of her 'liveners': triple gin and tonics.

'It's just . . . nuts. Isn't it?' Julie said.

'Oh yeah. It's nuts all right.'

'We should just stop this before it gets out of hand, shouldn't we?'

'God, no.'

'Sorry, Ethel?'

'Seems better to me than the alternatives.'

'The alternatives?'

'Finding some other poxy job like the one you just had. Do I get a gun?'

'A gun? I . . . well, I suppose so.'

'What kind?'

'I don't know! Look, we're not going to hurt anyone.'

'Just threaten them?'

'Well, I suppose we'll have to, yes.'

'*Really* threaten them?'

'If we have to, yes.'

'Brilliant. I'm in. Now come on. Sun's over the yardarm and all that.'

Ethel turned her wheelchair away from the bench and started trundling off in the direction of the pub. Julie watched the wheelchair-bound octogenarian she had just enlisted to join forces with the Zimmer-frame and oxygen-assisted octogenarian in an armed robbery heading down the hill. She got up to follow and sighed to herself. 'I must be losing my mind,' she said.

Jill Worth woke up the next morning to a ringing phone. It was a full minute before she could get Linda calm enough to get the words out. 'Oh, Mum. It was the worst yet. We had the ambulance out at three o'clock this morning. I thought this was it.' She collapsed into heaving sobs. 'The doctor in the A&E, he started talking to me about "facing certain realities"!'

'What realities?' Jill said.

'In terms of "time frame". Oh, Mum, he's going to . . .'

And Jill did what she always did. What she'd been doing these past few years. She made her reassurances and said all the things she knew how to say. And when the call was over, and her daughter had calmed down a little, Jill Worth put her head in her hands and wept for her grandson. Then she got up and crossed the hallway to the kitchen, to where she had left her Bible by the radio. She often picked it up and opened it at random when she was in need of guidance or inspiration. She did this now and got Proverbs 11:14 — *'Without good direction, people lose their way; the more wise counsel you follow, the better your chances.'*

Jill thumbed on. Stopped again. James 1:3 — *'For you know that when your faith is tested, your endurance has a chance to grow.'*

Meh. Best of three.

Matthew 19:26 — *'Jesus looked hard at them and said, 'No chance at all if you think you can do it yourself. Every chance in the world if you trust God to do it.'*

Good enough, Jill thought. She dialled the number quickly, the damp tissue clutched in her trembling hand. 'Susan?' she said. 'It's Jill.'

TWENTY-THREE

Friday, late afternoon, an overcast mid-June day on Beecham Crescent, and inside number 23 an unlikely gathering was in progress.

Everyone was gathered in Susan's living room, clustered around a coffee table covered in tea things, cakes, biscuits and sweets. Nails put his teacup down and, with the usual difficulties, stood up and cleared his throat. He was wearing a double-breasted suit that would have been considered the height of fashion around 1982, which was in fact the last time it had had an outing. Behind him was a large A2-sized flip chart on a stand that Susan had bought that very morning at the big Staples up near the bypass. On the first page was a drawing of the basic layout of the bank. Susan, Julie, Ethel and Jill stopped chattering and looked at him.

'Right, girls. Like a natter, don't we? Good old chinwag. Well, unless you fancy doing all your gossiping down on the bloody cock farm I suggest you shut your faces and pay attention.'

'Cock farm?' Jill said, puzzled.

'Prison,' Susan whispered to her. 'Anything you don't understand probably means prison.'

'First things first,' Nails went on. 'Job descriptions. Julie and Susan –' he pointed to them – 'staff and vault. Ethel and . . . what was your name again, love?'

'Jill.'

'Jill. Ethel and Jill, crowd control. Whoever is in there waiting to pay in their bloody cheques or whatever you've got to keep 'em shtum. No one goes out and no one comes in. Right?'

Ethel and Jill nodded.

'Which leaves old Nails here driving the motor. Now, tools of the trade. Susan love, can you clear some of this off?'

Susan moved cups, plates and sugar bowl while Nails reached down under the coffee table and, with great effort, hauled out a large canvas holdall. It was about the size of a tent and filthy, covered with clods and streaks of earth. He clanked it down on the table, unzipped it, and began taking things out: an automatic pistol, a revolver, a vicious-looking sawn-off shotgun, a World War II Mills bomb hand grenade, all of them somewhat rusted and pitted.

'Oh my goodness,' Jill said, her hands going to her mouth.

Ethel reached over and picked up the automatic.

'Careful, Ethel!' Susan began, but Ethel had already worked a catch or lever on the weapon with her thumb, causing the magazine to drop out of the grip and into the waiting palm of her left hand. She pulled the slide back and checked the chamber was empty before squinting expertly down the barrel and then letting the slide ratchet back into place, cocking the gun. She levelled the sights at the clock on the mantelpiece.

'You got a good eye, love,' Nails said. 'That's the pick of the bunch. Browning nine –'

'Nine millimetre semi-automatic,' Ethel said. 'Standard issue sidearm to British Army officers from the 1950s onwards.' She squeezed the trigger, dry-firing the weapon with a metallic 'click' as the others looked on amazed. 'But the action's stiff and the barrel grooving's ragged. Leading me to believe that this is a deactivated gun that someone's made a half-arsed job of reactivating.' She turned to see Susan, Julie and Jill looking at her, open-mouthed. 'It's a hobby really,' Ethel said.

Nails looked at her, impressed. 'I'll tell you what, this old gal's got some spunk in her, eh?'

'Yes,' Susan said. 'I shouldn't wonder.'

Ethel levelled the pistol at Jill and cocked the hammer.

'ETHEL!' the women all screamed. Ethel pulled the trigger again, saying 'BOOM!' as she did so and cackling as Jill shrieked.

'Right, enough buggering about,' Nails said.

Ethel laid the Browning on the table and ran a hand over the sawn-off. 'This is a bit more my speed, I think . . .' Nails was taking more stuff out of the holdall, a pair of thick metal bars, about three feet long.

'What are those for?' Julie asked.

'All in good time, love . . .' Nails rummaged around in the bottom. 'Ah, here we go. Right, pass these out, pick one and stick with it.' Susan took from him a pile of black woollen balaclavas. She passed them around, each of the women taking one. Julie held hers up. The word 'HATE' had been emblazoned across the forehead in white gloss paint. 'Why on earth . . .?' Julie said, looking around. Susan's balaclava had the word 'FEAR' written in the same manner.

'Two reasons, love,' Nails said. 'One, it makes it easier for you to identify each other. Two, if you've got something mental written across your forehead then that's where they're looking. Not at your eyes. I've known blokes get made from just the eyes.'

'I am *not* wearing this.' They all turned to see Jill holding up a balaclava with the word 'PAIN' on the forehead. 'It . . . it's just horrible.'

'I'll swap with you if you like, Jill,' Ethel said cheerfully. They all turned to look. Ethel was already wearing hers. The word 'FUCK' was embossed across it.

Nails looked at her admiringly. 'Mrs Fuck. Nails likes it.'

'Susan, can I swap with you?' Jill said. 'I'd rather have "fear" than "pain".'

'No!' Susan said. 'I like "fear".'

'Oh please.'

'Right, shut it!' Nails said. 'Who gives a monkey's what —'

Suddenly the doorbell rang — a bright, cheerful, comical *ding-dong*.

They all looked at each other. 'You expecting anyone?' Nails said, his eyes narrowing.

'I . . . no.' Susan moved towards the net curtains and peered out. What she saw caused her heart to travel half a foot up her chest and lodge in her throat. She felt her knees give.

A police car.

Parked right in front of her house.

She turned back to them. 'It . . . I . . . it's the police.'

Pandemonium.

Jill started crying. Nails started gibbering. 'Facking Jesus. The filth. Pigs. Bacon. Rozzers. Old Bill. Someone's stitched us up . . .'

'Everyone, just calm down,' Julie said, looking around the room, at all the guns, the balaclavas, the flip chart and the photos of the bank.

Ding-dong.

'Dobbed us in. Shopped us. Grassed us up . . .' Nails went on.

'I KNEW THIS WAS INSANE!' Jill shrieked.

'Susan —' Julie said, struggling to be heard.

'How the fuck —' Ethel said.

'Can everyone please stop swearing?!' Jill shrieked.

'This is it,' Nails said. 'Nails ain't going back inside. No way. Not again. FACK IT!' He fell to his knees, grabbed the revolver off the coffee table and stuck it under his chin. 'I'M COMING HOME, MA!' he screamed.

'For God's sake,' Julie said, snatching the gun out of his hand before he could pull the trigger. Nails toppled over on his side on the carpet, hyperventilating. 'Susan! Just go and answer the door and stall them for a minute.'

'How?' Susan said.

Ding-dong. Ding-dong.

'Just . . . use your bloody initiative!'

Susan hurried towards the hall. Julie turned back to the others. 'Jill, calm down and help me with this. Quick.'

Susan took a deep breath and opened the front door. DS Boscombe and DC Wesley were standing there, Boscombe wearing a fixed, idiotic grin. It took Susan a moment to place them. 'Sergeant . . .'

'Boscombe! Yes, and you'll remember Detective Constable Wesley?'

'Afternoon, Mrs Frobisher.'

'Yes, good afternoon.'

'Sorry to keep ringing your bell like that,' Boscombe continued. 'It's just that we saw your car and it looked like someone was in, so –'

'Sorry, Sergeant, I am rather busy. Was there something in particular you –'

Boscombe held up a clear plastic evidence bag. Inside were Barry's wallet, watch, keys, mobile phone and loose change. 'Your husband's personal effects. Normally we'd call and notify you that they're ready for collection but I thought that, given all you've been through lately, we'd just bring them out to you.'

'Oh, that's very kind . . .' Susan reached out to take the bag. Which Boscombe immediately withdrew.

'I just need you to sign a couple of forms.' Boscombe looked past her hopefully, into the hallway. 'If we could just . . .'

'Yes. I really am rather busy at the moment, Sergeant.'

'It won't take a moment.'

'It's really not convenient. I was just going out.'

Suddenly music became audible from inside the house. Boscombe looked at her. 'Entertaining, are we?'

Susan swallowed. 'Yes, I am actually. I was just out of . . . sugar. Was going to pop to the shops.'

'Well, as I say. It'll only take a mo—'

'Have you got a . . . a warrant?'

'A warrant?'

'Yes. Don't you need a warrant to come in here?'

Boscombe looked at Wesley confused, then back to Susan. 'Ah, not if you invite us in we don't.'

'Why wouldn't I invite you in?' Susan said.

'I don't know,' Boscombe said. 'So can we?'

'Can you what?'

'*Can we come in?*' Boscombe was beginning to wonder if this woman wasn't touched in the bloody head.

'Everything OK, Susan dear?' Julie shouted cheerfully from the living room. 'We could use your help in here.'

'Oh, very well, Sergeant. Do come in,' Susan said, opening the door for them.

'Thank you very much,' Wesley said.

She led them down the hallway and, taking a deep breath, opened the door to the living room. The music, a tango, was immediately louder and Susan and the two policemen were greeted by a strange tableau: Julie was tangoing Nails around the centre of the room, watched by Ethel and Jill. Jill had a fixed grin on her face. Ethel was happily clapping along to the music. Boscombe nodded politely to the old lady in the wheelchair covered with stickers. There was no sign of the weapons and the flip chart had been turned over. On the fresh page, Susan saw, Julie had hastily written some dance steps: a diagram of feet with various arrows indicating movements. The song finished and Ethel led the applause, with Boscombe and Wesley joining in. 'That was much better, Bert!' Julie said to Nails. 'You led wonder-fully!' She pretended to suddenly notice the two detectives. 'Oh! Goodness! Company!'

'Having a little dance class, are we?' Boscombe said.

'Indeed. Bert here is one of my most promising pupils.' Julie indicated Nails. Nails looked as though he were on the verge of a major coronary. Bullets of sweat were trickling down his face and his jaw was locked in a demented smile as he extended his hand for Boscombe to shake. 'Pleased to meet you, Bert. Detective Sergeant Boscombe, CID.'

'Fuunnghhrrr,' Nails said.

'He had a little stroke a couple of years back,' Julie whispered, stepping closer to the officers and very subtly twirling her index finger in the air near her right temple. Boscombe smiled and nodded kindly to Nails.

From behind them Susan made a strange, high-pitched squeak. Boscombe turned to look at her. Ethel noticed what Susan had been looking at – the barrel of the sawn-off shotgun was protruding from underneath her. 'Sorry,' Susan said as Ethel deftly covered the gun with her shawl, 'just a frog in my throat.'

'We were just returning some things to Mrs Frobisher here,' Boscombe said. 'Sorry to interrupt you.'

'Oh, not at all,' Julie said. 'We were just working on our tango.'

'Lovely, eh, Wesley? To see people of, well, advancing years keeping active. Keeping interested in things.'

'Yes, Sarge,' Wesley said.

'Well, thank you, Sergeant,' Julie said. 'You know, we can always do with a few more able-bodied young men like yourself at our classes!'

'Is that so?' Boscombe said. 'You know what? I've always fancied learning that there tango as a matter of fact. I love a bit of *Strictly*!'

*　　*　　*

A quarter of an hour later Wesley sat dunking a custard cream into his second cup of tea while he watched his boss dip Julie down into a reasonable, if strained, facsimile of the finishing position of the tango. The music stopped and everyone burst into applause.

'Excellent, Sergeant!' Julie said.

'Oh, he's quite the mover!' Ethel added.

'Don't half put a strain on the old back that last bit!' Boscombe said, not quite as sensitive as he could have been here to his partner's feelings.

'Well, Sergeant,' Susan said, 'if you have those forms . . .'

'Oh yeah, of course. Sorry.'

A few moments later Boscombe was putting the keys in the ignition of their car while Wesley buckled up his seat belt. 'Does you good, doesn't it, Wesley? To see them enjoying themselves like that.'

'Yeah, Sarge.'

'I only hope I'm that active when I'm their age.' He turned the key and pulled away.

Susan watched them go from behind her net curtain. She turned round and sat down on the floor, exhaling heavily.

'Well!' Ethel said, removing the sawn-off shotgun from under her bum. 'That got the old blood flowing!'

'Fack me,' Nails said, puffing gratefully on his oxygen mask.

TWENTY-FOUR

Later that night, in the same room, Julie and Susan sat sipping their tea in silence. They'd spent the rest of the day going over and over Nails's plan in detail. Timings, positions, code signals. Finally Susan sighed and put her mug down.

'This is just . . . nuts. Isn't it?'

'Completely,' Julie said, staring into the fireplace.

'We're going to end up in prison. Or worse.'

'Mmmm.'

'I mean, there's a chance, running around with guns and stuff, there's a chance someone will get hurt, Julie. Isn't there?'

'It's possible. Do you want that last piece?'

'No, you have – Julie! I'm trying to talk us out of this. You sound like you couldn't care less.'

Julie picked up the last slice of buttered toast and munched on it. 'You know something?' she said. 'I don't think I do any more. When the salon went under I was only what, twenty-nine or thirty? You don't even think about it in terms of failure at that age. You just think, "Oh well, I'll try something else." Then, with the bistro, when that went down, I was forty-five. And that *was* hard. Starting again at that age. But these past few years, with the boutique . . . I always thought I was an "upwards and onwards" kind of person, Susan. But now, at sixty, I just can't do it again. I can't start all over again at this age. So if this is a short cut, and we're not going to hurt anyone, then fine by me. Because anything – *anything* – has to be better than what I've got at the moment.

'Even the "bum-palace"?'

'Look at you. You played it safe your whole life and where have you ended up? Ending your days in Tom and Clare's spare room on a state pension? Was that how you saw "retirement" when we were younger?'

'You know what?' Susan said. 'When I thought of that word I always imagined somewhere warm and sunny. Tropical. Stretched out by a swimming pool. Going out every day for nice lunches.'

'What happened to that idea?'

'Barry wasn't keen on the heat.'

'Barry's dead.'

The two friends looked each other in the eye. Julie raised her mug and said, 'To the bum-palace.'

Susan brought her mug up to meet Julie's. 'The bum-palace.'

TWENTY-FIVE

The Lanchester Bank, Wroxham.

2.05 p.m. on the last Tuesday in June.

It was, fittingly, the hottest day of the year so far.

The digital thermometer on the counter showed 31 degrees as Sally looked out at the line of five customers. Her blouse was sticking to her and she felt sleepy after lunch. Oh well, less than three hours till closing time. 'Will there be anything else today, Mrs Trent?' she asked.

'Oh yes, I wanted to open an account for my grand-daughter. Do you have the forms for —'

Sally's eyes widened as she looked past Mrs Trent to the doorway, where three figures in navy boiler suits were walking in, all wearing balaclavas with something written on them. Her first thought was — students. That it was some rag week thing. But they didn't have collecting buckets in their hands. They had . . . were they . . .

'RIGHT, EVERYONE GET DOWN! THIS IS A ROBBERY!' one of them was screaming, the tallest one, nearest the counter, the one with 'FEAR' plastered across the forehead. The customers screamed as the last robber came bursting through the door. Well, 'bursting' would be pushing it. 'Trundling' would be more accurate. Trundling in on a wheelchair, wearing a balaclava with the word 'FUCK' written on it and producing a double-barrelled shotgun from beneath their tartan shawl as they came in.

One of the customers, the last man in the line, laughed and said, 'What's this? Red Nose Day or something?' Ethel smacked him very hard in the balls with the butt of her shotgun. The man went down groaning as Ethel levelled the weapon at the others and yelled: *'DOWN ON THE FLOOR, YOU FUCKING SLAGS, BEFORE I TURN YOU INTO FUCKING TEA BAGS.'* She pulled the trigger and emptied both barrels with a CRACK – blowing out the CCTV camera above the counter.

That did it. Screaming. People throwing themselves on the floor. Sally, panicking, instinctively palmed a button on the counter, causing the metal shutter to begin slamming down. But Susan and Julie were already there, already wedging Nails's three-foot iron bars in the sides, stopping the shutter halfway down, levelling their guns at the crying girl. 'OPEN THE DOOR. NOW!'

Sally hit another button and they slipped into the back room. Taking Sally at gunpoint, they made their way along a narrow corridor where they met Alan Glass, on the way out of his office to see what that great bang had been. Susan shoved her revolver straight in his face and grabbed his lapel. 'The strongroom,' she said, in the closest thing to a man's voice she could muster.

Glass burst into tears.

Two hundred yards up the street Nails sat sweltering behind the wheel of his 1988 Ford Granada. The one with the dummy plates he'd dug out of the attic. He had his balaclava up his head like a woollen cap, ready to be pulled down when he got the signal. He looked at the walkie-talkie on the passenger seat. Three or four minutes they'd been in there now. Ten tops he'd told them. 'Jesus. Jesus fucking Christ,' Nails panted, trying to control his breathing. 'Cool. You're cool, Nails. Cool as a cucumber. You drink boiling water and piss ice cubes. Fucking ice cream. Fucking . . .' He looked across the street and saw that there was indeed an ice-cream van parked there, in front of the supermarket at the top of the high street. Nails licked his lips as a salty bead of sweat coursed down his forehead and into his eye, stinging.

'Ohgodohgodohgod,' Jill was whispering to herself, her hands shaking as she tried to keep her gun level on the cowering customers. 'What's taking them so long?'

'Please,' one of the women on the floor sobbed. 'Please don't hurt us.'

'We're not going to hu—' Jill began.

'SHUT IT!' Ethel hissed at them, ejecting the spent cartridges from her shotgun, thumbing two fresh ones into the side-by-side barrels. 'If any of you so much as lifts their head up I'm going to unload this thing right in your bloody face.'

All of the guns except Ethel's were, of course, already completely unloaded. The shotgun cartridges Ethel was using had been filled with the traditional farmer's mixture of rock salt. At very close range the cocktail might be enough to kill but Ethel had no intention of firing it at anyone at close range. It was perfect, however, for taking out the CCTV cameras and, at a range of twenty yards or less, would deliver a stinging blast across the arse.

In the back Glass was punching the code into the lock for the strongroom while chanting his mantra of 'pleasedon'thurtmepleasedon'thurtmepleasedon'thurtme'.

For God's sake, Julie thought. *Show a little leadership!*

A beep, a light going from red to green, and the door opened. Julie and Susan herded all four staff into the room. There, in the middle, were half a dozen metal Securicor boxes all waiting to be loaded into the safe. While Julie kept the staff covered Susan opened the first box and started stuffing fistfuls of notes into their large canvas holdall.

The notes were all fifties. Banded in packs of one hundred notes, each bundle then was worth five thousand pounds.

There were *a lot* of them.

'He's just a blowhard, Wesley,' Boscombe said, slamming the car door. 'Seriously, Ted Pritchard? Detective Inspector? My bloody arse in parsley.'

'Wilson likes him,' Wesley countered.

'Wilson likes anyone who'll kiss his bloody arse.'

They came out of the small car park and onto the top of the high street.

'Bloody scorcher today, Sarge, eh?'

'Not half, lad,' Boscombe squinted into the glare. 'Here, hold up. Tell you what — you let your old boss treat you to an ice cream, eh?'

'Nice one, Sarge,' Wesley said.

They started heading towards the bright yellow van parked outside the supermarket.

'Hurry up!' Julie growled, looking at her watch. Five minutes since they came in the door.

'Mmmmmmm!' Susan said, not wanting to speak.

'You'll never get away with this,' one of the staff said. Julie leapt over and pointed her gun at him. More screaming. 'Be quiet!' Glass shrieked. 'Just let them do what they want. That's the policy in these situations.'

Susan was onto the fourth box.

There wasn't much room left in the holdall.

Nails's mind had wandered. Again. It kept doing this these days. In his head he was at the seaside as a boy. Down at Margate or Southend.

Lovely times, with his ma and da.

He looked across the street to the ice-cream van once more. Then back down the high street. What was he doing here? Something important, he was sure of that. He just couldn't quite remember what. And he was so bloody hot. It'd only take a minute, wouldn't it? Nothing could be that urgent that he couldn't have a bloody ice cream. Could it? Slowly he got out of the car (and whose car was this?) and tottered across the street. Leaving the walkie-talkie on the passenger seat.

'Mmmm!' Susan motioned to Julie to come over so she could whisper to her. Julie came across and knelt down, not taking her eyes or her gun off the staff. 'What?'

'I can't get any more in!'

Julie looked at the crammed holdall, at the one box remaining. And then at her watch – six minutes now since they came in. 'Fuck it,' she whispered. 'Let's go.' She grabbed a couple of handfuls of banded fifty-pound-note bundles and shoved them into her pockets. Susan picked up the holdall. Or tried to. 'Jesus,' she said. They took a handle each and edged their way out of the door and into the corridor. Julie kicked the door shut and it automatically flashed back to red, locking the staff inside.

Susan took the walkie-talkie out of her pocket and keyed it. 'Fear to Wheels. Fear to Wheels, come in. We're ready to roll.'

On the passenger seat of the old Granada her voice reverberated out of the walkie-talkie and around the hot, empty car.

Nails was queuing for his ice cream. Two fellas in front of him. One of them turned round. 'Oh, hello there!' he said. Nails looked at the man, confused. He'd never seen this geezer before in his life. 'Look, Sarge, it's Mr . . . you know. From the dance group.'

Boscombe turned now too, his large 99 in his hand. 'Oh yeah. Bert. How are you?' Boscombe smiled kindly, the way you do at simpletons. Bert? Who the fuck was Bert? Nails wondered. What the fuck was all this? But something was making alarm bells ring in Nails's brain. Sarge. Hold on. What the fuck . . . Nails remembered what he was doing here.

The girls came out of the front of the bank, Ethel bringing up the rear, holding her shotgun under her blanket, levelled at the still cowering customers. Susan looked around. Nothing. '*Where is he?*' Julie said. Terror sparking through her, Susan hissed into the walkie-talkie again, forgetting all protocol now, saying, 'Nails – where are you?' People were starting to stop and point at them. Susan looked up the street. A few hundred yards away she could see an ice-cream van.

In a sharp moment of focus Nails realised that a) he was a criminal, b) he was here on business and c) that the man standing in front of him was a policeman who had somehow rumbled him. 'Fancy an ice cream, do you?' the copper was saying. 'Here, on me.'

He was handing Nails his 99. 'Give us another one, would you, son?' the copper was saying to the kid working the van. Nails looked at the ice-cream cone now clenched in his fist. 'Hot old da—' the copper began. Fucking toying with him he was. Taking the piss out of old Nails. The fucking liberty of it. Go back to choky? No way. No fucking way.

Nails smashed the ice cream into Boscombe's face.

Then he turned and broke into a run. Well, 'run' would be pushing it. Although everyone — judge, prosecution, defence, jury — would later agree that it had been an astonishing effort for someone of his age, testament to what the human body could achieve when in extremis. Nails had once again slipped into being 1972 Nails, who could fight and outrun policemen. He had forgotten that he was pushing ninety and needed a puff on his oxygen tank to pick up the remote for the TV. He had also forgotten that his vision was limited to about twenty feet in front of him.

Wesley, Boscombe — who had ice cream dripping from his face and the words 'What the fucking fuck' forming on his lips — and several other witnesses watched in astonishment as the ancient man turned on his heel and ran twenty feet or so — smashing full force into the plate-glass window of the Morrisons supermarket.

Julie and Susan turned in the doorway of the bank, hearing the explosion of glass from the other end of the high street. 'Look!' Ethel shouted behind them. She was pointing across the road — at the Cancer Care minibus, parked there. Empty. The driver's door open. The bunch of keys visible in the ignition from here. Susan became aware of a rhythmic panting noise close to her — Jill crying.

This was a nightmare. What had happened? Where was Nails? What now? Where —

Susan's interior monologue was terminated by the

piercing note of the alarm going off. Somewhere within the bank, one of the staff had finally hit the button.

Wesley turned from regarding Nails scrabbling around, trying to get to his feet amid a hundred thousand tiny jewels of broken glass, bleeding quite badly, and squinted down the high street, into the sun. He saw it immediately — two hundred yards away, three figures in overalls, wearing balaclavas, holding . . . Jesus Christ.

'SARGE!' *he shouted.*

Boscombe stopped advancing towards Nails, wiped ice cream and broken bits of wafer from his face, and turned to follow Wesley's gaze towards the distant sound of a fire alarm. He saw them too.

'LET'S GO!' Ethel screamed, already wheeling herself towards the minibus. Its back doors were open and the platform for loading and unloading wheelchairs was already at street level. 'QUICK!' Julie yelled, pushing Susan after Ethel, grabbing Jill by the arm and pulling her behind them. They piled into the bus, Susan and Julie throwing the huge holdall onto a row of seats. Julie went to clamber over into the driver's seat only to see that Jill had jumped in there. She was panicking, crying and screaming 'OHMYGODOHMYGOD!' over and over as she tried to turn the key.

'COME ON!' *Boscombe yelled, taking off at a sprint, Wesley following.*

As Susan slid the side door of the Cancer Care minibus shut, she heard a low humming noise, and looked towards the rear of the vehicle to see Ethel magically ascending on the checkered steel platform. 'GET US THE FUCKING FUCK OUT OF HERE!' Ethel was yelling over her shoulder. From where she was sitting on the back of the bus, framed in the open doors, Ethel had a perfect view of Boscombe and Wesley sprinting towards them, shouting 'STOP! POLICE!'

They were about a hundred yards away.

Now eighty.

Now seventy.

'TELL THAT STUPID BITCH TO DRIVE!' Ethel yelled again.

Julie leaned forward and screamed in Jill's ear: 'DRIVE, JILL!'

'What the fuck!' a voice very close to them said and Susan turned to see, through the passenger-side window, the very angry driver of the minibus, coming out of the Cancer Care office.

Fifty yards.

Now thirty.

Ethel could see the sweat on Wesley's face. The ice-cream-spattered forehead of Boscombe.

'AAGGHHHHHH!' With a scream Jill finally got the key to turn and the engine growled beneath them.

Boscombe was upon them. With a roar he launched himself up onto the platform at the back, right at Ethel. Ethel dropped the spent shotgun and picked up her grabbing stick.

Two things happened simultaneously.

1) Jill crunched the bus into gear and hit the accelerator. Well, to say 'hit' would be engaging in hyperbole of the highest order. If Jill Worth wasn't the most cautious driver in the world she was certainly in the top five. More accurate to say she pressed gingerly down on the accelerator and moved off at a speed of about five miles an hour.

2) As he came at her Ethel shot out her grabbing stick

and took an absolutely perfect – and robotically strong – hold of Detective Sergeant Boscombe's testicles. He fell backwards off the platform but found he was still tethered to the moving minibus by the vice-like grip of the grabbing stick. In order not to have his balls ripped off Boscombe suddenly found he was having to run quite fast after the minibus.

Jill turned the corner and headed up Court Street, the one-way running off the high street. Her driving was being hampered not only by the fact that she was crying but also by the deafening roar of Julie and Susan screaming behind her, urging her to go faster. She tapped the accelerator and took the van up to a speed approaching ten miles an hour. 'Straight over the roundabout!' Julie was yelling. 'Head for the dual carriageway!' As the roundabout came into view Jill was aware of a keening, high-pitched scream. She crunched up to second and nudged the pedal a little more, hitting fifteen miles an hour.

Wesley gave up and stopped running. He watched his boss in astonishment. Boscombe was *hurtling* after the bus, going full pelt just a few feet behind it, his legs just a crazed blur. From his vantage point directly behind him, Wesley had no way of knowing that, rather than suddenly discovering superhuman reserves of speed, his boss was simply being pulled after the minibus by his very scrotum.

'JILL! FASTER, FOR GOD'S SAKE!' Julie was screaming.

'WE'RE IN A TWENTY!'

'YOU'RE NOT EVEN DOING TWENTY!'

'IT'S A LIMIT – NOT A TARGET!'

'ARE YOU FUCKING KIDDING M—'

Jill found third gear and the needle on the speedometer passed the 20 mph marker.

Usain Bolt has been recorded running at speeds of just over twenty-seven miles per hour. To do this requires incredible levels of musculature and training, levels well beyond the fifteen-stone frame of DS Hugh Boscombe, who was now looking in astonishment at his own madly blurring legs while screaming his head off. With the incentive of retaining his testicles to help him, he was somehow managing to run at just over twenty miles an hour. He looked back up – into the merciless eyes of Ethel, staring at him through the slits of her balaclava, the word 'FUCK' glaring in white capitals across her forehead.

She was sitting in a wheelchair, Boscombe realised. He glimpsed a bumper sticker fixed to the front: 'WHERE'S THE BEEF?' Somewhere in his agonised, screeching mind this rang a bell.

'JESUS CHRIST, JILL!' Susan screamed. 'WILL YOU PLEASE PUT YOUR BLOODY FOOT DOWN?!' *Right, enough*, Julie thought.

She clambered over into the front seat, threw herself down on Jill's lap and mashed the accelerator to the floor.

The van rocketed off across the roundabout just as Ethel tore the grabbing stick from Boscombe's nuts, making a *riiipppppping* sound, tearing the front of his trousers open in the process.

Boscombe screamed as he watched the leering, wheelchair-bound figure disappear into the distance. He also had a split second to register disbelief at how fast he was still running – much like the cartoon character whose legs are still frantically pedalling in mid-air after they've run off a cliff edge – before he rocketed into a parked Ford Fiesta at twenty-five miles an hour, cracking the windscreen and knocking himself senseless in the process.

Mayhem in the minibus: Ethel wheeling herself further back into the boot area, the wind whistling through the open doors, Susan screaming to take the dual carriageway, Julie sitting in Jill's lap, driving, Jill crying and screaming and trying to wriggle out. *Well, this beats* Lovejoy *repeats and digestives at four o'clock,* Ethel thought to herself as Julie tugged the wheel hard to the left and they went careering down a ramp towards the dual carriageway. Ethel just had time to register the 'NO ENTRY' sign they'd just passed.

'Oh fuck,' Susan said flatly as they saw the first car coming towards them.

Wesley came screeching down the high street in their car. He'd barked garbled instructions to the two uniforms who'd been loading the battered and bleeding Nails into the back of a squad car ('assaulting an officer, malicious damage') before slapping the blue light on top and hitting the siren. He took the corner onto Court Street fast and was about to accelerate again when he saw Boscombe stumbling into the middle of the road. Jesus Christ — what the fuck?

Wesley hit the brakes hard and came skidding to a halt six feet in front of his boss. Boscombe looked like he'd been smashed to pieces. The crotch of his trousers had been torn open. He came round to the driver's side.

'Sarge,' Wesley began, 'what happened to —'

'Shift,' Boscombe said, already getting in the driver's door. Wesley scooted over.

'Are you OK?' Wesley asked. There was a good-sized gash in Boscombe's scalp and his face and hair were matted with blood.

'Pensioners. Dancing,' Boscombe said, already pulling off, his

face a grim mask of blood and determination, staring straight at the road ahead.

'Ah, Sarge?'

'My balls, Wesley.'

'Are you – '

'Tried to rip them off.'

'Are you sure –'

'Pensioner.'

'Are you sure you should be driving?'

'SHE TRIED TO RIP MY FUCKING BALLS OFF!'

He seemed pretty sure, Wesley thought.

All four women were screaming as they hurtled towards the oncoming estate car, the car frantically beeping its horn and flashing its lights.

'OH GOD OH GOD OH GOD!' Julie was chanting.

'AHHGHGHHHH!' said Susan.

'HELP ME, JESUS!' Jill screamed.

'FUCK ME!' Ethel shouted.

They could see the faces of the occupants of the estate car now – a man and a woman. They were screaming too, the righteous terrified screams of people legitimately taking the off-ramp from the motorway only to see a Cancer Care minibus screaming towards them at seventy miles an hour.

Julie yanked the wheel hard to the right and they crunched onto the hard shoulder, missing the car by inches, causing the driver, a Mr Leslie Hough, to soil himself.

Boscombe came over the roundabout at eighty, cars slamming their brakes on, siren blaring, blue light flashing, The Sweeney theme pumping in his smashed mind. As they came up the elevated section onto the second roundabout that allowed you to join the dual carriageway, Wesley looked to his left. He saw the minibus.

It was about a mile away. Heading west. On the hard shoulder. On the wrong side of the carriageway.

'LOOK!' Wesley yelled, pointing.

Boscombe followed his finger. He saw the minibus too and emitted a low growl.

'Fucking hell,' Wesley said. 'They're gonna kill someone. We better get some help —' He picked up the mike for the radio and was about to key the button when Boscombe smashed it from his fist.

'Eh?' Wesley said.

'Ours,' Boscombe said.

'We need to —' Wesley stopped talking as he realised what Boscombe was doing. He was taking the 'NO ENTRY' ramp, taking the hard shoulder, following the van.

'SARGE! NO!'

'MY FUCKING BALLS!' Boscombe screamed, his eyes glittering and mad, like a pair of marbles with fire inside them.

Even more screaming in the minibus — Julie nudging the speedometer towards ninety, honking the horn and flashing the lights as they tore along the hard shoulder, the oncoming traffic passing them on their left, the faces of the people in the cars in the slow lane just a mad blur of open mouths and wide eyes. 'GET US OUT OF HERE!' Susan screamed. Behind her she was aware of a hooting noise and turned to see Ethel: punching the roof and barking with joy and excitement as there came another noise in front of Susan, honking and rhythmic — Jill, vomiting into the front-passenger footwell.

Boscombe floored it — coming down the hard shoulder of the off-ramp, his siren blaring and blue light strobing. Traffic scrambling to give him a wide berth. Indeed it would be the actions of the driver of a low-slung Porsche Carrera trying to get out of his way a few hundred yards along the dual carriageway that would prove to be so catastrophic. Being sat so low to the ground, the driver (a Miss Daisy Welling, a 32-year-old marketing executive) couldn't really see what was happening up ahead as she moved into the slow lane in preparation for taking the off-ramp to Wroxham, the ramp Boscombe and Wesley had just come down at eighty miles an hour. Miss Welling just heard police sirens and saw brake lights coming on and traffic slewing out of lane. Panicking she made the appalling decision to pull over onto the hard shoulder. She glanced in her rear-view mirror as she did so, to check there was no one coming up the hard shoulder behind her. She never for a moment factored in what might be coming down the hard shoulder in the opposite direction, against the traffic.

'JESUS CHRIST!' Wesley screamed as he saw the silver Porsche pull directly into their path. Boscombe was trying to press the pedal through the rubber mat at this point, through the floor, onto the tarmac, his eyes fixed on the white minibus in the distance, with its back doors flapping open, the hunched, hooded figure of the woman in the wheelchair still just visible. Boscombe saw the Porsche pull into their path less than a hundred yards away. He knew that he was doing close to a hundred miles an hour and had no chance of stopping in time. He realised that he had only two options open to him and — tuning out Wesley's screaming — that he had perhaps three seconds to choose between them.

Left into the oncoming traffic?

Or right, over the grass verge, into . . . what exactly?

Boscombe yanked the wheel hard right.

Somewhere up ahead Julie threw a right-hander too, hitting the brakes, leaving a strip of skid marks fifty yards long on the hard shoulder as she almost 360'd the minibus and took the (amazingly clear of traffic) exit ramp off the dual carriageway. Thirty seconds later they were over another roundabout and motoring down a quiet B-road as though nothing had happened. It was eerily quiet, just the sound of Susan breathing hard with her eyes shut. Jill had fainted. 'Oh Lord,' Ethel said from way in the back. 'That was fucking *brilliant.*'

When retelling the story in the years ahead, which he would be asked to do often — down the pub, at retirement dos, at Christmas parties — Wesley would stress the strange feeling of weightlessness, of the brief absence of something as fundamental as the laws of gravity. The grass verge acted as a sort of natural ramp. Their 2.5-litre police Rover took it at ninety-two miles an hour, that speed being lessened slightly as the front bumper was torn off and splintered beneath them.

Then there was blue sky all around them.

Here Wesley found himself thinking of the last words of Donald Campbell, driver of the Bluebird, *as he attempted to break the world water speed record. 'I'm flying!' Campbell said, as the craft's nose rose out of the water.*

At the wheel Julie was experiencing the backwash of an adrenalin blast she hadn't felt since perhaps 1972, specifically December 1972, when she was seventeen years old and in the front row when T. Rex ran onstage in Poole. The adrenalin was pumping a clarity of thought through her. 'Susan!' she said over her shoulder. 'SUSAN! Is the money safe?' Susan patted the seat next to her, feeling the stuffed, zippered holdall. Julie saw her nod in the rear-view mirror. 'Right,' she said. 'We need to ditch this van . . .' Julie started scanning the hedgerows for a turning, thinking about barns, woodland, anything.

As all survivors of terrible car wrecks will tell you, time stood still for a moment. There was just a whooshing noise. Wesley even found he had a moment to turn his open-mouthed face to his right and behold Boscombe, staring straight ahead, still uselessly turning the steering wheel. It occurred to Wesley that he would quite like to punch his boss in the face. In terms of his last actions on the planet, this seemed like it would be a fairly reasonable one. Then gravity was back with a vengeance and they were plummeting down. In his peripheral vision (he was still staring hatefully at Boscombe) Wesley became aware of water.

The heavy Rover smashed nose first into the duck pond, sending a spray of water thirty feet into the air and activating the airbags, which punched both of them softly in the face. Luckily for Boscombe and Wesley it had been a hot day and their windows were down. The shock of the cold water rushing in was balanced by the fact that this allowed the water pressure on each side of the doors to equalise, so that both of them could open their doors.

They swam to the side and lay there panting, watching the boot of the Rover point skywards as it sank slowly.

In the distance they could hear sirens approaching.

TWENTY-SIX

Julie stopped the van. A single-track lane led off the B-road. A wooden, hand-painted sign on it said 'DENSMORE COTTAGE'. She looked down the lane – leafy, overgrown, secluded. *What the hell*, she thought. *Ditch the van in a hedgerow and continue on foot if need be.* She turned back and looked at Susan. 'What do you reckon?'

'We've got to get out of these clothes.' She'd ripped her balaclava off. Her face was slick with sweat. Julie nodded and took the turning. Susan leaned over into the front seat and brushed Jill's hair from her face. 'Is she OK?' Julie asked, steering the minibus slowly down the bumpy lane.

'I think so,' Susan said. Jill was beginning to stir.

'Oh God,' Julie said, 'have we still got the pass—'

'I got 'em,' Ethel said, patting a small canvas knapsack tucked inside her wheelchair. It contained all their passports, their means of getting out of the country.

'Here.' Ethel's gnarled fist appeared over the seat behind

Susan's head, holding her pewter hip flask. 'Give her a belt on that.'

'I don't think just yet,' Susan said, taking the flask. She was about to take a nip of what smelt like brandy when Julie abruptly threw them into reverse, causing Susan to nearly spill the liquid all over herself. 'Careful, Ju—' she was saying.

'Look!' Julie said, pointing as she backed up.

Susan and Ethel turned. Julie was pointing to a pretty Edwardian cottage. It had a double garage attached to it.

'What?' Susan said. 'You want us to go in and say "Hi there! We just robbed a bank. Can we hide out here for a while?"'

'No. *Look*,' Julie said. 'The doorstep.'

'Well, I'll be . . .' Ethel said.

'Where are we?' Jill said, sitting up, groggy.

'What is it?' Susan said, looking at what appeared to be a perfectly ordinary doorstep, well, ordinary save for the fact that there about a dozen bottles of milk on it.

'It's what we call "a break", love,' Ethel said.

Julie was already reversing the minibus, preparing to take the turning into the driveway. 'What are you doing?' said Susan, still not getting it.

'Someone forgot to cancel the milk,' Julie said.

'Eh?'

'Fucking hell,' Ethel said.

'Ethel! Language!' Jill hissed automatically, not yet fully awake.

'Ah. They're on their holidays,' Susan said.

A moment later, the minibus off the road and the gates closed behind it, Susan and Julie stood on the front doorstep, ringing the bell. Behind them Jill was sitting on the step of the open passenger-side door. She had her head in her hands and was muttering a kind of numb, looped mantra, something along the lines of *'What was I thinking . . . prison . . . dear God, help me . . .'*

After the fourth ring Julie said, 'Definitely not home.'

'So what now?' Susan said.

'Well . . .' Julie said, already eyeing up windows and drainpipes.

'Please don't tell me,' Jill said behind them, 'you're actually thinking about breaking into this poor person's house.'

'Jill,' Julie said, 'we just robbed a bank. I think a little light breaking and entering is neither here nor there at this point.'

Jill moaned.

'But how . . .?' Susan said, looking up at the cottage, which looked pretty well fortified.

'You know what they say,' Julie said. 'Imagine you've lost your keys and you ask yourself "How do I get in?"'

'Yes, but what if there's a burglar alarm or something?'

'Let's just go to a police station and give ourselves up,' Jill said.

They ignored her. 'Maybe,' Julie said, 'if we –'

There was a noise from somewhere inside the house and they both stiffened.

'Oh shit,' Susan whispered.

They took a step back from the door as, incredibly, it began to swing open.

'Wotcha, shaggers,' Ethel said, sitting there in the hallway in her wheelchair. 'Went round the back. They'd left a key under the mat. Lovely country simpletons. Come away in. Kettle's on.'

She trundled back off down the hall, whistling. Julie and Susan looked at each other. 'She's a one-woman crime wave,' Susan said.

It felt surreal, Susan thought moments later, to be sitting around the table of a farmhouse kitchen, listening to a kettle coming to the boil while Ethel, with surprising calm and efficiency, motored around gathering tea things, mugs, teapot, spoons, etc. Somewhere behind her Susan could hear Julie muttering to herself as she took bundles of notes out of the holdall. She was counting. 'Ooh, here's posh . . .' Ethel said, reaching up into a cupboard with her grabbing stick and bringing down a large box of fancy Marks & Spencer's chocolate biscuits. 'Ethel!' Jill said. 'You can't steal their biscuits!'

'This is silly,' Susan said. 'I mean, these people could be home any minute. We should –'

'Easy, sweet cheeks,' Ethel said through a mouthful of chocolate. 'No one's coming home soon.'

'What makes you so –' Jill began.

Ethel answered by tapping something on the wall next to the Aga with her grabbing stick. Susan and Jill looked up to see a calendar (a National Gallery calendar, a collection of Impressionist paintings) on the wall. In there, among various kids' birthdays, dentist appointments and so forth, was the word 'TUSCANY'. There were two arrows coming out from either side of the word, spanning the dates 15–29 June. 'Not home for a week yet,' Ethel said. 'So can everyone just relax. We'll have a nice cup of tea and figure out what to do next. Oh, first things first. Susan? You should go out and put the minibus in the garage. Just in case anyone drives by.'

'I . . . yes. Good thinking, Ethel.'

'Jill?' Ethel went on. 'There's a couple of sets of car keys up there. Go and have a look in the garage. Hopefully there's a motor out there that goes with one of them.'

'I'm not helping you steal someone's car!' Jill said, standing up, banging her tiny fists on the table. 'This has all gone too far! We —'

'Jill,' Ethel said, 'do you really want to go to jail? We're going to lay low here until it's dark then we can —'

'Ah, guys?' Julie said.

The three of them turned to look at her. She was holding up a banded bundle of notes. She had taken a lot of the money out of the holdall and stacked it up in little towers on the kitchen counter. There was still quite a lot in the holdall itself.

'These are fifty-pound notes. There are a hundred of them in each of these bundles.'

'How many bundles did we —' Susan said.

'A little over eight hundred,' Julie said. 'Maybe more. I think a few fell down inside the minibus.'

'But, that, that means . . .' Susan began, trying to do the arithmetic in her head.

'Yeah,' Julie said. 'A little over four million quid.'

There was a pause, silence in the kitchen.

'We're all millionaires,' Ethel said.

'Fuck,' Susan said.

A huge crash interrupted their reverie.

Jill had fainted again. It was suddenly lovely and quiet.

TWENTY-SEVEN

It was quiet too in Chief Inspector Wilson's office. He took a deep breath and looked around the room. Sergeant Tarrant stood to the side of his desk. Wesley and Boscombe were sitting opposite him, Boscombe looking like he'd gone a few rounds with a fairly talented boxer. (A scenario Wilson would have paid good money to see.) Wilson pressed his fingertips together and leaned forward.

'So, Boscombe,' he said. 'To recap.' Tarrant swallowed. This was a very bad sign indeed. 'Having actually walked in on the robbers planning the heist and yet failing to notice that anything was amiss – indeed you went so far as to dance a . . .' He scanned the report in front of him.

'A tango, sir,' Tarrant said.

'Yes, thank you, Tarrant, a *tango* with one of them, you were then bested in hand-to-hand combat by a wheelchair-bound octogenarian before engaging in some kind of crazed, *Miami Vice*-inspired high-speed pursuit along the hard shoulder of the A23. A pursuit you lost to a gang of OAPs driving a Cancer Care minibus and somehow destroying a £50,000 patrol vehicle in the process?'

'Yes, sir, but —' Boscombe began.

Wilson held up a finger, silencing him, and turned to Tarrant. 'Sergeant Tarrant, make sure the mugshots and licence plates go out to media and all stations ASAFP please.'

'Yes, sir.'

'The thing is, sir —' Boscombe tried again.

Again Wilson silenced him. This time simply by shaking his head, closing his eyes and emitting a low, strangulated moan. 'Boscombe,' he continued, 'if these ladies escape then I am afraid we will become that most dreaded of clichés — "the laughing stock of the entire force". You understand that this is not the note I wish to sound prior to my retirement?'

'No, sir.'

'However, before retiring, I can promise you that I will find the time to make certain that you spend the next ten years back in uniform policing non-league football matches. Are you with me, Boscombe?'

'Yes, sir.'

'Dismissed, gentlemen.'

Wesley and Boscombe stood up. The front of Boscombe's ripped trousers fell open and hung down in a loose panel, exposing his crotch. His tired, purple Y-fronts glared a few feet in front of the chief inspector's face. Wilson found himself staring at this sight with incredible, unfathomable sorrow.

Boscombe followed his gaze. 'I . . .' he began.

Wilson waved a hand limply. 'Get out, Boscombe,' he sighed.

TWENTY-EIGHT

The reactions to the news that all four of them were now millionaires was as varied as their individual characters. Ethel found a bottle of gin and began singing football songs, displaying particular energy and relish on a simple number that consisted of one line, endlessly repeated, that went 'MY OLD MAN SAID BE AN ARSENAL FAN. I SAID FUCK OFF, BOLLOCKS, YOU'RE A CUNT.' This would ordinarily have been enough to send Jill into a screaming fit. Mercifully, however, she was in the garden praying to God for forgiveness, so Ethel's songs were not, currently, a problem. Julie's mind was going a mile a minute. 'Right, stay here tonight, get home early in the morning, book the cruise, day ashore in wherever, money in a suitcase under the bed, find a nice place to rent, ooh I've been looking in the Algarve by the way, for three thousand quid a month we'll get an absolutely *gorgeous* place, pool, jacuzzi, four bedrooms, mind you, if we're taking it long-term and offer to pay in advance in cash we'll probably get an even better deal, say 2,500 a month? That's what – about thirty grand a year? Three hundred grand over the next ten years between the two of us, barely 150,000 each out of a million, Susan! Or we could . . .'

Susan was thinking, staring at the money, stacked in neat piles on the counter, a mini Manhattan skyline of cash. She looked at Julie.

'. . . go further south, somewhere more remote, you'd get even more for your money, but would you want to –'

'Julie?'

'What?'

From along the hallway they could faintly hear Ethel, now singing the words *'You root through a dustbin for something to eat, you find a dead rat and you think it's a treat, IN YOUR LIVERPOOL SLUMS!'*

'What about Nails?'

'What about him?'

'What happened to him?'

'Oh God, who knows? He fell asleep, wandered off, whatever. All I know is that we're both a few hundred grand better off because of it.'

'Hmmmm.'

'What are you worrying about?'

'If he got arrested . . .'

'He'd never tell them anything. He's old school.'

'Yes, Julie, he's also completely demented. Who knows what he might say?' In the kitchen they heard Ethel turning the TV on, getting what sounded like MTV, some pop-dance number. She started singing along. Surprisingly her voice was sweet and she knew all the words.

'Look, darling,' Julie said, coming over and sitting next

to her on the low Laura Ashley sofa, 'we didn't get arrested. We've hidden the bus. We have a safe place for the night. No one knows who we are and within forty-eight hours we'll be long gone from this miserable bloody country with a million quid each to see out our lives with. So will you please cheer up?'

Right on cue there was a crash, the door swinging open, and Ethel came trundling into the room, suddenly looking very sober. 'Turn the telly on. Now.'

Susan grabbed the remote and jabbed the 'ON' button: a property programme, a soap opera, flipping through the channels fast, getting to BBC1, the news at six and the announcer saying, '. . . *in a daring daylight robbery of the Lanchester Bank in Wroxham this afternoon. One of the robbers was apprehended during the raid while two of the others are believed to be a Mrs Susan Frobisher, aged fifty-nine, of Wroxham . . .'* A picture of Susan, taken from the programme of last year's Wroxham Players production of *The Merry Wives of Windsor*, came up on the screen and she screamed. Susan actually screamed.

In their flat in Crouch End, Tom and Clare Frobisher were just sitting down to their tea when the same image appeared on the screen. Tom dropped his plate of lasagne and teetered backwards.

'. . . *and a Mrs Ethel Merriman . . .'* A photo of Ethel came up, taken from her resident's file at the care home. 'Oh, I hate that fucking photo,' Ethel said. (And she pictured the relish with which Miss Kendal surely handed it over.) '. . . *believed to be in her late eighties and until recently a resident of Glade Side retirement home, Wroxham.'*

In the rec room at Glade Side a huge cheer went up

among the more sentient of the residents as Ethel's face replaced Susan's on the screen.

'OH MY GOD!' This was Jill, who had just walked back in from the garden to see Ethel's face on the screen.

'SHHHHH!' Julie yelled. 'SHHHH!'

'. . . *two other unidentified persons are also being sought in connection with the crime. They were last seen driving this vehicle* – here a photograph of the Cancer Care minibus in happier times flashed up – '*in a southerly direction on the A23 outside Wroxham this afternoon. If you have any information regarding the whereabouts of these people, or the vehicle, Dorset police are urging you to please come forward and call the number at the bottom of the screen. Members of the public are advised not to approach the suspects as they are believed to be armed and extremely dangerous. Sports now, and in . . .*'

Julie turned off the television, leaving only the sound of Jill crying. Susan had her head in her hands.

'Oh Jesus,' Julie said.

'Well,' Ethel said, 'that's certainly put the rapist among the virgins.'

'We're going to jail,' Jill wailed. 'I knew it! I knew I shouldn't have listened to you lot! I was just trying to help Jamie. Oh, Jamie, I'm sorry, love. What have I done?'

Susan got up and paced up and down near the window. A beautiful evening out there, swallows darting, willows weeping.

'What are we going to do?' Julie said.

'We need to get out of the country,' Ethel said.

'How? You saw that,' Julie said. 'They'll be watching the airports, ferry terminals, everything. It'll be a . . . whaddya call it, in the films? An APB?'

'Well, we need to think, love,' Ethel said.

'What's there to think about?' Jill cried. 'We're finished.'

'How did they get you two and not us?' Julie said.

Susan strode across the room and picked up her purse. In the folds she found what she was looking for. She turned to the others. 'Jill, get a hold of yourself. We're not going to jail. Julie, go and check that estate car in the garage has petrol in it. As soon as it's dark we're getting out of here. Now, one of you, give me a fucking phone.'

The three of them looked at her, astonished.

TWENTY-NINE

Terry Russell sipped his gin and tonic and looked out of the clubhouse window over the eighteenth green, dusk just beginning to creep over the shorn grass and his golfing partners' chatter providing a pleasant background burble. It had been a good day. He'd made a nice up and down out of the bunker on fifteen, sunk a fifteen-footer early on, on four, for a birdie, and split the tenth fairway with a huge, booming drive. Some nice moments to add to the highlights reel all golfers carry in their heads. On top of all this he'd banked a profit of almost fifty grand this morning on that load of refrigerator parts they'd shipped to Murmansk. A very nice earner the whole thing was turning out to be. As the gin flowed pleasantly through his veins, the steaks were ordered and the scorecards totted up, Terry took a moment to reflect: life was good.

A vibration against his left thigh interrupted this meditation. Discreetly, below the table (no mobiles in the clubhouse), Terry slipped his phone out and looked at the screen. An unknown number. Mmmm. Chances were it was another one of those fucking automated sales calls. *'Barclays, HSBC . . . have you been mis-sold payment protection?'*

But it might be one of the Russians. A problem with the load? Or customs? In Terry's view it was always better to know than not know. 'Excuse me a second, lads,' he said, standing up. He thumbed the green 'answer' button as he stepped through the French windows onto the patio and said, 'Hello? Terry Russell.'

A little over three minutes later Terry hung up, thinking to himself *well, I'll be damned.* You never knew, did you? When it came to women, you could always be surprised. And this one, oof. What? – over forty years he'd fancied this one. He checked the time on his huge IWC chrono-meter, a fiftieth birthday present to himself. (And could that really be a decade ago? Where did it go once you got past forty?) Doable. Very doable. Smash his ribeye down, tell the boys something urgent had come up at the office, pick up some champagne on the way. Might even have time to swing by the house and grab a little blue tab of Viagra from his bedside drawer. Well, Terry reasoned, she'd sounded fucking keen. And at his time of life you didn't want to take any chances. Had Terry just turned his head the other way a few moments ago when he was sipping his G&T, had he looked across the bar to where the local news was playing silently on the big TV screen, rather than looking out across the golf course, he might have rethought things. But such are the teeny blips of serendipity that make life so interesting.

THIRTY

Boscombe sighed and leaned back in his chair. Wesley took a tiny sip on a plastic cup of coffee that had long gone cold. They both regarded Nails, sitting across from them in the interview room, his arms folded, a bloodstained bandage turbaning his head.

'I told you, copper,' Nails said. 'You won't find these gels. They gone bye-bye. *Adios*. Nails trained them himself.'

'Who were the other two?' Boscombe asked again. 'Julie Wickham? Julie Wickham was one of them, wasn't she?'

The first two had been easy enough. Ethel, that old bitch in the wheelchair, well, he'd never forget that sticker, or those mad eyes, fixed on his as she tried to rip his balls off. Susan Frobisher? As soon as he'd placed Nails he'd remembered her house that day. A swift search warrant this afternoon, kicked the door in, neighbours staring in amazement, and they found a bunch of it in a drawer: photos of the bank, drawings of the layout. But the other two . . . the other two who'd been there that day, with the dancing thing. One of them they had no idea. She'd been a mousy type. Forgettable. The other one, Boscombe was pretty sure, was this Julie Wickham.

The woman at the care home – right old boiler called Kendal – said Wickham and Ethel were thick as thieves. She'd resigned a few days back. Thrown a bucket of piss over Kendal into the bargain. Fitted the description of the woman who'd pretended to be holding the dance class that day too. But fucking Wilson wouldn't let them officially add her name to the list of suspects until they had something concrete. Too scared of getting sued probably.

'Fuck yourself, copper,' Nails said.

'Why do they call you Nails?' Wesley, changing tack.

'Gangland thing,' Nails said. 'See these?' He held his hands up, showing them the palms, with two white scar marks in the centre of each one. Wesley nodded. 'I crucified myself once.'

'Why?' Boscombe said.

'Had to prove a point.'

Wesley frowned. 'How did you get the second nail in?'

Nails thought for a moment. 'It wasn't easy, son.'

'What was the point?' Boscombe asked.

'What point?'

'The point you were trying to prove.'

'Old Nails can't remember.'

'You can't remember why you crucified yourself?'

'Who crucified himself?' Nails said, puzzled.

Boscombe banged his head on the desk.

THIRTY-ONE

'*The look, of love, bum ba ba . . .*' Terry sang along softly to Burt Bacharach on the Bang & Olufsen as he busied himself around the cabin of *The Geraldine*, getting things ready. He'd named the boat after his second wife. Ironically, it had been one of the very few things she hadn't wanted in the divorce. She'd hated the sea, Gerry. He'd always meant to rename the boat, but it was a bit of a palaver and it seemed to be destined to be one of those things he never got around to. He was wearing only a short kimono and his hair was wet from the shower. (If she found all this just a little too much too soon he had his backstory all ready: *I got here early and decided to just dive over the side for a quick night swim in the harbour. Well, it's such a beautiful evening. The water of the Channel this far south is lovely, but why don't you help yourself to a glass of champagne while I go and put some clothes on? Unless . . . maybe you fancy a swim too? Then we could jump in the hot tub to warm up? The contrast is wonderful.*) He turned the bottle of Perrier-Jouët in the black plastic bucket, scrunching it further down into the ice, cold beading forming nicely around the neck now. He turned the music down slightly and the lighting up a little. Didn't want to be *too* obvious.

The walnut panelling in the twenty-foot-by-twelve lounge shone softly, the lighting was still low enough to be flattering to the off-cream velour upholstery, to not show its multitude of sins, the *CSI*-style stories it could tell of previous conquests. He loved it on the boat. She was a fify-footer with twin outboard motors and could make fifteen knots easily. Terry had taken her as far down as San Sebastián, him and a couple of business colleagues, a weekend of drinking and tapas.

He opened the folds of the kimono a little at his chest, exposing the mat of silvery hair – it was a warm night, the sea breeze coming in gently from the window he'd just opened – and was just beginning to worry that she'd misunderstood his very clear directions to the mooring (maybe he should have waited until she actually got here until he popped the Viagra) when he heard the glass door somewhere behind him begin sliding softly open. Terry turned, a smile already on his face and the words 'Hello, Susan . . .' already forming on his lips.

He stifled a scream.

There, framed in the doorway, leering at him, was an ancient woman in a wheelchair. She licked her lips, staring straight at his crotch as Terry instinctively belted the kimono tighter, covering his rapidly shrivelling erection. 'Come on, love,' the leering hag said, 'let the dog see the bone.'

'What the fu—' Terry began.

Susan Frobisher appeared behind the woman. 'Terry! I'm really sorry –'

'Jesus Christ, Susan, what on earth –'

'Hi, Terry!' another woman said brightly, a woman he vaguely recognised, stepping into the cabin now too. 'Julie? Julie Wickham? We were in chemistry together? In fourth year? Mr Edwards's class?'

'I . . . what?' Terry stammered.

'I'm terribly sorry for the intrusion,' a fourth woman was saying as she too, incredibly, stepped inside. 'What a lovely boat.'

Susan was coming towards him now, stepping across the thick carpeting, saying, 'I really am very sorry, Terry, but I need to ask you a favour.'

'A favour? What? Who are these people? What the fuck is going on, Susan?'

'Language!' he heard one or other of the women say in the background.

'I need you to take us all to France. Now. Tonight.' She was standing right in front of him, looking him straight in the face. Christ, she was still beautiful.

'FRANCE?' Terry said, the words registering. 'Are you out of your mind?'

He heard the whine of an electric motor, the trundling of tyres on carpet from somewhere behind Susan and suddenly the barrel of a shotgun appeared and was levelled at his face.

'We really have to insist,' the woman in the wheelchair said, cocking the weapon. Terry's eyes widened and his hands instinctively went up in the air. 'Please,' he said. 'Please don't kill me.'

'For God's sake, Ethel! Stop that!' Susan said, slapping the shotgun away.

'All right, calm down,' Ethel said. 'It's not even loaded.'

'You haven't seen the news then?' Susan asked.

'No . . .'

'Come on, let's have a chat.'

She took the bewildered Terry's elbow and led him through the doorway down to the bridge of the boat. From behind her as she closed the door she heard the crack of a champagne cork.

Ethel.

THIRTY-TWO

'Fuck, Susan. I mean, *fuck*. Jesus fucking Christ.'

They were sitting in the two big swivel chairs in the bridge and Susan was pouring him a second brandy. 'Yes, you already said that, Terry. It's not very helpful.'

'What were you thinking?'

'I really don't know. I couldn't possibly explain it.'

'And now you want me to help you out? To run you to France? You couldn't enter a port legally. You'd have to be dropped somewhere off the radar. I mean, you're fugitives. Proper bloody fugitives. No, forget it. Then I'm caught up in all this too. You're going to get caught anyway, you know. You may as well turn yourselves in and give back the money to try and offset your sentence because –' He paused. 'How much did you get anyway?'

Susan was staring out at the moonlit water, not really listening to him. 'Terry?' she said.

'What?'

'Why did you come to Barry's funeral?'

'I . . . I wanted to pay my respects.'

'Rubbish. You couldn't stand him. Even at school.'

'That's not true! I . . .' He trailed off, not really having the heart for a spirited defence of Susan's late husband. 'I just thought you could have done better than Barry Frobisher.'

'You were right. It's just a pity it took me a lifetime to find that out.' She stared into her brandy, swirling it in the balloon.

'Come on,' Terry said. 'Your life isn't over yet.'

Susan looked up at him. There was this sharpness, a kind of cunning, in her gaze that he'd never seen when they were younger. 'No, it bloody well isn't,' she said. 'Now listen, getting to France? That isn't the half of it. How dodgy are you, Terry?'

'What?'

Susan slapped him across the face.

'JESUS!' Terry yelped. 'What was that f—'

'Stop being coy. You're the richest man I know and you got rich doing something utterly nebulous called "import and export", something no one who knows you really knows anything about, so I'm assuming, I'm hoping, you've rubbed up against some pretty rough sorts along the way. We are in a life-and-death situation here and I need you to be honest with me and try to help me. We need new identities, passports, so we can get out of France somehow.'

'And go where?' He rubbed his stinging jaw.

'I'm not sure yet. Maybe South America.'

'Why do you think I'd know anyone like that?'

'Money.' Susan shrugged.

'Eh?'

'To answer your earlier question, how much did we get? Roughly 4.2 million pounds. We'll pay you a hundred grand for the ride to France and another hundred if you can put us together with someone who can help us out with the passports. Come on – two hundred grand for a quick trip across the Channel and a phone number?'

Terry gestured around him, at the yacht. 'Do I look like I need money, Susan?'

'No. I don't think you'll do it just for the money.'

'Why then?'

'Well, because you have a massive crush on me and you have had since you were fifteen years old.' Susan took a big gulp of brandy, shuddering just a little as it went down. She really was acquiring a taste for the stuff. 'That's why.'

'You've changed,' Terry said, smiling.

'Good.'

They sat there in silence for a moment, just the sound of the water lapping at the hull.

Finally Terry sighed. 'God help me. There's a jetty outside Le Havre. Private beach belonging to a friend of mine. I can drop you there. If we leave soon we'll be there around dawn.'

Susan smiled at him and raised an eyebrow as if to say 'Go on . . .'

'And . . . there's a guy I know. Down in Marseilles. Russian. I can put you in touch. I'd be surprised if – properly compensated of course – he couldn't help you out on the passport front.'

'There's also the question of how we get the money out of France and into South America . . .'

'Well, in my experience, in the import and export game,

no one tends to care too much about what you take *into* South America. But you'll need to watch yourself, Susan. With the Russians? These are genuinely scary people.'

'So am I,' Susan said, draining her brandy and smacking the glass down. 'I'm Mrs Fear.'

Terry laughed, shaking his head. 'Well,' he said, 'this certainly wasn't how I saw this evening going.'

'How *did* you see it going?' Susan asked.

'You know . . .' Terry grinned.

Susan stepped close. 'Play your cards right. It's a long trip, isn't it? I'm assuming there's a cabin somewhere on board this thing?' She pecked him on the cheek. 'Right, I'm just going to check on the girls.'

Terry swallowed and poured himself another brandy.

THIRTY-THREE

'Boscombe?' he slurred.

Detective Sergeant Hugh Boscombe had been woken by the ringing phone just after dawn on the day following the robbery. He'd fallen asleep at his desk, after another gruelling interview with Nails had failed to yield a single plausible lead. (It had occurred to Boscombe that Nails wasn't so much hard – which would have been a more credible explanation of his nickname than the self-crucifixion story – as completely deranged. From minute to minute he literally didn't know if it was New York or New Year. Didn't know whether he wanted a shite or a haircut.)

The chain of events that led to the phone ringing went as follows . . .

At 5.15 a.m. a local beat officer in Sands, a PC Graham Denning, had noticed a navy-blue Mercedes estate parked on a side road near the marina. The interior light was on as someone had failed to close the rear passenger door properly. On closer investigation he noticed the keys were still in the ignition. He called the car in and discovered that the licensed owners were a Mr and Mrs Torbet of Densmore Cottage, Buttcombe, near Wroxham and that the car had not been reported stolen.

Denning might ordinarily have left it there – who was to say that the owners had not simply been enjoying a lively night out at the marina club and had left their keys in the ignition and been a little careless with closing their doors? It was their battery to run down as they saw fit after all. But something made him think twice. 'Wroxham'. News of the bank job there had been all over the area yesterday. As had two CCTV clips currently enjoying huge viewing figures on YouTube: one of an old-age pensioner running full tilt into the plate-glass window of a Morrisons supermarket and the other of this Dorset CID bloke screaming his head off as he got dragged by his nuts behind a Cancer Care minibus. Then Denning noticed something on the floor of the rear seat, behind the driver's seat. Something pink and waxy – a single fifty-pound note.

At 5.25 a.m. Denning rang the cop shop in Buttcombe and suggested someone swing by Densmore Cottage and see if either Mr or Mrs Torbet were home. Around half an hour later, at approximately 6 a.m., a PC Willard did just that and discovered that they were not in residence. But a glance through the garage window revealed a vehicle that most definitely did not belong there – a Cancer Care minibus.

Beyond himself with excitement, Willard rang Wroxham CID and asked to be put through to the detective in charge of the Lanchester Bank robbery investigation.

And so, at 6.10 a.m., Boscombe found himself yawning and saying 'Boscombe' into the phone.

He listened.

He scribbled down a licence plate and an address.

He ran across to Wesley's desk and thumped him awake with the words 'Come on, Wesley! We're on!'

THIRTY-FOUR

Julie woke up with an ugly, thumping headache and looked around her. She and Jill had both fallen asleep at either end of a long, L-shaped sofa. Jill had fallen asleep long before Julie had of course. The reason for Julie's late night was snoring like a bandsaw, slumped upright in her wheelchair across from her, still cradling a near-empty bottle of gin. Christ, where did Ethel put it? Did it go into those huge, surely hollow, legs? Or perhaps into an unspeakable reservoir hidden somewhere in the wheelchair itself? Julie knew that Ethel came from a hard-boozing generation – drinks at lunch, pre-dinner cocktails, nightcaps and so on – but even so, it was impressive. Julie surveyed the four empty champagne bottles on the table, the opened bottles of vodka and gin, and tried to reconstruct the night before.

When it had become clear that Terry was going to have his hands full driving the boat and Susan had sloped off to bed early, she and Ethel had gone a bit nutty and made free with their unwilling host's (extensive) drinks cabinet.

Even Jill had accepted a couple of small sherries, for 'her nerves'. What was the last thing she could remember? Her and Ethel dancing to 'Do Ya Think I'm Sexy'? Julie spinning Ethel around in her chair?

She picked up a bottle of water near her and drained it, sluicing it around her cracked, sandy mouth, feeling the steady motion of the big boat, the rumble of the engines somewhere beneath them.

She looked out of the porthole and saw a pale band of pink light on the horizon, the sun about to come up. Feeling guilty she reached into the pocket of her jeans and took out a roll of fifties. She counted off ten of them and put them on the low coffee table. Should about cover what they'd drunk. She smiled. When had she last been able to do something like this? Drop five hundred quid on booze? Fifteen years ago or so, during the brief heyday of the boutique? Or even further back maybe, in London, in the eighties, when she'd been hostessing . . .

'Bloody hell,' a voice said. Julie looked up to see Susan in the doorway, looking fresh as dew. 'What happened in here?'

'Ech. All got a bit celebratory, I'm afraid. I'll tidy up in a sec.' But Susan was already advancing into the room, picking up glasses and straightening chairs.

'I'll do it,' Susan said. 'Why don't you go and have a shower? We're nearly there.' She was humming a little song to herself while she tidied, all brisk, businesslike and cheerful.

Julie looked at her, narrowing her eyes. 'What's up with you?'

'What?' Susan said.

Julie kept looking at her.

'What?'

'Something's up. You're a bit . . . cheery for someone on the run.'

'Can't someone wake up in a good mood?'

But Susan was colouring a little, plumping up cushions, keeping herself busy, not meeting Julie's gaze. There was something almost . . . girlish about her.

'NO WAY!' Julie exclaimed.

'Shhh! Shhhh! Shurrup!' Susan came at her, flattening a hand over her mouth, pushing her back into the sofa.

'Susan Frobisher! You dirty —'

'SHHHHHH!'

'Filthy —'

'*Please,*' Susan begged.

'OK, OK. Get off me.' Susan let her go and they looked at each other for a moment. Then they both burst out laughing, Susan burying her head in her hands. 'Details,' Julie said. 'I want details.'

'Oh, later. OK?'

'You and Terry Russell . . .'

'Oh God . . .' Susan said.

'I bet it was something after Barry . . .'

'Right, enough. You'll wake the others.

'Wait till Ethel hears about this. Oh, this is huge.'

'Oh, do shut up,' Susan said, sitting down next to her and blowing some hair out of her face. They continued talking in whispers, even though Ethel's snoring would have drowned out a shouting match between two drunken town criers. 'I just thought, what the hell. You know? And you know something else, Jules? I woke up this morning thinking, what the hell. Not just about Terry, but about all of it. It's done. No one died. We're not in jail. Yet. So, let's just take it as it comes.'

'Bloody hell. New Susan, new danger?'

'Something like that. Come on, you,' Susan said, standing up. 'Shower. Blow the cobwebs away.'

'What about this pair?' Julie gestured to their sleeping colleagues.

'Oh, let's give them another fifteen minutes. Ethel needs it and Jill's probably going to start crying again the minute she wakes up.'

'So what are we doing? I mean, where are we going?'

'I've got it all figured out.'

'Oh, really? How so?'

'I'll tell you over breakfast in Le Havre.'

'You and Terry Russell. Bloody hell.'

Twenty minutes later the four women were standing on a small wooden dock in the chill dawn wearing fleeces, jeans and trainers (except for Ethel who had a tartan shawl over her lap) they'd purloined from Densmore Cottage. The money was now in two smaller holdalls – again both courtesy of Densmore Cottage – which were hanging from Ethel's wheelchair. (It had surprised Susan how much money you could fit in a fairly small space. You could easily carry a million pounds in fifty-pound notes as part of your baggage allowance on most airlines.) Ahead of them the jetty led to a shallow beach, which gave onto a forest, where a path led up through the trees. Terry made sure the stern line was tied tight and walked towards them, wiping seawater off his hands on the backs of his thighs. Susan had crouched down and was rooting through her bag for something or other so Julie put her hand out and he took it.

'Sorry for, you know . . .' she said, amazed to feel she was fighting to keep the smile off her face. What was she – fifteen again?

'Yes, been an odd . . . reunion,' Terry said.

'Thanks, Terry,' Julie said, thinking, *I bet it has*.

'Christ,' Ethel said from somewhere behind them, 'was I drinking petrol last night?'

'Yes, thank you very much, Terry,' Susan said, oddly formal suddenly as she stood up.

'Are you heading straight back?' Julie asked him.

'Nah. You have to file a route plan with the harbour master. I thought, for your sakes, just in case anyone comes asking, that it might be best if I didn't answer that completely truthfully. I said I was taking her down to Cowes for a few days, so I'd better show up there at some point . . . shit.'

Susan was holding out a housebrick of fifties.

Terry looked at the money and smiled. 'No,' he said. 'You keep it.'

'Please, Terry,' Susan said. 'It's the least we –'

'Honestly, no.'

'Why ever not?' Julie asked.

'Well, for one, I don't know that it's a great idea for me to have a hundred grand in stolen banknotes on me –'

'They're used. Unsequenced,' Ethel piped up. 'Totally untraceable.'

'And two,' Terry continued, 'I think you girls are going to need every single penny you've got, whatever happens.'

'Are you sure?' Susan said.

He nodded. 'Just follow that path there.' He pointed to

the treeline. 'Takes you up to the main road, then you're a mile or so to the outskirts of Le Havre.'

Julie got a little peck on the cheek before she turned round and started pushing Ethel off up the dock, towards Jill. Susan smiled at Terry, the sun rising behind her, making her hair glow golden. He handed her a piece of paper. There was a name, 'TAMALOV', in block capitals and a Marseilles phone number underneath it. 'Like I said, watch yourself. These are pretty serious guys.'

Susan nodded. 'Thank you, Terry. Look, if there's any comeback on this, if anything happens, just tell them we stuck a bloody shotgun in your face and made you do it.'

'Never,' Terry said. 'They'll never break me.' They shared a laugh. 'See you round,' Terry said.

'Sure,' Susan said as she embraced him.

THIRTY-FIVE

'Yeah, lemme see. Yeah, here . . .' The man pointed a pudgy, bacon-fat-smeared finger at an entry in the ledger on his desk. 'Just one. *The Geraldine*. Owned by a Mr Terry Russell. She went out at 1.15 this morning.' With a title like 'Harbour Master' Boscombe had been expecting something a little more grand: a sea-captain type, in his sixties, in uniform. Not this fat boy of about thirty in a sweatshirt and jeans, a half-eaten bacon roll in his fist and a can of Monster energy drink at his elbow. They were in an office on the top floor of the marina, with a grand view of the rows of boats tied up at the wooden dock, their masts bobbing and swaying gently in the soft breeze. Boscombe could see Wesley through the window, walking along the dock, nosing around.

'And who was on board?'

'Come on, mate. What do you think this is? Captains don't have to file passenger lists with us, just routes.'

'So where was it going?'

The guy consulted the ledger again. 'Ah . . . Cowes.'

'Where's that?'

'Isle of Wight.'

'Right. And what do you know about this Terry Russell guy?'

'Eh? How do you mean?'

'I mean, where's he from? What kind of man is he?'

'God, I don't know. No idea where he's from. I've seen him around. Silver-fox type. Rich enough I should think. Lives in Sands.'

'Can you get on to your oppo at Cowes and see if the boat arrived there?'

The guy sighed through a mouthful of bacon and bread. Christ, Boscombe was starving. It was after nine now. They'd been on the go since six and not had a bit of breakfast. Not even the offer of a cup of tea from this shiftless, greedy bugger in front of him. The same shiftless, greedy bugger who was now saying, 'I *could* do that. Are you telling me I have to?'

Right, Boscombe thought. That was about enough. 'Listen, *mate*,' he said, leaning down closer to the guy. 'The people I'm after are wanted in connection with a very serious armed robbery. If I have to I'll get a court order and have five officers down here up your chuff all day while they tear this place apart. I might also pass your details on to the audit section of the HMRC for a laugh. I'm hoping I won't have to do any of that because I'll be so pleased with how you went out of your way to help us.'

'OK,' the harbour master said, suddenly quiet and offended. 'There's no need to threaten me. I'll call them.'

'Thank you very much.'

He started dialling and Boscombe walked over to the other side of the room and looked back down at the harbour. He could see Wesley, talking to an old boy who was loading fishing gear into one of the smaller boats. The guy was pointing up along the dock. Wesley had the notebook out. Boscombe looked out to the green swell of the sea. Beautiful day it was shaping up to be – as hot as yesterday probably. *They were here*, Boscombe thought. He knew it. He had a hunch . . . fuck Wilson – sometimes you just *knew*. Something caught his eye and he looked back down to see Wesley was waving to him to come down to the dock, making a thumbs-up gesture and pointing to the old guy. In the background fat boy was saying, 'OK. I see. Ta, Chris . . .' Boscombe made a 'gimme two minutes' gesture through the glass to Wesley and turned round as the phone clacked back down into the cradle. 'No,' the harbour master said. 'Not arrived yet.'

'How long would a trip like that normally take?'

'Well, depends how keen you were to get there. A boat like *The Geraldine*, two big engines . . . if you wanted to you could do it in five or six hours.'

'Where else could you go from here in that time?'

'A bunch of places. Up the coast to Scotland. Across to France . . .'

France.

'OK. Thank you for your help. I'll be back in a minute. Could you dig out this Terry Russell's contact details for me? Thanks.'

Without waiting for an answer Boscombe turned and went out of the door into the fresh air, into the cries of gulls, and started down the wooden staircase that led to the dock. He took his mobile out and rang the station, getting old Sandra. 'Sandra? Find out whatever you can about a Mr Terry Russell from Sands. Yeah, Terry like Chocolate Orange, Russell like Harty. Great. Ta.'

'This is Mr Amerhill,' Wesley said, indicating the kindly old man smiling beside him as Boscombe marched over, hanging up. 'He slept on his boat last night.'

'Did you now?' Boscombe said.

'Yeah. Woke me up they did. Around midnight. One of them was in a wheelchair.'

Boscombe smiled and looked out to sea.

THIRTY-SIX

Had Detective Sergeant Hugh Boscombe been able to see far enough, if he could have gazed right across the English Channel and over the small private beach, through the trees and down the road to an outside table at a cafe on the outskirts of Le Havre, he would have seen the following . . .

Jill Worth: stirring her tea, ignoring her fruit cocktail and looking around twitchily, nervously, as if she fully expected a mob of policemen to descend upon her at any second. Ethel Merriman: hung-over, taking a break from greedily attacking a huge plate of steak and eggs to slather butter onto yet another piece of toast. (Indeed she seemed to be challenging the very physical laws regarding the amount of butter a piece of toast could hold.) And Susan Frobisher: working on her second (delicious) *café au lait* while she studied the map of France spread out on the table in front of her. After Susan had laid out the basic plan – to get to Marseilles and obtain new identities from Terry's guy, dropping the unwanted and unsuspected Jill off at an airport somewhere en route – Julie had grabbed a croissant and headed off to take care of their transport needs. They'd seen a big second-hand car dealership back along the road, near the little bureau de change where they'd changed a couple of thousand pounds into euros.

'Something inconspicuous,' Susan had stressed.

She stared down at the map. There seemed to be two possibilities to get to Marseilles from here . . .

They could either head south-east towards Paris and then straight down to Provence, through the interior of the country, or go directly south from here, past Le Mans, until they picked up the coast road around Rochefort, then down towards Bordeaux before heading east past Toulouse and Montpellier. The Paris route was faster, but would take them closer to big cities and major roads. The coastal route was more indirect – about thirteen or fourteen hundred kilometres as opposed to one thousand – but more discreet. Lovely scenery too, Susan imagined. It'd probably be Nantes airport for Jill if they went down the coast and Lyon if they went through the interior. Either way it was at least a two-day drive. Then, when they got to Marseilles, even if they hooked up with this Tamalov right away, it'd take, what? – probably a couple of days to arrange new identities for her, Julie and Ethel. She couldn't see them getting out of France for at least four or five days. Possibly longer if . . . but no. She was getting ahead of herself. Just deal with getting south for now and the rest of it would all unfold. She was surprised at how calm she felt. It was like she'd told Jules – right now they had the money and they weren't in jail. They'd take it from there.

Susan put the route dilemma to the group. The response was predictably diverse.

'Ooh, let's take the coast!' Ethel said. 'So beautiful. I haven't been down that way in years.'

'Oh, for goodness' sake!' Jill snapped. 'Can't we just go the fastest way? I feel sick to the pit of my stomach every single minute.'

'You should eat something, love,' Ethel said, punting another huge forkful of near-raw meat glistening with egg yolk into her mouth.

Jill turned away and said, 'Yes, and some of us might want to be a bit more careful about what we put *into* our bodies . . .'

'You know what I'd like put into my body?' Ethel said.

'Ethel . . .' Susan said warningly.

'Don't,' Jill said. 'Just don't.'

'A great, big . . .'

'No!' Jill squeaked, stuffing her fists in her ears.

'. . . massive, hard . . .'

'Ethel . . .' Susan on autopilot, not even looking up from the map.

'CO—

TOOT TOOT! Two short blasts on a car horn caused the three of them to turn round.

'Goodness,' Jill said.

'Ding-dong,' Ethel purred in Terry-Thomas fashion.

'What the fuck?' Susan said.

'Language!' Jill said.

There was Julie, sitting grinning at the wheel.

The wheel of a bright red Porsche Cayenne 4x4.

'What the fucking fuck?' Susan repeated, coming towards

her and sticking her head in the open passenger-side window, the car reeking softly of expensive leather. A top-of-the-range satnav screen glowed in the middle of the dashboard. Julie, in her sunglasses, one arm resting on the sill of the open driver's window, looked like Susan hadn't seen her looking in years, since the glory days of her late forties, when she was bombing around town in her SLK.

'It was a steal, honestly!' Julie said. 'Two years old. Only 20,000 miles on the clock.'

'Not the money, Julie – I said *"inconspicuous"*.'

'It's got tinted windows,' Julie offered helpfully. 'And we needed something with enough boot space for the wheelchair. And look!' She pulled on the handbrake and pressed a button. The satnav image switched to a local TV channel. 'It's got a telly and everything!'

'A telly!' Ethel shouted in the background.

'Great,' Susan muttered, walking around the gleaming car, taking it in. 'We can watch some French TV while the arresting officers go about their business . . .'

'Oh, don't be such a killjoy,' Julie said.

'Can we please just get going?' Jill said. A few other diners were staring. For once Ethel found herself in complete agreement with her.

'Yeah,' Ethel said, folding her last piece of steak up inside a slice of bread and stuffing it first into a napkin and then into her handbag. 'Let's fucking rock. Oi! *Garçon! Le addition see vous play!*'

THIRTY-SEVEN

Two hours forty-five minutes.

That's how long it had taken. Just two hours and forty-five minutes from first contact with the police to full confession.

Terry had been surprised to see the police car already waiting at the end of the jetty as he tied the boat up in Cowes that afternoon, just after breakfast time, at 10.04 a.m. He'd sailed north-west from Le Havre, running the twin diesel engines pretty near full, making the crossing to the Isle of Wight in just over four hours. The local officers had immediately placed him under arrest (suspicion of aiding and abetting fugitives) and taken him to the main police station along the road in Ryde, there to await the arrival of the CID detectives from the mainland, the detectives who were now sitting across from him in the interview room. Boscombe and Wesley had arrived at 12.11 p.m. After Terry tried to stonewall them for a while the older, fatter one revealed that they knew he came from Wroxham, that he'd gone to school with two of the women and that an eyewitness had seen them boarding his yacht the previous evening. Then he mentioned (among other things) the possibility of involving the HMRC if he didn't tell them everything he knew right now.

That did it. Those four letters were far more terrifying to Terry Russell than any threat of prison. His personal tax arrangements were a byzantine labyrinth of illegality that would have made Bernie Madoff himself crap his pants. At 1.49 p.m., just after lunchtime, his belly rumbling, he fell forward onto the interview table and started sobbing.

'They stuck a bloody shotgun in my face . . .' Terry wailed.

THIRTY-EIGHT

'Lunch lunch lunch lunch, lovely lunch, wonderful lunch . . . lunch lunch lunch lunch, lovely lunch, WONDERFUL LUNCH! Lunch lunch lu—'

'For God's sake, Ethel – will you PLEASE SHUT UP?!' Susan screamed in the front passenger seat. Jill had her fists in her ears. Only Julie, smiling quietly to herself at the wheel as miles of French motorway slid by, seemed impervious to Ethel's constant demands for lunch, expressed here by simply singing the word 'lunch' over and over again in the manner of 'spam' from the Monty Python song. (A reference that only Julie understood. Susan and Jill both just thought she'd gone mad.) They were heading south on the E402, towards the forest d'Ecouves. They still hadn't resolved the east-then-due-south or the due-south-then-east dilemma.

'Oh, come on!' Ethel said. It's gone two! It's time for *lunch.'*

'I suppose we could stop at a services . . .' Julie said, looking sideways at Susan for approval.

'Fuck that,' Ethel said.

'Ohhh . . .' Jill moaned in the manner of someone who has been burned with a hot needle.

'I want a proper lunch,' Ethel said. 'With *wine*. I want a cassoulet, a soufflé, coq au vin, pommes doff-in-fucking-vase. In a restaurant or pub. I mean, look at the gorgeous bloody day. We're in *France* and you buggers want to go and sit in some sordid *petrol station*. Are you all mental?'

'We're on the bloody run, Ethel,' Susan said.

'Have you any idea how big this country is?' Ethel said. 'I mean, I still can't believe we got out of Britain, but we did. Now? Now they're looking for a needle in a haystack.'

'She's got a point,' Julie said.

'I am rather hungry . . .' Jill piped up. She'd hardly touched her breakfast.

'OK, OK, fine,' Susan said. 'Let's take the next turn-off and see what we can find then . . .'

'Yes,' snarled Ethel, smacking a fist into her palm.

'Okey-dokey,' said Julie, flipping the indicator on, getting into the right-hand lane as a sign saying 'Courtomer' came up ahead. 'I have to say,' she added, cornering, taking the bend at a good clip, 'this baby handles like a *dream*.'

Fifteen minutes later, less than ten kilometres up the road, they saw a big restaurant, with lots of tables outside, families, kids playing, many trucks and cars parked in its dusty gravel car park.

'This do?' Julie asked the group.

Shortly after that and a second round of drinks was appearing on the table – red wine for Ethel and Susan, mineral water for Jill, a Coke for Julie – while they all attacked their food. They were at a wooden table outside, the warm sun coming through the fabric of the umbrella above them. Susan took a sip of wine and managed to convince herself for a second that they were all on a lovely holiday. 'Oh God,' Ethel said, wiping her mouth, 'you should all try this rabbit. How often do you see rabbit on a menu back home these days?'

'Ugh,' Jill said.

'The chicken of the fields, love,' Ethel said. 'How's your salad? Your nice, safe, boring –'

'I don't think it's boring to eat healthily actually,' Jill said, blowing her nose.

'What's that you're having?' Ethel asked Susan.

'Chicken?'

'For Christ's sake, you two. Boring. You could have had the steak frites rare then I could have got in on it when you didn't finish it.'

'You shouldn't eat all that red meat,' Jill said, pouring herself a glass of Badoit. Ethel was making good inroads into the house red.

'Bollocks,' Ethel said. 'I'm what – twenty years older than you? I eat what I like and I'm never ill. Look at you. You eat nothing but lentils, kale and blueberries and you're forever broken in two with some dreary cold or other.'

'You're never . . .' Jill said. 'Ethel, you're in a *wheelchair* because you're so fat.'

'Oh, you're having a go at the disabled now?' Ethel said. 'I have luxurious bones.'

'Bones? Your problem is –'

'Will you two cut it out?' Susan said, catching herself on the verge of saying 'you kids are driving me crazy'. 'Julie, we need to figure out a route to get Jill to an airport and get her money into that account for Jamie.' No response. 'Julie?' Susan said, turning.

Julie was staring intently across the picnic area to a table quite far away, right by the fence bordering the car park. There were two people at the table: a man and a girl. The man was in his fifties, unshaven, with greasy hair. Swarthy. Greek or maybe Spanish. He had mirrored shades on and was wearing a black leather waistcoat over a T-shirt that looked stuck to his body. His food lay untouched in front of him as he drank pastis. The girl was very beautiful, very *French*, Julie thought, with her black, bobbed hair. She was wearing denim shorts and a skimpy vest top. She was attacking a plate of frites hungrily. She was also, maybe, seventeen years old. His daughter? The man reached for the bottle of pastis on the table and poured a splash into her glass, adding a little water. There was a rucksack at the girl's feet too, Julie noticed. She also noticed the wolfish way he looked at her when she bent her head down towards her food. No, probably not his daughter . . .

'Julie!' Susan smacked her on the leg.

'Ow! *What?*'

'What are we going to do about getting Jill's money for Jamie back?'

'We need to do five transfers of 9,999 each, to avoid the revenue, remember? So we'll need to find five Western Union type places between here and Marseilles and do it that way.'

'Oh God, that sounds like a lot of . . . exposure,' Susan said.

'She could always just get on a plane with fifty grand in her handbag,' Ethel said.

'You know what?' Jill said. 'I don't care about getting caught. As long as Jamie gets his operation I don't care what happens to me after that.'

'All right, Spartacus . . .' Ethel said, signalling the waiter, holding up the empty bread basket.

The man was Spanish. She had a little Spanish but he spoke with a thick regional dialect and she couldn't understand most of it. She was grateful for the food though and kept her head bent down over her frites. The liquor burned in her belly as she caught him saying something about the border, about dropping her off near there. It would do, it would be far enough. She had a little over seventy euros on her. Enough for a night or two somewhere cheap en route and a bite to eat here and there. What . . . what was he . . . topping her glass up again? She didn't refuse. It would help. She smiled back and said, 'Merci.' He, oh. She stiffened at his touch but she didn't pull away. From here to past Toulouse for free? She couldn't pass that up. Not that it would be exactly 'free' of course. What was?

No. Definitely not her dad, Julie thought, cutting into her chicken, stealing sidelong glances, only half listening to the chatter of the others. Touching her leg under the table like that? Definitely *not* a fatherly gesture. Julie felt the hair on the back of her neck prickling. There was something in the way the girl was reacting – about the way she was neither encouraging nor repelling the attentions of this man who was, now she thought about it, surely old enough to be her grandfather – that was gradually enraging her. It was the fact that she seemed to be acquiescing. Reluctantly and with a weariness far beyond her years, she was simply acquiescing. Beside her Susan had the map out again and was trying to pinpoint the names of a few likely towns between here and Marseilles, places big enough to transfer money but not so big that they'd have a major police presence. Oh, what now? He was . . .

The man was standing up and picking up the bill . . .

He muttered something about paying the bill and pointed over to the car park, to where a huge sixteen-wheeler truck was parked. She smiled and thanked him. He went off and she glanced around, suddenly feeling very young and vulnerable on her own at the table, out here in the world without an adult. So what? Fuck it. Grow up, Vanessa. She picked up her glass and tossed the last two inches of the liquorice-flavoured spirit down her throat, shuddering, hating the burn but needing it.

That look around — the neediness with which she pounded that drink. Julie recognised it. She saw herself, over forty years ago, 1972, 'Layla' on the jukebox and scared in a pub in Brighton. Nowhere to stay. And then later, in that terrible flat. She could hear the sea . . .

Needing the burn to get through that which lay ahead. To let her . . .

Enough.

Maybe it wouldn't be so bad. Maybe he . . . A shadow fell over her and she looked up. An old lady, maybe sixty, was standing there.

'Hello,' said Julie.

'Hi,' the girl said uncertainly.

'Do you speak English?'

She nodded.

'I saw your rucksack,' Julie went on, bright and friendly. 'My friends and I are sitting over there . . .'

The girl followed the wave of her hand and looked over to where three more old ladies were sitting under an umbrella at a wooden table. One of them, she was in a wheelchair, waved back cheerily.

'Anyway, we were wondering where you were headed?'

The girl looked from Julie to the other old ladies and back again. 'Uh, south . . .'

'Really? What a coincidence! Us too! How about we give you a lift?'

'A *lift*?'

'Sorry. A ride?'

'I already have a ride,' the girl said, nodding vaguely in the direction of the restaurant.

'Yes,' Julie said. 'I really don't think that's the kind of ride you want, darling.'

Who was this mad old cow? 'What do you know about it?' the girl said, an edge in her voice.

'Well.' Julie reached over and picked up her empty glass. She sniffed it. 'I think I might be in a better position to judge than someone who's drinking spirits at two o'clock in the afternoon. Do we normally drink at lunch? Or are we trying to get our courage up?'

The girl looked away. She went to say something and hesitated. 'He . . . he said he's a nice guy.'

'Really?' Julie said. 'Because you know by law they're obliged to tell you they're rapists and paedophiles before you get in the truck.'

The girl didn't quite understand the sarcasm here. But she caught the key words in the sentence – 'Rapists. Paedophiles.'

'I'm old enough,' the girl said. 'I know what I'm doing.'

'Really?' Julie said again as there came a grunt from behind her, another shadow falling over the girl, and then the man was standing there, a fistful of change in his hand. '*Que?*' he said to them.

'Hello!' Julie said, extending her hand. He did not take it. 'I'm an old friend of her mother's. Thank you so much for your kind offer but she's going to come with us.' Julie again jerked her thumb towards their table and the trucker glanced over towards Susan, Ethel and Jill. 'Go on,' Julie said to the girl. 'Scoot over there.'

The trucker stepped in closer to Julie. 'Hey,' he said, English now, with a thick Spanish accent. 'Fuck off, Granny.' Something about the edge, about the urgency of the menace in his voice, seemed to make the girl's mind up for her. She grabbed her rucksack. 'Go on now . . .' Julie said to her. 'Take these.' She handed the girl the keys to the Porsche, 'and give them to the lady about my age, with the blonde hair, and tell her to go and start the car . . .'

The girl bolted off towards the other table.

The trucker took another step towards Julie. He might only have been seven or eight years younger than her. What were they thinking, these men? 'Right,' Julie said. 'That's enough.' She stepped towards him, both of them very close now. She could smell the pastis on his breath. She'd noticed the bottle was half empty. 'I think you're very lucky if she's fifteen,' Julie whispered. 'Do you really want to make a scene? Here? With all these people?' She gestured around them, at all the families. 'You really want me to call the gendarmes? When you've been drinking prior to taking a minor in your truck? Are you sure?' The guy's English was weak, but he caught enough. *Gendarmes* was enough. He stood there. Staring her down, saying nothing. 'OK then,' Julie said. 'Drive safely.'

She turned on her heel and walked off towards the car park, to where she could see the others already clambering in, Susan starting the engine.

Julie closed the door behind her and turned round. The girl was in the back between Ethel and Jill. 'You've met everyone?' The girl nodded, smiling for the first time. 'Good. I'm Julie by the way. What's your name?'

'Vanessa. Nice car.'

'It certainly is, Vanessa,' Susan said. 'Now, buckle up.' Susan nudged the accelerator and, with a splash of gravel, they were out of there.

THIRTY-NINE

Now this was the business, Wesley thought. *This was what you joined the fucking force for.* They were in the back of a Hampshire Police car, doing ninety along the coast road out of Ryde, the Solent flashing by on their left, the siren whooping and gulping, blue lights strobing. Boscombe was next to him, on the phone to Wilson, having to shout.

'That's what he said, sir, near Le Havre. Seems like they kidnapped him.'

Wilson had Boscombe on the speakerphone in his office, Tarrant sitting opposite him. 'OK. Listen, the French police will meet you,' Wilson said. 'They have jurisdiction obviously –'

'What, sir?'

'I said – Oh, for Christ's sa— WILL YOU TELL THEM TO TURN THAT BLOODY SIREN OFF?'

'Siren? Oh, hang on.' Wilson could hear a muffled conversation then, mercifully, the siren stopped. 'Sorry, sir?' Boscombe said.

'The French police have jurisdiction. They've assured me of their full cooperation, Boscombe – they're issuing descriptions to airports, stations, hotels and the like – but they'll have to make any arrests and then we'll have to follow the normal extradition procedures. Do you understand?'

'Of course, sir.' Boscombe turned to Wesley and made a face, both of them getting thrown to their left as the car pulled off the main road, cornering at speed, turning inland, away from the sea.

'You are simply there to provide a positive identification on the suspects and to assist with inquires. One other thing, Boscombe . . .'

'Yes, sir?'

'For goodness' sake try to remember that you're representing your country while you're over there, will you?'

'Of course, sir. I'm not –'

'Goodbye, Boscombe.' Wilson hung up.

'Fucking . . .' Boscombe said, giving the finger to the silent mobile phone.

'Here we are, Sarge,' Wesley said, excitement in his voice.

Boscombe looked up to see they were pulling up on a grass airstrip, next to a gleaming red-and-white, two-engine Cessna, the pilot already in the cockpit, wearing Aviator shades and headset, flicking switches above his head.

'Now this is a bit more like it, eh, Wesley? *This is a bit more bloody like it!*'

FORTY

Susan followed the bend round the corner, driving slowly in the dark (Julie was right, it was a *lovely* car to drive), as the rain that had moved in over them came down sideways through the headlight beams. She was listening to the harsh, robotic voice of the satnav, telling her – again – to do a U-turn and wondering how she could have got so lost. According to the map the motel they were looking for should have been right back there. (Only fifty euros per room per night the guidebook had said.) She glanced around the car – everyone was fast asleep. The car clock said 9.03 p.m. It had been a long day though, and next to no sleep the night before. No, for the *two* nights before. '*Re-routing*,' the posh, clipped male voice said to her again.

'Oh, will you shut your bloody face?' Susan hissed at it, pulling over onto the grass verge – a field on one side of the road and a brick wall with a large black metal gate on the other.

'Mmmm?' Julie stirred sleepy-eyed in the passenger seat.

'Oh, sorry, love. I didn't mean to wake you . . .'

'Where are we?' she said sleepily, stretching. 'Christ. It's pissing down.'

'You're telling me. We're somewhere off the . . .' Susan started scrolling back and forth through screens on the satnav.

'I'm bursting for a slash . . .' came Ethel's voice from the back.

'Understood, Ethel, we're just a tiny bit lost at the moment,' Susan said.

Jill yawned and opened her eyes too, leaving only Vanessa, their waif and stray, asleep between her and Ethel. 'Poor lamb must be exhausted,' Jill said.

Julie was now looking at the map she had spread out on her lap. 'Oh, how have we wound up here? This is nowhere near that motel!'

'Goodness, I'd love a bath,' Jill said.

'I don't know!' Susan said. 'This bloody thing kept telling me to do a U-turn and then saying it was re-routing and then –'

'You should have –'

'I didn't want to wake you!' Everyone tired, gritty and crotchety.

'I am bursting for the loo . . .' Ethel said.

Vanessa began to stir.

'Oh,' Jill said dreamily, absently, 'doesn't that look lovely?'

'What looks lovely?' Susan said irritably, easing the hand-brake off, preparing to pull away.

'There,' Jill repeated, pointing through her window, wiping condensation off it.

The others followed her pointing index finger, squinting through the rain. Just across the road, on the brick wall, so overgrown by ivy that it was almost invisible, was a brass plaque. On it, in elegant black script, were the words 'L'Auberge du Château' and, below them, five magical stars. Susan pressed the handbrake on with her foot. Jill was actually pointing through the black metal gate next to the plaque. Just visible through the bars and the rain was a long gravel drive, leading to the soft lights of a huge country house, just visible in the distance, in the dusk. Jill sighed, yawned, and said, 'Wouldn't it be lovely to be able to afford to stay somewhere like that?'

The others just turned and looked at her.

'Oh, you daft cow,' Ethel said.

A little less than an hour later and a very jolly scene was playing out in suite 14 of L'Auberge du Château.

Julie and Vanessa — champagne flutes in hand — were dancing to Motown blaring from the wall of matt-black hi-fi equipment hidden discreetly in a huge oak armoire. Susan was bouncing up and down on an enormous four-poster bed while Jill moved around cooing and ahhing over various pieces of antique furniture. Ethel presided over all of this from her power corner of the jacuzzi, where she was, for the third time in thirty minutes, torturing room service: up to her fleshy neck in hot bubbling water, a telephone clamped to her ear, a glass of neat gin next to her and — fairly incredibly — a large Cohiba cigar clamped between her teeth.

'No,' Ethel said. '*Non.*' She removed her cigar. 'It was two lobster, one salad and two steaks. You're out of the

Beluga? Dearie me. OK, I suppose we'll make do with the Sevruga. Great, thank y— Oh! Do you have any oysters? Great, we'll have two dozen. And you'd better bring us a couple more bottles of champagne. Yes, 14, thank you. *Merci!*' She hung up and raised her glass to the dancing Julie.

Oh, I've missed this, Ethel thought.

FORTY-ONE

'Christ, Sarge,' Wesley said, 'my neck's as stiff as a bloody board.' He craned his neck, turning his head slowly in circles, trying to loosen up the muscles.

Boscombe grunted, in no mood for pleasantries. He returned to staring at the noticeboard in front of them at Le Havre police station, the usual stuff: Rabies, Pickpockets, Smuggling. What the hell were they doing keeping them waiting this long? Didn't these French bastards know he was pursuing dangerous fugitives? He looked out of the window, into the dawn glow of a beautiful morning, the streets and trees still soaking wet.

Despite its promising start, their glamorous trip hadn't quite panned out as they'd hoped. The light aircraft had flown into very heavy weather somewhere over the Channel. A torrential rainstorm had settled over north-eastern France, making it impossible for them to land here in Le Havre. They'd had to fly nearly a hundred miles north up the coast to get around it. Then the driver assigned to them had been given the wrong instructions and had taken them to Calais by mistake. By the time they realised this it was one in the morning.

They'd had to spend the night sleeping in the cells at the cop shop (the bloody cells!) before a drive down here in the first rays of dawn. They were both tired and cranky and the only sustenance they'd had was a sticky bun and a cup of what Wesley said was very nice coffee at 5 a.m. (Boscombe would take his word for it – it just tasted like bloody coffee to him.) And what the fuck was going –

Ah, a door opening and a guy was coming out, looking at them. He was handsome in that uselessly French way, tall and slim, wearing a nice, well-pressed suit, in stark contrast to the wrinkled and rumpled English detectives in front of him. 'Detectives Wesley and . . . Bostock?' he said in a thick French accent.

'*Boscombe*. Detective *Sergeant* Boscombe,' Boscombe corrected the man.

'Ah, excuse me. I am Lieutenant Pourcel.' He extended his hand and they shook. 'Please come into my office.'

About bloody time, Boscombe thought to himself.

They settled themselves in front of Pourcel's desk (the desk, like the office, was spotlessly clean and tidy) as he apologised for their delayed arrival here and offered them more coffee, which Wesley gratefully accepted.

'To move on to the matter in hand . . .' Boscombe said.

'Ah yes, of course,' Pourcel said, opening a file in front him. 'Your . . . robbers.' Here he allowed himself the flicker of a smile. *Cheeky fucker*, Boscombe thought. 'I must say, it is quite a story, no? These old ladies.'

'Yeah, that's not the word I'd use . . .' Boscombe said.

'*Oui oui*. I have seen your video. On YouTube?' Pourcel pursed his lips, making an 'Ow!' expression. 'Are you . . . is everything OK with you?'

'Yes, everything's fine thank you, Lieutenant.' *That fucking video. How could he get it removed?* 'As I say, to return to the matter in hand, you have their descriptions there, so what we going to do?'

'In terms of?'

'In terms of stopping them. Have you plans to put officers at stations and airports? Or . . . or checkpoints on major roads?'

'Checkpoints?' Pourcel almost laughed. What did this guy think this was? *The Day of the Jackal*? 'Well, let's be reasonable, gentlemen. These women have a twenty-four-hour lead on you at this point. From where they landed, in twenty-four hours you could go almost anywhere.' Pourcel gestured to the large map of the region on his wall. 'North towards Belgium, or east to Germany, or south into Spain. Indeed, if they got to a border or an airport before we received the information that they were even in France then there's a very good chance they're not in the country any more. I should tell you that this is the view my superiors are inclined towards . . .'

'Eh? Why?' Boscombe asked.

'Extradition, I suppose,' Wesley said, slurping his *café au lait*.

'Exactly so,' Pourcel said. 'Extradition from France to the UK for non-French citizens wanted in connection with a crime is a very straightforward matter, just paperwork really. From here, however, you can get to any one of a number of countries where the extradition procedure is a great deal more difficult.'

'Yes, of course, obviously, obviously,' Boscombe said. *Fucking smart-arse Wesley, showing him up.* 'I mean, it just seems a bit premature of them to be jumping to any conclusions just yet.'

'Well, you know the powers that be, Sergeant. The cost of doing something like you suggest would be enormous. It would be something that would only be considered in the gravest of circumstances. Terrorism. National security. What have you.'

'I'm afraid in my country,' Boscombe said, trying to control his temper, 'armed robbery is considered a very serious crime.'

'As it is here. But let us talk frankly for a moment. These old women are not hardened professional criminals. They will slip up soon enough, no?'

'So that's it?' Boscombe said. 'You're going to . . . what? Just sit around and wait?'

Pourcel sat back in his chair and looked at the map again as he thought for a moment. 'I really don't see what we can do beyond what we're already doing, Sergeant. We're having your descriptions faxed to hotels, train stations and airports along all the major routes. You never know . . .'

Boscombe snorted. 'Sounds a bit bloody hopeful to me . . .'

'Well, hope is important, no?' Pourcel stood up and shot his cuffs, indicating that the meeting was over.

'And you'll still give us a car in the meantime?' Boscombe asked. 'To allow us to make our own inquiries?'

'But of course. It will be my pleasure.'

'Thanks for the coffee,' Wesley said.

'Fucking dirty bastard garlic-shovelling wine-guzzling collaborator Nazi Charles Aznavour-loving bastards,' Boscombe was saying a few minutes later as he stood in a distant corner of the police station car park looking at their loan car. It was possible that, at some point in its long history, Citroën may have made a smaller model than the one they were looking at now, but it was very doubtful.

Boscombe kicked a tyre and sighed. 'This is taking the fucking piss, Wesley. Taking the fucking piss.'

'Let's just make the best of it, eh, Sarge?'

'Sergeant Boscombe?' an English accent said from behind them. They both turned to see a woman and two men approaching. The woman was young, in her mid-twenties, and very attractive. One of the men was holding a fur-covered pill-shaped thing on a long pole, the other one had a very professional-looking video camera on his shoulder.

'Who wants to know?' Boscombe said.

'I'm Katie Slater.' The girl extended her hand, grinning. 'We're from Sky News. We wondered if we could have a quick interview about the old ladies you're after.'

'You came out from England for this?' Wesley asked.

'Nah.' Slater shook her head. 'We were up in Calais covering another story. Immigrants. But our editor asked us to come up here to try and get on this.'

'Interview, eh?' Boscombe said.

'Ah, Sarge,' Wesley said, 'maybe we should refer this to the press office back home, eh?'

'Oh, come on, guys!' Slater said. 'By the time we deal with all that . . .'

'Right enough, Wesley,' Boscombe said, already straightening his tie. 'With all the help we're getting from them bastards in there . . .' He jerked his head towards the police station in the distance. 'They get Sky in France, don't they?'

Slater nodded. 'Oh yes. Everywhere.'

'A little publicity might help,' Boscombe added, smoothing his hair out.

'I really don't think this is a good idea, boss,' Wesley said. 'Maybe we should run it by Wilson first. Put in a quick call. See what he says at least.'

'You seem to be under the illusion that this is a democracy, Wesley . . .' Boscombe was still irritated by the smart-arsed bugger's 'extradition' point back in the office. The guy hoisted the big camera up on his shoulder. 'Is here OK?' Boscombe asked.

'That's great, Sergeant,' Slater said. 'Aren't the French authorities being very helpful then?'

'You're joking, aren't you?' Boscombe said. 'Helpful? Listen, love . . .'

He went on, at length, blissfully unaware that the interview had officially begun.

FORTY-TWO

Julie poured herself some more coffee and sat back in the comfortable, deeply padded lounger to better admire the view from their balcony, though 'balcony' was perhaps underselling it. 'Terrace' would be more accurate. How she'd loved checking in last night, when the receptionist said they only had a two-bedroom suite available and it was 2,500 euros a night and Susan had airily waved a hand and said, 'That'll be fine.' In the distance, over fields and woodland, Julie could just make out the spires of the great cathedral at Chartres. A misted dawn hung over the fields, dew dripping from branches in the grounds. A huge spread of food lay in front of her, the continental breakfast buffet for five, delivered by room service: two great silver pots of coffee, beakers of orange and grapefruit juice, baskets of croissants, muffins and pastries, a fruit bowl glistening with perfectly ripe strawberries, apples, bananas, grapes and slices of mango on crushed ice. There were even a couple of splits of champagne and a jug of sieved peach juice to make Bellinis. It was strange, given everything – the crazy risks, the great danger they were in, the uncertainty that lay ahead of them – but she felt happier at this moment than she'd felt in years.

She turned as she heard the door sliding back behind her. Vanessa was there, sleepy-eyed and wrapped in a huge towelling robe much too big for her, her tangled, thick black hair a very close match to Julie's own. (*Yes, admit it. She looks very like you imagined she'd look, doesn't she?*) 'Morning, gorgeous!' Julie said. 'Come and have some breakfast.'

'*Merci.*' Vanessa took a pastry from the nearest basket and sat down cross-legged on the nearest lounger. 'Ooh, my head!' she said as she nibbled it.

'Oh, stop it,' Julie said. 'You're too young to have a hangover. But, yes, quite a party, wasn't it?' Behind them, in the living room, an array of bottles and plates covered much of the available surface space. At the prices she'd clocked when tearing things out of the minibar last night Julie reckoned they'd easily spent the cost of the room again in extras.

'*Oui,*' Vanessa nodded. 'Thank you, Julie. For the rooms, the food and everything.'

'Our pleasure, love.'

Vanessa nodded at the food, the view, everything, and said, 'You must have very important jobs back in England, you and Susan, no?'

'Well,' Julie said, 'I had a little bit of a career change recently.'

'What do you do?'

Julie thought. 'I'm in . . . asset redistribution.'

Vanessa nodded thoughtfully, chewing.

'So,' Julie said, taking a plump strawberry, 'my turn. What do you do?'

'This and that . . .' Vanessa grinned.

'I see. And where are you headed exactly?'

'To Cannes. A friend of mine is working there, as a dancer, in a nightclub. She's making a thousand euros a week!' Vanessa's eyes widened at the very thought of this inconceivable amount of money.

'Really?' Julie said, taking a bite of the strawberry, looking out over those fields. 'She must be a very good dancer . . .'

'*Oui,*' Vanessa said, nodding innocently. They both sat and chewed in silence for a moment. 'Julie?'

'Mmmm?'

'Why did you come over to me? At the restaurant?'

'Well,' Julie said, smoothing out her robe, 'let's just say I got into the wrong car myself a few times when I was your age. Which brings me on to my next question . . . how old are you?'

'I'm seventeen.' Vanessa held her gaze. Julie waited. 'Next birthday,' Vanessa said, looking down. In a slightly edgier voice she added, 'I suppose you want to know what I'm doing away from home.'

Julie sipped her coffee and took a moment. 'I think, when you want to, you'll just tell me.'

They took the view in for a moment. The birdsong. 'My mother,' Vanessa said. 'She ran away when I was little. I live with my dad. He works all the time.'

'Does he know where you are?'

'He thinks I'm staying with some friends. He won't even notice I'm gone.'

'I'm sure that's not true.'

'He wants me to get a job, to bring some money in.'

'Is that why you're going to do this . . . dancing thing?'

Vanessa shook her head, picked at her croissant. '*Non*. I want to go to college next year. To art school? But he says we cannot afford it. I thought if I did this for the summer, saved some money . . . I could get a place of my own.'

'Chriiisssttt,' a voice said behind them. They turned to see Ethel, wheeling herself into the doorway. 'I feel like I've been gang-banged by the Foreign Legion. Come on, coffee. Now.'

Vanessa and Julie laughed.

Meanwhile, in the bedroom, Susan was on the phone. '*OK*,' the thick Russian accent on the other end said. '*The day after tomorrow. Call me again when you're in town.*' Click.

It had been a very short conversation. Thirteen words in total on his part, if you added the gruff, suspicious 'Hello' he'd said when he answered. Susan replaced the receiver on the bedside phone. She walked through the living room, smiling slightly shamefully at the two maids who were cleaning up the considerable mess from last night, and out onto the balcony where Julie, Vanessa, Jill and Ethel were gathered around a spread-out map of France. 'Well,' Susan said, 'I just spoke to our Mr Tamalov.'

'And?' Ethel said.

'Not the friendliest chap in the world. He said he'll see us day after tomorrow. I've to call him again when we get to Marseilles.'

'Great,' Julie said. 'I've got it all figured out. Basically –' she pointed to a main road heading south on the map – 'if we keep on this road until we get to Lyons and then follow signs for the Riviera and Cannes we can –'

'Cannes?' Susan said.

'Yeah, that's where this little one is headed . . .' Julie indicated the grinning Vanessa.

'Ah.' Susan hesitated. 'I really think we need to get to Marseilles as soon as possible.'

'It's fine,' Julie said. 'It's not much more than a couple of hours out of our way.'

'Yes, Julie, but you seem to be forgetting that –'

A knocking on the door interrupted her. Susan walked back through the living room towards the door. *Bloody hell! Am I the only one who gives a shit that we're on the run with millions in stolen cash?* She peered through the spyhole and saw another maid standing there. She opened it. 'May I check the minibar?' she said.

'Please,' Susan said, standing aside and holding the door open for her. She closed it and turned round to see Julie standing in the hallway, with her arms folded.

'What's the matter with you?' she whispered.

'Julie, I just think we need to keep our heads down and get straight to Marseilles.'

'It's a tiny detour!'

'Be that as it may, I just don't think we should be gallivanting all over the place. We're fugitives for God's sake!'

Julie stepped closer to her, shutting the door to the living room, to the maids. 'Look Susan, that kid is headed down there to a "dancing" job that I'm pretty sure involves the kind of dancing you do on your back. If we just –'

'Julie?' Susan said, taking her by the shoulders.

'What?'

'Is this, the reason you're so . . . is this to do with . . . you know?'

'What? No.' Julie looked away. 'No.' She bit her lip. 'I just . . .'

'Oh, darling.' Susan embraced her. 'Fine. We'll go to Cannes.'

'You're a doll,' Julie said. She pecked her on the cheek and hurried back to the balcony to pass on the good news.

FORTY-THREE

Tom and Clare Frobisher were preparing their evening meal, a spartan supper of baked potatoes, quiche and an undressed lettuce-and-tomato salad. The kind of unloved meal favoured by people who do not much care for food.

The past forty-eight hours had been about the most surreal of their lives. On top of still grieving over the untimely and sordid demise of his own father – dying in agony impaled upon a monstrous sex toy – there had been the police and then the reporters for Tom to deal with. The questions. Had he known his mother was an armed robbery mastermind? Did he have any words for her? Would he be sure and inform the authorities if she made any attempt to contact them? And so on and so on. There had even been the implication, from a surly, stressed, overweight detective, that he might have been in on it!

Clare went through to the sitting room carrying water glasses and jug (they rarely drank) to the tiny dining table set for two (they never entertained) and looked at the television, which was, as always, on with the sound turned down, and there he was, standing in what looked like a car park – the very detective who had implied that Tom might have known something about the robbery.

The words *'investigation into Wroxham OAPS bank robbery moves to France'* were rolling in yellow ticker across the bottom of the screen. 'Tom!' Clare cried towards the kitchen as she picked up the remote and thumbed the volume up. Tom entered just in time to hear Boscombe saying, '. . . *and I just want to say to the suspects, to these women, if they're watching this, give yourselves up now before things get out of hand . . .'*

'That's that cheeky bugger who interviewed me!' Tom said.

'Shhh,' Clare said, turning the volume up further as, on the screen, the image cut to a female reporter – young and pretty – saying, *'Earlier in our interview Sergeant Boscombe expressed some frustration with the cooperation of the French authorities in the investigation . . .'* and the picture cut back to the detective.

In his office at Wroxham police station Chief Inspector Wilson was taking care of some paperwork when Sergeant Tarrant knocked on the open door. 'Ah, sir,' he said, 'you might want to come out here and take a look at this . . .' Wilson sighed, laid down his pen, and followed Tarrant out into the main office area, where a group of uniformed officers were gathered around the television set that was usually tuned, with the sound down, to either BBC News 24 or Sky News. Several of the officers were looking expectantly, nervously, at Wilson, who was immediately displeased when he saw Boscombe's face on the big screen. Tarrant had paused the image using Sky Plus, catching Boscombe in mid-flow, his lip curled and his eyes half shut, the overall effect suggesting Boscombe was either about to sneeze or was in the middle of having a stroke. Wilson was only mildly disturbed by how entertaining he found the prospect of the latter scenario. This tiny shred of humanity towards the detective sergeant lasted as long as it took Tarrant to hit the 'play' button on the remote control and for Boscombe's voice to come rumbling from the speakers. '*Cooperation? Listen, love,*' he said, '*it's a joke. You know what this country would be without us, don't you? The German bloody Riviera, that's what. And another thing . . .*'

Wilson closed his eyes, tilted his head back, and began taking a deep breath in through his nose. Somewhere behind him he heard Tarrant say, 'I'd best get onto the press office right away, eh, sir? Start the old damage control.'

'Yes, thank you, Sergeant,' Wilson said in a voice slightly higher than his usual register.

FORTY-FOUR

Wesley couldn't believe it. The quality. There were crusty bread sandwiches with delicious fillings, bowls of crisps, leafy salad. There was a bubbling pot of coq au vin and several different types of cheese. All of it fresh, none of it sweating in cellophane and looking as though it had travelled four hundred miles down the M6. You could even, had you not been on duty, get wine or a glass of beer. All of this, right here in a service station! God, these people knew how to eat all right. '*Merci*,' he said as the man behind the counter finished spooning thick French onion soup into his bowl. Though over here, Wesley thought, they probably just called it onion soup.

'Here, Wesley, give us one of them pie things.' He turned to see Boscombe behind him in the queue, his tray loaded high with the closest things he could find to the food of his native land: three fat sausages, a mound of chips, a white bread roll and a can of Coke. He saw Boscombe was gesturing to a plate of game pies and dutifully passed one over. 'You sure you don't want some of this soup?' No wonder about 60 per cent of the sarge's diet consisted of Ex-Lax. That he munched Rennies like Tic-Tacs.

'That muck?' Boscombe said. 'Looks like bloody watery gravy.'

Wesley sighed. 'It's your colon, Sarge. Look at that mackerel pâté.'

'Oh, shut it, Nigella,' Boscombe said as his mobile started ringing. He jabbed a pudgy finger at the green button. 'Boscombe?'

'Can I speak to the racist halfwit who's made sure that I won't be leaving the office before ten o'clock tonight?'

'Sorry, sir?' Boscombe said, covering the mouthpiece and mouthing 'Wilson' at Wesley. 'I'm not following you.'

'THE GERMAN RIVIERA!' Wilson screamed. Boscombe pulled the phone back from his ear as though it had bitten him. 'ARE YOU OUT OF YOUR BLOODY MIND, BOSCOMBE?'

Boscombe gestured to Wesley that he should pay for the food and walked away quickly. 'Sir, if I may. I didn't know the sneaky bastards were filming then! I didn't think we'd started!'

'This is why you are *not allowed to talk to the press, Boscombe.*'

'I thought a little, um, exposure, might do the investigation good, sir.'

'Ah,' Wilson said. 'I see what's happened here. I see. You know where all of this went wrong, Boscombe? At exactly the moment you allowed yourself a "thought". Or whatever passes for thinking inside that hollow, redundant cavity you carry around on top of your shoulders. I don't even know why I'm surprised any –'

Boscombe pulled the phone away from his ear and did the 'yak yak' thing with his hand to it for the benefit of Wesley, who was looking over while making his way with their trays to an empty window seat.

'. . . and if I get one more surprise like this, Boscombe, I swear to God I'll —'

His phone started vibrating again. He looked at the screen, another call, on the other line. 'Sir?'

'Don't interrupt me, Boscombe! I've already had the superintendent, the Foreign Office and a couple of tabloid newspapers on the phone about all th—'

'Sir, I have a call on the other line. It might be about —'

'Any inquiries, interview requests, requests for state-ments, all of them go through the press office from now on. Got that, Boscombe?'

'Yes, sir. I'll call you later.'

'And Boscombe?'

Fucking hell. 'Yes, sir?'

'I want you to call your liaison officer there in France and make a personal apology ab—'

'Yes, sir. Bye.'

Boscombe hung up and punched the button for the other line. 'Hello?'

'Sergeant Boscombe? It's Lieutenant Pourcel.' Pourcel's tone was clipped and formal. 'We've had some information, regarding your ladies. Do you have a pen?'

'Sure, go ahead.' Boscombe uncapped the biro and hovered it over the back of his hand. When he had finished writing he said, 'Thank you, Lieutenant.'

'Yes,' Pourcel said. 'Good luck. We are not all so bad here on the German Riviera.'

'Ha. Look, about that, I –'

Click.

Touchy French bastard, Boscombe thought.

Brilliant. Just bloody brilliant, Wesley thought, hovering the second spoonful of soup under his nose, the vapour misting warmly on his face as he inhaled rich broth, cracked black pepper and melted cheese. Suddenly a hand was smacking on his back, sending the soup spattering all over the table, and Boscombe was saying, 'Come on, lad,' as he grabbed a couple of sausages off his own plate.

'Eh? What?'

'Just south of here, a couple of hours away.'

'B-but my lunch?'

'Have it in the car!' Boscombe said over his shoulder, already striding towards the exit.

'It's *soup!*'

'You should have thought of that before, Wesley, shouldn't you?'

Boscombe jumped into the driver's seat and they came tearing out of the service station car park. Well, 'tearing' as fast as the tiny engine would allow. Wesley screamed what he screamed every single time Boscombe took the wheel – 'SARGE! ON THE RIGHT! *ON THE RIGHT!*' Boscombe slewed the car back over onto the correct side, even managing the good grace to mutter a cursory 'sorry' this time.

FORTY-FIVE

A jazz station played softly, Stan Getz doing something or other, and Susan enjoying the peace and quiet as she drove. The sound of four different sets of snoring wove their way in and out of the music – little Vanessa's not much more than breathing, there in the middle of the back seat. Julie's an even, nasal rasp from the passenger seat next to her, her jacket bunched up and tucked under her head, against the glass. Jill emitted a tiny, regular whistle through her front teeth on the exhale while the entire concerto was underscored by Ethel's fat bass notes. They'd made very good time, hardly any traffic at all, straight down something called the N85, all the way south from Grenoble. Although she feared she might be a little lost now. What had the last sign she'd seen said – straight on towards Nice or a right towards Antibes? She'd turned the satnav off a while ago, to avoid waking the others with its strident barking. It was comforting in a way, all this snoring. She used to like it when she got up early and went about her chores on a Saturday morning while the sounds of Barry and Tom snoring drifted from their respective bedrooms. How long ago all that felt now. Another life. Well, this was her life too.

Didn't someone say that we do not have a single life so much as several different ones, several different stages of being? Well, yes. This was her life too and it – oh my goodness.

There it was, suddenly, right in front of her, sparkling.

The Mediterranean, and, down the hill in the distance, its white buildings nestling up against the sea – Cannes.

Susan pulled over. Lord, it was beautiful. 'Girls?' she said. 'Girls?' They stirred slowly around her.

'God,' said Julie sleepily. 'Look at that!'

'Ah!' said Vanessa.

'Are you allowed to stop here?' said Jill, looking around at the traffic gliding past them.

'Wow,' Ethel said. 'I haven't seen this view in a long, long time.'

'Have you been here before, Ethel?' Susan asked.

'Mmmm. I should say so. In '52 or '53? I was staying on a yacht belonging to a friend of a friend, just along the coast there. We'd swim all day and then take the little motorboat into the harbour and have dinner at one of the restaurants on the seafront. I met Picasso here, you know.'

'Really?' Vanessa said, settling back with her Evian.

'Oh yes. It was a glorious summer.'

'Oh, Ethel,' Jill said, everyone transfixed as Ethel peeled back the years, everyone trying to associate the person in the wheelchair and the heavy, egg-stained wool skirt with a lithe girl in a bathing suit, here, over half a century ago. Her voice was misty, had sepia in it. The sea breeze blew through the open car windows.

'I met a young man,' Ethel went on. 'Very rich. Very handsome. We'd walk on the beach at dusk. In the afternoons we'd drink mint juleps on the deck of the yacht. Then, at the end of the day, with the heat still coming off the water, we'd go downstairs into the cabin . . . and he'd fuck the bloody tits off me.'

Susan closed her eyes.

Vanessa sprayed mineral water right across the car.

'RIGHT! THAT'S IT!' Jill shrieked as she fumbled for the door handle. 'I SIMPLY WILL NOT LISTEN TO THAT KIND OF TALK!' Jill leapt out and stomped up and down the lay-by fuming, Julie, Susan and Vanessa all doing their best to make it look like they weren't laughing.

'I mean, honestly,' Ethel said, 'the package on this lad. It was like he'd stuffed a bag of sugar and a sockful of mince down there —'

'Ethel!' Susan said.

'It really doesn't get old for you, does it, Ethel?' Julie said, nodding at Jill, standing up ahead, arms folded tightly, staring at the sea, the radiation lines of fury almost visibly bristling off her.

'Oh, come on. Bloody Christians, that's what they're there for,' Ethel said.

'Right, so what's the plan?' Julie said, clapping her hands together. 'I'm starving.'

'Well,' Susan said, turning the key in the ignition, the huge Porsche thrumming into life around them, 'we're not due in Marseilles until the morning. I think we find a hotel for the night, don't you?'

'Only one place to stay when you're in Cannes . . .' Ethel said.

FORTY-SIX

All right for some.

Boscombe was taking in the grand, lobby of L'Auberge du Château – the lush potted fronds, tapestries hanging on the wall – while waiting for the manageress to come back. He shifted uncomfortably, trying to move something in his lower bowel. Maybe Wesley was right. Maybe his all-meat, all-carb diet did need reviewing. It felt like his digestive system had been plastered with Artex, with roughcast or pebble-dash. He wondered, maybe he could . . . could he fart his way out of the need for a toilet visit? No, here she was, the manageress, coming back with a young, nervous-looking maid trailing along behind her.

'This is Suzanne,' the manageress said. 'She was on duty this morning.

Boscombe produced his photographs of Susan Frobisher and Ethel, his testes-flaying wheelchair nemesis. The girl took them as the manageress said in French, 'Are these the same women who stayed in suite 14 last night?'

'*Oui.*' Suzanne was quick to recognise them. They had been so lovely. They had left such a big tip.

Boscombe felt a surge of adrenalin. 'Ask, ask her if they said where they were going.'

The manageress and the maid began a rapid-fire conversation in French. It was impossible to follow, but Boscombe was no stranger to reading body language. He sensed reticence on the part of the girl. There was reluctance in her shrugs and frowns.

'Tell her,' Boscombe said, moving closer, looking straight at the maid but talking to the manageress, 'that these women are very dangerous criminals.' The manageress translated and the maid's eyes widened. 'Tell her that if she doesn't tell us everything she knows then she might be leaving herself open to prosecution for perverting the course of justice.' The manageress didn't seem to understand this. 'Her.' Boscombe pointed at the girl. 'Jail. Prison. La Bastille.' The manageress frowned and more gibbered French followed, during the course of which Boscombe could see the girl's lip beginning to tremble. She remembered all right, remembered them all cheering when they said it out on the balcony. She started to speak while looking at the floor.

Wesley had the driver's seat cranked back, allowing him to doze at just above the horizontal position; he was almost falling over when his peace was shattered by Boscombe exploding back into the tiny car, into the passenger seat.

'Cans,' Boscombe said, panting from the thirty-yard dash from the lobby to the car park.

'Cans?' Wesley said.

'Cans. You know. Where the bloody film stars and all that go!'

'Oh,' Wesley said. 'You mean *Can*. The "s" is silent.' He started cranking his chair back up into the driving position, his knees already feeling like they were buckling against his chest.

'I'll silent you in a minute, professor,' Boscombe said, snapping his seat belt into place. 'They reckon it's a good nine hours from here. We should just make it before dark. You drive the first shift. Come on, let's get going, Wesley.'

'Shouldn't we radio on ahead to the local police? Get a description out? See what they —'

'One, Wesley, as we've seen the French police DO NOT give a shit about any of this business. And two, I am not handing my collar over to some bastard smirking collaborator turd, OK? You with me?'

'I'm with you, Sarge,' Wesley said, starting up the one-litre engine. Honestly — you might as well have had a couple of hamsters running on a wheel attached to the driveshaft. 'I mean, it's a fairly blunt point you're making.'

Oh well, Wesley thought. *Free holiday at the end of the day*. He'd always fancied seeing Cannes. Film stars and all that. He'd heard the food was great down there too. If he could just keep the gourmand here out of the local McDonald's . . .

FORTY-SEVEN

Bloody Hell, Susan thought, as they crossed the sunlit lobby. Her and Barry had stayed in some grand places over the years, four- and five-star hotels, and there had even been that one night at the Savoy for his boss's retirement party – she could still remember the vastness of the bed, the fluffiness of the towels – but this . . . this was something else: the Ritz Carlton was now – depressingly for Ethel – called the Intercontinental Carlton, and it was a vast expanse of cream-and-beige marble, ivory-white columns reaching up to the impossibly high ceiling with chandeliers dangling from it and everywhere, reading newspapers, sipping drinks, *rich people*. Very, very rich people. Susan was suddenly conscious of their motley dress as the five of them made the long walk from the colonnaded entrance to the reception desk. Of their rumpled, sweaty, ill-fitting clothes, unchanged for forty-eight hours now. They'd just washed their smalls out in the sinks at the Auberge. God only knew what was going on underneath Ethel's fulsome skirts, Ethel who was wheeling herself enthusiastically ahead of them. Ethel's head was reeling, spinning. She hadn't been in this place for what, sixty years? Grace Kelly had been staying here at the time. Lovely girl. Terrific figure. It had been darker then, the lobby. Less airy. They'd done a lovely job.

Claude, the receptionist they were headed towards, was, in his turn, thinking, *Mon Dieu*. Probably tourists who'd wandered in for an ooh and ah at the lobby. They might want tea or something. He moulded his features into a professional grin as the one in the wheelchair reached the desk. *'Bonjour!'* she said, surprising him with excellent pronunciation.

'Hi there,' Susan said, trying for a bright and casual tone. Jill was gripping her handbag tightly, looking like she was standing before God Himself. Julie wanted to slap her. You had to be nonchalant in places like this. This is what the rich were, nonchalant. Like Vanessa – she'd flung herself across a big armchair and was casually flicking through a magazine. That was style. 'We'd like a room for the night,' Julie said. 'Two rooms actually.'

Claude the receptionist stared at her for a beat. He hadn't been expecting this. 'Ah, madame,' he began gently, 'I am afraid we are fully booked.'

'Oh please,' Julie cut in. 'Look at the size of the place. You must have two little rooms.'

'I am afraid not. It is the height of the season. I can recommend some other hotels . . .'

'Sorry, Ethel,' Susan said, going to push her away.

'We understand,' Julie said. 'Perhaps if we . . .' She slid a fifty-euro note across the counter towards him. 'Could come to an arrangement . . .'

What was wrong with these old fools? Claude wondered.

'Ah, madame. It is not a question of —'

'Oh, come on,' Susan said. 'We'll just go somewhere else. Let's tr—'

'It cannot be!'

They all turned to see a tiny gentleman standing there, leaning on his cane. He was wearing what looked like a very expensive pale blue suit, which had almost swallowed him whole — for he was ninety if he was a day, made Nails look sprightly. His eyes blinked behind lightly tinted gold-rimmed sunglasses. He looked like a very well-dressed mole. 'Ah, sorry?' Susan said.

'I thought it might be, but, after all these years, and then I heard your name and . . . it cannot be . . .'

He continued to stare straight past Susan and Julie, staring straight at Ethel. 'Mademoiselle Merriman? Ethel Merriman?'

'*Oui,*' said Ethel as they all joined the mole fellow gazing at her. Claude behind the counter was suddenly starting to colour.

The man stepped closer. 'May I?' Ethel extended her hand and he leaned down to kiss it reverentially.

'My name is Armand Ferrat. I saw you dance at the Bamboo Lounge in Paris, just after the war. You were the most beautiful woman I'd ever seen . . .'

'Oh, get away, you daft thing,' Ethel said. 'Still, always nice to meet a fan.' The others were openly staring at her now.

'What brings you to Cannes?' Ferrat asked.

'Oh, my health. The waters.'

'Well, we'll be delighted to have you here with us.'

'Or not . . .' Julie said.

'I'm sorry?' Ferrat's brow furrowed.

'Ah, Monsieur Ferrat,' Claude the receptionist began,

'we . . . I was just explaining to the ladies that we are completely full.'

Ferrat straightened up and looked at the man. Suddenly he didn't look like a little old mole at all. Suddenly he looked like Michael Corleone with a hangover. 'I believe the Connery Suite is available.'

'The . . . but it is twelve thousand euros per –'

'You are quite right,' Ferrat said. 'It is an outrageous sum. You will give it to Madame Merriman and her party for the standard room rate.' He waved a hand. 'Bill the difference to my account. Now, show these ladies to their suite immediately. It is outrageous that they should be made to wait in this intolerable heat.'

'Of course, Monsieur Ferrat . . .' Claude was now simultaneously filling in a form, preparing room keys and ringing a bell. Porters seemed to appear from all sides.

'Mademoiselle Merriman,' Ferrat said, his tone softening as he bent to her once again, 'please let me know right away if there is anything we could do to make your stay more comfortable.'

The other four stared at Ethel in wordless amazement as the lift made its way up the building, the handsome young bellboy with their bags (not *the* bags of course. These were tucked into the spare wheel compartment of the Porsche, which was safely parked in the hotel car park) standing with his back to them watching the numbers slowly ascend. The lift doors pinged open and the bellboy started leading them down the corridor, across carpet as thick and lush as turf.

'Who was that man?' Jill whispered.

'God knows,' Ethel shrugged. 'Some crazed fan or other. Not many of them left now I don't suppose.'

'You were famous, Ethel?' Vanessa asked.

'Infamous, darling, infamous,' Ethel said.

'*Mesdames, mademoiselle?*' the bellboy said, sliding the key through the lock. He pushed the double doors open with a flourish as he said, '*Voilà!*'

'Oh. My. God,' Susan said.

The suite was *enormous*. Over one thousand square feet easily, with glass doors leading onto a balcony running all the way along one wall, overlooking the Croisette and the beach seven floors below. *Beats Wroxham on a wet Wednesday*, Susan thought.

'Cheers, my lovely,' Ethel was saying to the bellboy as she slapped a hundred-euro note into his hand.

'Anything you need, ladies, just call.'

'Oh, I love going first class,' Ethel said. 'No one messes with you.'

'It's like a film . . .' Jill whispered.

'Cocktail?' Julie said, turning round from the fully stocked wet bar at the far end of the room.

'Maybe later,' Susan said. 'There's something I thought we might do first . . .'

'What?' Vanessa said.

'Well, we're not short of a bob or two and we've been wearing these bloody clothes for nearly three days now . . .'

She and Julie looked at each other for a moment before – in chorus, like they had been doing since they were teenagers, for nearly fifty years now – they both trilled '*SHOPPING!*'

FORTY-EIGHT

Wesley sat in the passenger seat, moving his mobile phone around, trying to get a signal, trying to reactivate the satnav app he'd downloaded. It was pitch dark outside now, the only light coming from the tiny screen. He glanced back up the path towards the tiny hotel. The sarge was taking his time. Probably working his winning way with the locals with his aggressive blend of English and commonplace French. It was almost touching in a way that, despite repeated evidence to the contrary, the sarge never lost his faith in the concept that repeatedly shouting the same phrase in English, gradually increasing the volume and the level of gesticulation as you went, would eventually result in some sort of osmotic translation from English into French occurring. That the listener's face would suddenly light up in recognition as they said, 'AH! Yes, of course. Here is the thing you asked for, kind sir.'

How had they got so lost? They'd taken the turning the device had told them to take off the E15, heading east, supposedly in the direction of Cannes, now here they were: somewhere on a B-road in Aix-en-Provence, past midnight, both of them absolutely shattered and still miles from Cannes. This was the fourth hotel they'd tried. Summer. Height of the tourist season.

Wesley heard a gate slamming and looked up to see Boscombe coming through the night into the headlights of the car, sourly frugging his head from side to side, gesturing downwards with his left thumb. Shit.

'Full,' he said flatly as he crumped down into the passenger seat of the tiny car, before adding, inevitably, 'fucking collaborators.'

'Bollocks,' Wesley said. 'What now?'

Boscombe yawned and looked around at the dark hedge-rows, the night sky. He reached up, turned the interior light out and began the process of cranking his seat back into as close to the horizontal position as it would go. He turned onto his side, his back to Wesley, and pulled his mac tighter around him. 'Night, Wesley,' he said.

Christ, Wesley thought. Somewhere off in the distance an owl hooted mournfully – the saddest sound. The saddest sound for a moment or so at any rate, until Wesley sensed Boscombe's body stiffening in the dark as he raised himself very slightly before emitting a shrill, high-pitched fart directly at Wesley.

'Fucking *hell* . . .'

'Sorry,' Boscombe said sleepily. There was not one trace element of sincerity in his voice.

Now came the moment of terror – of seeing the mush-room cloud on the horizon, but being incapable of compre-hending the damage the blast wave will do when it finally reaches you. Four seconds later the true horror began as the vaporous evidence of his boss's recent diet began to fill the scant few feet of cubic space: city rubbish heaps, festering landfill, cabbage that had been boiled for days in sour milk, corpses.

'Oh fuck me, fuck me, fuck me . . .' Wesley gagged as he wound his window down and began craning his neck for relief. *What the fuck had he been eating?* Actually Wesley knew very well what he'd been eating – pies, sausages, burgers, hotpots, stews, cheap steaks, bacon sarnies: the all beige diet, the spackled abattoir of his boss's bowels. But it actually smelt worse than all that, like his food intake consisted solely of neat sulphur.

'Jesus Christ, Sarge . . .'

But Boscombe was already fast asleep.

FORTY-NINE

What a day it had been, Ethel thought, propping herself up on the mass of thick pillows. Jill was snoring lightly in her bed, far away on the other side of the enormous bedroom. They must have spent a fortune in those shops – Chanel, Versace, Gucci, Hermès. They'd bought things for pleasure – clothes, shoes and bags – and some things that would be essential for phase two of the plan: a large new make-up kit for Susan, a very loose-fitting summer suit cut for the larger gentleman, and some wigs. Julie also picked up two cheap mobile phones in case 'we need to split up'. 'Burners' she'd called them. She watched too much detective stuff on TV Susan thought. Ethel looked down at the side of her bed where her new Prada slippers nestled. Julie had insisted she had them. At one point Susan had started to get a bit uncomfortable about all the spending, making the point that if they were caught then giving back as much of the money as possible would help their case, but in the end she was overruled. Then on to dinner at a very fashionable restaurant on the Croisette, which the hotel manager had arranged for them, doubtless at the urging of Monsieur Ferrat who had also arranged for a magnum of iced champagne to be on their table when they sat down. My goodness they'd put it away. Even Jill was drinking a bit now, which you never saw her do back home in Dorset. (Dorset! How far away and dreary the very name sounded now.)

Ethel looked over to the huge velvet curtains covering the window and tried to guess the time of morning by the strength of the crack of light coming between them. It was weak and pale – maybe between five and six?

She wasn't even tired, hadn't even the trace of a hangover, even though she'd put away a useful train of brandies after the meal, back here, sitting out on the terrace after the others had gone to bed. This was one of the few upsides of age, Ethel often thought, the ability to function perfectly well on four – or even three – hours of sleep. As long as she got her afternoon nap in, which she was planning to do today on the drive to Marseilles. Anyway, she wasn't going back to sleep right now, that much was clear. Coffee. There was a machine in the little kitchenette they had, off the main living area. Give that a go. If the machine wouldn't play ball she could either call room service or go down to the restaurant if it wasn't too early. She swung her legs out of the bed and snuggled her toes into the luxuriant lining of the new slippers. She pulled her wheelchair as close to the bed as she could and – with great effort – hauled herself into it. Oof. Bastard knees, riddled with gout. Still, what were you going to do? Live on water and kale? Not in this bloody lifetime. She glanced at the clock by her bedside – yep, 5.45 a.m.

Ethel came trundling out of the bedroom into the hallway, softly closing the door behind her so as not to wake Jill, and rolled straight into young Vanessa.

'Oh!' Ethel said. 'You're up ear—'

Then she took it in. Vanessa was fully dressed, with her bag hooked over her shoulder and a guilty expression on her face. 'Well,' Ethel said. 'I see.'

'Ethel, I . . .'

'I'm not much on big goodbyes myself, Vanessa.'

Vanessa looked at the floor and pushed a strand of hair out of her face. She looked incredibly young. 'Say goodbye to the others for me, Ethel.'

Ethel nodded. 'Off to your big dancing audition, are you?'

'*Oui.*'

'Good luck to you, love. I'll just say this: in my experience there's two kinds of dancing gigs. There's dancing A, the kind that involves, you know . . .' Ethel started miming a sort of disco hand-jive while she sang, '*I love the night life, I love to boogie, on the disco ah-hhh* . . . actual dancing. Then there's dancing B. Which is the kind that tends to involve having a stranger's willy in your mouth.'

Vanessa frowned. 'Willy? I – oh.' The penny dropped. 'Look, I can handle myself, you know?'

'I'm sure you can, darling,' Ethel said, trundling closer to her. 'But remember, no matter what anyone tells you, or what you tell yourself, it takes something away from you. And you never get it back.'

Vanessa met Ethel's gaze.

'Do you understand?' Ethel said gently. Looking into her eyes Vanessa could see it all there, shining softly, many,

many years of it, of moments in hotel rooms and apartments and cars. Experience.

'I understand,' Vanessa said, nodding.

'Good girl, here . . .' Ethel was holding out a thick roll of euros. Vanessa shook her head. *'Here . . .'* Ethel said, stuffing the notes into the pocket of her denim jacket. 'Be one less thing on my conscience, OK?'

'Thank you, Ethel.' The girl leaned down and kissed her. She really was something, Ethel thought. So beautiful. Yes, tough times ahead for this one and no mistaking.

Ethel watched her leave and rolled on down the hall, towards that coffee machine.

Vanessa came down the steps of the Carlton, smiled shyly at the uniformed doorman who tipped his hat to her, and turned right onto the Croisette, which was almost deserted in the dawn, apart from two men who were standing on the pavement beside their tiny Citroën car. They were discussing something in English, she recognised the word 'bollocks', from hearing Ethel say it. Tourists.

Vanessa turned up a side street and started heading away from the sea and into the town of Cannes, towards the address her friend had given her. It really wasn't far.

'Bollocks,' Boscombe said again, casting a glance at the departing back of the young girl before turning back to survey the empty Croisette and the beach beyond it. 'Blackpool with bloody palm trees, Wesley.'

'Don't go much on the finer things, do we, Sarge?'

'Right, here's the plan. We're about in the middle. I'll go to the far end up there –' Boscombe pointed up the street – 'you go to the other end. We'll check all the hotels and meet back here in a couple of hours. In front of that one.' He pointed to the Carlton.

'How about a bit of breakfast first?' Wesley asked. 'I'm bloody starved.'

'There's half that pasty thing left in the glovebox if you fancy it.' Wesley shuddered. 'Come on, lad. Let's get on with it. We're here to work. It's not some gourmet trip at the taxpayers' expense, you know.'

Chance would be a fine thing, Wesley thought.

FIFTY

'For God's sake, Ethel! Why didn't you stop her?'

'Julie, love,' Ethel tried gently.

'God knows what kind of people she's getting involved with!'

'You can't force people to –' Ethel tried again.

'She's only a bloody kid!'

Jill and Susan said nothing, letting it run its course. Julie was as angry as Susan had ever seen her. 'I mean "dancing"? Jesus, Ethel . . .'

'And what were you like when you were her age, eh? Exactly the same, I'll bet.' Ethel was getting angry now too. 'The same as we all were – you thought you knew it all. She's got to make her own bloody mistakes.'

Julie turned on her heel and clicked off along the marble floor towards her bedroom. They heard the heavy door slam shut. 'Fucking hell,' Ethel said.

'Language,' Jill countered automatically, without energy, as Ethel went to wheel along the hallway after Julie.

'No, Ethel,' Susan said. 'Just leave her, love.'

'What's all that about?' Ethel said.

'It's . . .' Susan thought, remembering back nearly thirty years, holding Julie's hand in that sad, terrible room, both of them weeping as Julie said, 'Well, that's that,' over and over again. 'Nothing, Ethel.' Susan grabbed her towel. 'Just leave it for now. Come on, let's go down and have a quick swim before we get back on the road, eh?'

Seven floors below them and about half a mile to the west, Boscombe was thrusting his photographs at another bewildered concierge. At the same moment, approximately half a mile to the cast, Wesley was coming out of the fourth successive hotel where he had met with confusion and then blank looks. He came down the steps onto a little terrace and, dear God, that smell, that heavenly smell. What was th . . .

Wesley found he was overlooking the restaurant.

Under pale ivory umbrellas wealthy-looking holiday-makers were breakfasting and Wesley took it in via a series of close-ups, moving from table to table to the buffet itself: scrambled eggs and coffee, pitchers of ruby-orange juice with beads of iced water running down their sides, crisply fried slivers of bacon, perfectly golden omelettes, a whole side of poached salmon, bowls of sliced fresh fruit on ice: papaya and watermelon and strawberries and kiwi fruit.

Wesley found that saliva was cascading into his mouth and, before he quite knew what he was doing, he was pulling out a chair at an empty table for two, while signalling to a waiter. *Fuck it*, there was nothing that couldn't wait half an hour. If Boscombe wanted to alternately play the martyr and then stuff his face with processed meat products that was his lookout. *Oooh*, Wesley thought, watching a waiter carrying a silver tray with two brimming champagne flutes on it. *I might even have one of them Mimosas.*

Julie was lying on the bed, crying. The thought came: this is stupid. When had she last got like this over something that had happened so long ago? Only when she was really drunk, late at night. Ethel was right of course, she knew that. But, still, she'd thought she might be able to . . . oh God knows. *It had been so small, the tiny thing.* She reached for a fresh tissue, choking back a sob in her chest, feeling that salty expansion in her ribcage, when she heard a soft knocking at the door and then it was being pushed open and Vanessa was in the room, crying too, and Julie was coming up from the bed and folding her in her arms and they were crying together, neither one knowing why the other was crying, until Julie pulled her hair out of Vanessa's hair and wiped the tears from her eyes.

'Vanessa . . . shh . . . what's wrong? What happened?'

Vanessa looked at her and wailed, 'It was dancing B!'

Boscombe looked at his watch. *Fucking lazy, slow-arsed Wesley. Taking the piss.* Here he was, in front of the Carlton, bang on time, and where was laughing boy? Nowhere. He'd give him a few minutes.

He sat on the wall in front of the great white building and took out his cigarettes. He lit one and stared at the sparkling water across the street, the sun already high and hot at 9 a.m. It was famous for something, this hotel. Wesley had mentioned it in the car. What was it? Oh, yeah. Elton John. The video for one of his songs, 'I'm Not Standing' or something, was filmed here. Wesley — mine of useless bloody information that lad was.

'It's OK, love. It's fine,' Julie said, savouring the warmth and smell of the child, 'it'll all be fine. Not quite what you expected, eh?' She felt Vanessa shaking her head fiercely into her chest.

'I lied to you, Julie,' Vanessa said, her voice coming muffled from somewhere south of Julie's chin.

'Oh yeah?' Julie said. 'How so?'

'I'm only fifteen.'

'Ah. I see. Oh well. Never mind, darling.'

Vanessa was getting her breathing under control now, pulling away from her, wiping tears and wet hair from her face. Julie handed her a fresh tissue and, as she took it, Vanessa seemed to notice Julie's own red eyes and streaked make-up for the first time.

'Why were *you* crying?' Vanessa asked her.

'Oh, that,' Julie said. 'Well. I was just thinking about something that happened a long time ago.'

'What?'

'Nothing. Honestly. Anyway, what are your plans now?'

Vanessa shrugged and laughed.

'Fair enough,' Julie said. 'Tell you what, let's grab our swimming costumes and go and join the others down at the pool. We can have a chat and decide what to do from there, eh?' Julie clapped her hands together and got up from the bed, crossing over to the wardrobe.

'Oh, Julie?' Vanessa said.

'Mmmm?'

'What *do* you do for a living? You know, the thing you lied to me about?'

'Oh. That. Right. OK.' Julie thought for a second, biting her lip. 'Well, here's the thing . . .'

Bugger it. Check this one and then find soft lad.

Boscombe flicked his cigarette away and walked up the hot steps and into the huge, cool lobby. Fucking hell. How the other half live. He looked around at the knots of wealthy holidaymakers, sitting chatting, strolling in and out, and motioned to one of the staff to come to him. The concierge looked at Boscombe oddly, momentarily thrown by his cheap, sweat-soaked clothes and florid, malnourished complexion. The thought *le vagabond?* briefly crossed his mind and he approached Boscombe with some caution.

'Monsieur?' the concierge said.

'Can I speak to the manager please?' Boscombe said.

The concierge looked him up and down again. 'Per-aps I can help?'

Boscombe sighed as he produced his identification for the umpteenth time that morning. The act of pulling it from his inside pocket provided an uncomfortable reminder that there was what felt like a paving stone lodged in his bowels. How long had it been since he . . . before they got the plane over? No, surely not? That was two days ago. 'Just get the manager,' he said, flopping the CID badge out. The cheeky beggar actually took the ID from Boscombe and looked at it thoroughly.

'English police?' he said.

'*Oui,*' Boscombe said sarcastically.

The concierge continued to scrutinise the ID. Finally, inevitably, Boscombe's paper-thin patience burned through. 'Look, pal,' he said. 'I'm here on official police business. I have a letter of cooperation from your government and I need to see your register of guests right now. *Comprende?*'

The concierge stared Boscombe down, completely unruffled. Here was someone used to dealing with hung-over studio moguls and oligarchs in a hurry. A pissant policeman was nothing and the instant suspicion he'd had about Boscombe had hardened in a matter of moments into a fairly robust dislike. 'May I see it?' he said.

'See what?'

'This letter. I am afraid your English police credentials do not mean anything here, Detective . . .' he squinted at the ID again, 'Balls comb.'

The vein in Boscombe's temple started pulsing as he rooted through his jacket. 'Look, what's your name, mate?'

The concierge pointed to his brass lapel badge, where the word '*Charles*' was writ in elegant black script.

'Charles, right. I'm making a note of that.'

'As you wish. I am afraid we must protect the privacy of our guests. May I?' He held up Boscombe's ID and letter.

Boscombe: 'Oh for fu— yes! Go on then.'

'Wait here please.'

'But chop-chop. I'm in a hurry.'

'Of course,' Charles smiled weakly.

The arrogant bugger, Boscombe thought as he watched the guy go clicking off across the quarter-acre of marble. He sat down heavily in a deeply cushioned wicker chair, again feeling the heft of what felt like a seal pup wedged in his rectum. Might have to get some Ex-Lax or something. And, God, despite this, he was hungry too.

Maybe Wesley was right – they should have eaten.

He picked up a newspaper – *Le Monde*. Fuck it. Just look at the pictures.

Instead of taking a left towards the manager's office Charles the concierge took a right towards a door marked

'EXIT'. He went down a short corridor and opened a fire door out onto a back loading dock. He tucked Boscombe's ID and letter into his pocket and lit up a Camel.

Arrogant English asshole. Let him wait.

Wesley burped happily. My God, that was good. The flakiness of the croissant, the perfect sun yellow of his scrambled eggs. And the coffee. He was, even now, signalling to the waiter for another cup. He checked his watch. Yeah, running a bit late for sure. Fuck it – he'd just tell Boscombe it had all taken longer than he thought. He was going to enjoy the one decent meal he'd had on this trip.

'*Merde!*' Vanessa said once again, her eyes wide. Julie hadn't stopped talking for nearly five minutes: all the time it had taken them to find their swimming costumes and get the lift down to the lobby. Julie had pretty much taken her from Barry's death up to this morning, with a full account of the robbery thrown in. 'And where will you go now?' Vanessa asked.

'Well,' Julie said, watching the numbers on the lift blip down – 6, 5, 4 . . . 'I think it looks like South America for me, Ethel and Susan. We've got to get Jill home.'

'It . . . it's incredible!'

'You got that right,' Julie said. 2 and 1.

Bing.

They came out into the lobby and commenced the short walk from the lift to the changing rooms.

Boscombe yawned, looked up from *Le Monde*, some bollocks about the ex-French President Sarkozy, some fit bird he was –

His yawn stiffened and froze.

Fuck me.

There she was – the one who had tricked him into doing that bloody tango. She was strolling across the lobby about fifty yards away.

Boscombe looked like he was finally having the stroke so devoutly wished by his superior officer.

Julie and Vanessa went into the ladies' changing room. '*Merde!*' Vanessa said. 'So this is why you must go to Marseilles? To get new identities?' She sat down on the wooden bench and took her top off, stripping quickly down to her vest and knickers. The air was thick with expensive lotions and perfumes.

'Yep,' Julie said. 'A friend of Susan's hooked us up with this gu—'

The door burst open.

Vanessa and Julie – the only people in there – turned to see Boscombe advancing into the room, grinning savagely, his eyes locked on Julie's.

'Well, well, well . . . the *dance* instructor,' Boscombe said.

Julie started backing away from him as Vanessa instinctively stood and placed herself between them. 'Who are you?' she said. 'You can't come in here!'

'Detective Sergeant Hugh Boscombe, British CID, love,' Boscombe said, not looking at Vanessa, not taking his eyes off Julie as he added, 'Game over, sweetheart.'

Now Vanessa spoke to Julie without taking her eyes off Boscombe. 'Run!'

'No, love,' Julie said quietly. 'Don't get inv—'

'RUN, JULIE!' Vanessa said, shoving her hard as she took a deep breath and unleashed an eardrum-shredding *scream*.

Out in the reception area several guests jumped as the scream's treble cut through the doors and walls. Claude the guest clerk jumped too. Recovering his composure he immediately signalled for two security guards while, inside, Julie took off running for the back exit to the pool. Boscombe went to follow but his path was blocked by Vanessa throwing herself at him. Boscombe was trying to remove the tiny French girl from his chest in the manner you might use to get a feral cat off you, while, all the time, Vanessa's screaming increased in pitch and intensity.

'GET OFF ME!' Boscombe yelled. During the struggle Vanessa very deftly reached down and found Boscombe's zip. She tugged hard and had a quick scramble around.

'What the fuck!' Boscombe yelled.

'AHHHGHHHHHHHHHHHH!!' Vanessa screamed. 'HELP ME!'

Boscombe started flattening a hand over her mouth. 'Shhh, shut up! Shut up! I'm a policeman!'

'MMMMPHH! UHHUNNNNN!' Vanessa said.

The door burst open for a second time as Claude charged in flanked by the two guards. They took it all in: the red-faced, sweating, tramp-like Boscombe with his hand clamped over the mouth of a very young, very half-naked girl. Vanessa fell to the floor sobbing and the following exchange took place very quickly and, apart from Boscombe, entirely in French.

Claude: 'What the hell is all this?'

Vanessa: 'He . . . he . . .' (More sobbing.)

Boscombe, reaching for his ID: 'Easy, lads. Easy. I'm a policeman.'

Vanessa: 'He tried to make, make me . . .'

Security Guard One: 'Step back from the girl.'

Boscombe, finding pocket empty, realising: 'Fuck.'

Vanessa: 'HE TRIED TO MAKE ME TOUCH HIS THING!'

Then all three of the men looked down, to see Boscombe's flaccid, terrible penis dangling from his open flies.

Later it would be hard for Boscombe to recall who threw the first punch. Either way, a couple of minutes later, guests arriving at the Carlton were stunned to hear sirens ripping through the summer air as two police cars pulled up at the hotel just in time to meet the departing Detective Sergeant Hugh Boscombe, British CID. He was being carried – struggling and screaming – by four security guards now. He had a black eye and a cut, bruised face. Security had got a bit carried away. 'LET ME GO! *LET ME GO, YOU FUCKING BASTARD CUNTS!*'

Two policemen joined the hotel bouncers in trying to bundle the berserk, flailing Boscombe into the first patrol car.

'*Qu'est-ce que c'est?*' a bellboy asked Claude who was overseeing the operation.

'*Le pédophile,*' Claude replied quietly.

'*Mon Dieu!*'

'YOU FUCKING CUNNNTTTSSSSS!' Boscombe screamed.

This scream marked Boscombe's last real contribution to the fight as the lead policeman shrugged, stood back, drew his taser, and fired a full charge into the good sergeant's arse.

'Urrrnnnnn,' Boscombe said as he went limp.

Almost immediately the air was filled with a terrible stench as 400-odd volts of electricity achieved what superhuman doses of Ex-Lax hadn't been able to touch the sides of.

'Jesus,' one of the policemen said, turning his face away.

Five hundred yards along the Croisette, Wesley was contentedly savouring the last of his third cup of delicious *café au lait* when he heard the police car go screaming past, sirens blaring, blissfully unaware that his unconscious boss was sprawled flat across the back seat with two or three pounds of mayhem caked in his pants.

'Go on, lads,' Wesley said, raising his coffee cup in salute. 'Give 'em hell.'

FIFTY-ONE

'But don't . . . don't you have *security*? To make sure this
sort of thing doesn't happen?' Susan spluttered. She was
finding it surprisingly easy to muster a good level of faux
indignation.

'Madame, I . . . I can assure you . . .' Claude spluttered
in return. He was standing in the doorway to their suite,
flanked by the two guards who had just thrown a fairly
decent beating into Boscombe. Behind Susan, in the background, Vanessa was still sobbing in Julie's arms on one of
the enormous, overstuffed sofas, flanked by Ethel and Jill.

'I mean, we come to stay here, paying goodness knows
how much money and –'

'I do not know how ziz man came to be in our hotel
but I can assure you . . .' Claude went on, detailing how
thorough their search was going to be, how no stone would
be left unturned, how they would be prosecuting the
disgraceful pervert to the full extent of the law. Claude's
investigation would have had a great deal more clarity,

would have been far more simple, had he known that at that very moment, seven floors below, having enjoyed two Camels on the trot and a lengthy phone conversation with his mistress arranging an assignation for later that evening, Charles the concierge had wandered back into the lobby having completely missed the whole altercation. Unable to find the rude, badly dressed English detective he had simply assumed he had wandered off for a moment. Charles patted his inside pocket, checking Boscombe's identification and letter were still there, and joined a couple of members of junior staff near the main entrance where they were discussing all the excitement Charles had just missed. Something about a sex offender wandering into the ladies' changing rooms.

'I don't know,' Ethel said, trundling forward in her wheel-chair, stopping beside Susan as she prepared to play their trump card. 'I really think I need to have a word with Monsieur Ferrat about all of this.'

The mention of the dread name stopped Claude mid-babble. '*Mesdames*,' he said with tremendous gravity, 'firstly let me assure you that you will be receiving no bill in connection with your stay here. Secondly –'

'IT WAS HARD!' Vanessa wailed in the background.

'God knows what the press will make of all this,' Julie said.

'Secondly,' Claude swallowed, 'I would like to extend these terms to allow you to stay with us here as long as you like.'

Ethel and Susan looked at each other. 'Thank you,' Susan said, 'we'll think about it. Now, please, if we could just have some peace and quiet for a moment . . .'

'But of course. If there is any –'

'Thank you,' Susan said, closing the door as Claude retreated, palms spread out before him in a gesture of supplication.

The moment the heavy door closed Vanessa stopped crying, looked up at the others and gave a sheepish grin. There was a moment for the collective sigh of relief before Ethel said, 'Yeah. Ladies? Let's get the fuck out of here.'

FIFTY-TWO

Approximately one hour behind all of this, back on good old British Summer Time, Chief Inspector Wilson was having lunch at his desk. It was a basic affair that would surely have offended many Frenchmen: a tuna-salad sandwich and a few grapes accompanied by a bottle of still mineral water. The wife was always on at him – and not without reason – about the cholesterol, the blood pressure. Part of the reason for the blood pressure, and the whole reason why he was having lunch at his desk, rather than down the Joiner's Arms or at the Fox, towered to his right elbow: a teetering stack of paperwork. As he ate Wilson took the top sheet from the pile, glanced over it, and then either signed and placed it in his 'OUT' tray or frowned and placed it in his 'ACTION' tray if it was something that merited further discussion. It was an archaic system – most of his peers spent the day peering at screens of emails – but one that Wilson had been using since the late 1970s and that worked well for him. He had tried to go down the electronic route but found that he needed a piece of paper in his hand in order to properly concentrate. Subsequently he had ended up just printing off all the emails he received and adding them to his 'PENDING' tray, which, as his eldest daughter said, rather defeated the whole point.

He took a document from the top of the pile and saw that it was a bill for several thousand pounds for the charter of the light aircraft used to take Detectives Boscombe and Wesley to France a couple of days ago. With only a tremor of the eyelid, a slight increase in the heart rate, Wilson scribbled his signature in the box marked 'Approved'. Just as he did this, at the very moment his eye was still hovering on the dread word 'Boscombe', there was a knock at the door. 'Come!' Wilson shouted, not even needing to look up to know that it would be Sergeant Tarrant.

'Ah, sir, do you have a moment?'

'Out with it, Tarrant,' Wilson said, not looking up. He hated preambles and throat-clearing.

'It's about Sergeant Boscombe . . .'

The slight tremor of the eyelid, the feeling of blood being pumped a little faster through his heart.

'Yes?'

'Well, he, I don't quite know how to put this, sir.'

'Oh, do get on with it, Tarrant. What's he done now? Urinated on the Arc de Triomphe?'

'Ah, not exactly, sir, no. He's been arrested in the South of France for sexually assaulting a fifteen-year-old girl.'

Wilson looked up. He was conscious of a light-headedness, of spots dancing in the periphery of his vision. 'Ah,' he said simply, setting his pen down and leaning back in his chair. 'I see.' He sat there, motionless for a moment. Tarrant shifted uncomfortably in the doorway, still holding the email he'd received from Cannes Gendarmerie. He'd printed it off, as per his boss's preferred modus operandi. His boss who was now sitting there, quite still, seeming to look through Tarrant, through the outer office, all the way to France itself.

'Sir?' Tarrant said after what felt like a very long time. He noticed that colour seemed to be gradually returning to CI Wilson's face. Indeed, perhaps a little too much colour . . .

'Just give me a moment please, Tarrant,' Wilson said, sounding distracted, as though he were focusing on a much greater, more pressing problem.

Another moment passed before, far away in the outer office of Wroxham police station, the rest of the staff collectively jumped as they heard Wilson's voice roaring *'BAAAASSSTAAAARRRRDDDDD!!!'* at an inhuman pitch, the roar accompanied by a metallic clang followed by a thud that only Tarrant knew was made by Wilson booting a metal wastepaper basket across the room and into the wall of his office.

FIFTY-THREE

Marseilles, a little less than two hours' drive from the mani-
cured beauty of Cannes and home to one and a half million
souls. The seaport was also home to much of the wretched
villainy that passed through this part of Europe. The Mos
Eisley of France indeed. Since antiquity the underbelly of the
world had been flocking here to trade commodities as diverse
as silks, spices, drugs, guns and humans.

And now it was – briefly – home to one and a half
million and five souls.

At Susan's insistence they had taken far less grand lodg-
ings here: a three-star hotel on a shadowy backstreet
near the Old Port. It was here that they stashed the money
and the bag containing Nails's guns underneath a few sweaters
in the bottom of the wardrobe and went over their plan
again.

Someone would always remain in the room with the
contraband. As Susan and Julie were meeting Terry's Mr
Tamalov at a nightclub he owned (which was, unpromisingly,

called 'Le Punisher') and Ethel and Vanessa were 'starving', Jill was taking first shift guarding the weapons and cash while the oldest and youngest members of the team slurped bouillabaisse near the seafront.

In the morning Jill was going to take a taxi to Nice airport and get the first available flight back to England. In a day or two they would wire the thirty thousand Jill needed for Jamie's operation to an account she would open back home. Then, using their new identities purchased from Tamalov, Susan, Julie and Ethel would board a flight to a South American destination yet to be agreed upon. The only other point yet to be agreed upon was exactly how they were going to get several million in cash out of the country.

It was this subject Susan and Julie were discussing while they sat in the empty nightclub waiting for Tamalov. 'Could we buy something big and hide it inside it and then have it shipped to wherever we're going to be?' Susan asked.

'Ooh, don't know about that,' Julie said. 'You fancy chancing that?'

'No. Stupid idea. Sorry.'

Around them cleaners were hoovering and staff were collecting glasses, their feet making a ripping, Velcro sound as they trod across the sticky carpeting. Some of the cleaners were blasting air-fresheners into the darker recesses, trying to overpower the odours of alcohol, tobacco, sweat and desperation. Nightclubs weren't called nightclubs by accident, Susan thought. They worked in the dark: pounding neon chambers, impossible paradises of music, seduction and sophistication. By day they were revealed for what they were – tawdry sex abattoirs. Not her environment. Julie, on the other hand, felt perfectly at home here. She watched the cleaners with some affection, having done similar jobs many times, in London, Sydney, San Francisco.

'Or how about –' Susan began again, but whatever she was about to say was cut off by a loud voice booming 'LADIES!' They turned to see a figure coming across the deserted dance floor, looming out of the semi-dark.

Tamalov was, in some respects, exactly what you'd expect of a middle-aged Russian man of dubious business background. (And, let's face it, that 'dubious background' could apply to pretty much all Russian businessmen. A country that went from wheat and dung beetles to the greatest military superpower in the world in thirty years? That later went from full-blown communism to crazed full-bling capitalism in less than twenty? There had to be a certain moral flexibility afoot here.) He had a silvery beard and a drift of (thinning) white hair. A gold chain as thick as clothes-line rope hung around his neck. His watch, Julie thought – as he came into their booth, grinning, urging them not to stand up, extending his hand to shake theirs, getting their names straight, and urging them to call him Alexei – it looked like a dial prised from the control panel of a nuclear submarine and then encrusted with enough jewels to make a supermodel vomit. He wore a Ralph Lauren Polo shirt (stretched taut over a thrusting pot belly), chinos and brown leather loafers without socks – the uniform of the wealthy in hot climes. The only jarring note was that he appeared to be exactly five feet high. Tamalov slid into the banquette across from Susan, next to Julie, who did her best to slink down against the wall in order not to tower over him. 'So!' he said. 'You are the friends of Terry's?'

'Yes,' Susan said.

'Old friends,' Julie stressed.

'Very good, very good. I have not seen Terry in, oh, five or six years. We first did business together back in the early nineties. Shipping Range Rovers into the former Soviet Union. A lot of money. A lot of money. Anyway, we –' He stopped and frowned, looking at the table, seeming to notice something for the first time. 'But you have no drinks. Many apologies. This is terrible.'

'No, no, we're fi––' Julie began.

'Please, some champagne?'

'Oh, that's very kind. But maybe just a Coke, thank you,' Susan said.

'COKE!' Tamalov barked. 'Coke is for children! Come, please, I have some excellent Pol Roger.'

'I could go for a glass of champagne,' Julie said.

'Very good!' Tamalov said. 'This one here –' he smacked the table in front of Julie – 'she has a look. In the eye. Much trouble, I think.'

'You've no idea,' Susan said.

'DOMINIC!' Tamalov shouted. A guy of around thirty, tanned and handsome, appeared from around the bar, his teeth glinting white in the murky neon of the club. 'Champagne. From my office. Not the syrup you sell behind that fucking bar. Excuse me, ladies. So, Terry is well, yes?'

'Very well,' Susan said. 'He sends his regards.'

'And you must give him mine. The old bastard! Do you mind?' He had produced a pack of Sobranie, the cigarettes pastel-coloured, in greens and pinks, yellows and blues with a gold band near the filter, which he surprised them by breaking off.

'No, please,' Susan said.

'Actually, do you think I could have one of them?' Julie asked. Susan looked at her. 'Oh, when in Russia,' Julie added.

'Ha. Of course. Please.' He took a green one and passed it to her, holding out his lighter. Julie lit it and inhaled the thick, rich smoke.

'Oooh . . .' she said.

'I have them sent by the case from back home. Before you go, I will give you a carton.' Tamalov puffed on his unfiltered cigarette, then pulled a strand of tobacco from his teeth.

'Oh God no. Don't tempt me.'

'Julie,' Tamalov said, 'you do not look like you need much in the way of temptation.'

Julie giggled coquettishly. *OK*, Susan thought. *Down to business*. 'Mr Tamalov, Alexei, we –'

But he was there before her. 'Yes, yes. The reason you came to see me. Of course. I will take the liberty of assuming, ladies, that if Terry has pointed you in my direction, then you are not here because you need cigarettes. So, please, let us all speak frankly. What *do* you need?'

Julie and Susan looked at each other. Julie nodded.

'Passports,' Susan said.

'Which nationality?' Tamalov said without blinking, as though they had indeed just asked him for some cigarettes and he was enquiring after the brand.

'British,' Julie said.

'How many?'

'Three.'

'Ah! Excellent, thank you, Dominic,' Tamalov said, spying the approaching ice bucket, the green neck of the bottle protruding, the three flutes. 'Pol Roger. Your own beloved Winston Churchill would drink it every day.' Dominic set it down and immediately retreated as Tamalov set about the foil and the wire. 'Three British passports . . .' Tamalov repeated to himself as he twisted the cork. 'Three British . . .' *CRACK!* He popped the bottle open smoothly, professionally, still holding the cork in his right hand, a whisper of smoke appearing to curl from the neck. (As she did whenever champagne was opened Susan had to fight a girlish urge to go *'Oohh!'*) Tamalov poured and said, 'I can help you with this.' Julie and Susan glanced at each other again, fighting smiles. 'However, nowadays, with the terrorist sons-of-whores everywhere, you must have only the best work. Anything less and, well, I am afraid you might have a short trip. And, as I am sure two refined, cultured ladies know, the best never comes cheap.' He passed them their drinks, the champagne very cold, already beading and misting the glasses.

'How much?' Susan asked.

'Twenty thousand euros,' Tamalov said, taking a sip of his wine.

'Twenty thousand?!' Julie said, nearly spitting hers out.

'That is per passport of course.'

'Sixty thousand?!' Julie said. 'We bought a bloody Porsche for less than that!'

'Mmmm.' Tamalov toyed with the base of his glass, turning it on the table. 'I fear your Porsche will not take you as far as you need to go.'

'Thirty thousand for three,' Julie said.

Tamalov smiled. 'This is not the fish market.'

'How soon can you get them?' Susan asked.

'Maybe a week.'

'No,' Susan said. 'By tomorrow.'

'Tomorrow?' Tamalov laughed now. 'Forget it.'

'If you can get them by tomorrow we'll give you sixty thousand *plus* the Porsche. Otherwise no deal.'

'Susan!' Julie nearly screamed.

'Year, model and mileage?' Tamalov said.

Susan looked at Julie. Julie glared back. *'Julie,'* Susan said.

'This is . . .' Julie said hopelessly. 'Oh, right, fine. It's a 2012 Cayenne. Just under 20,000 miles on the clock.'

Tamalov's brow furrowed as he did some maths in his head before saying, 'I believe we can do business on those terms.'

'I bet you can!' Julie said, already grieving for the loss of the Porsche.

'I'll have my man begin preparatory work. He'll need to work through the night on this, you understand? You will need to come back as soon as possible with photographs.'

'Of course,' Susan said.

'Excellent,' Tamalov said, taking the bottle from the bucket again, topping them up. 'Well, ladies, a toast. To living well. It is the best revenge, no?' Julie and Susan raised their glasses, the latter more enthusiastically than the former.

Moments later, on the street in the hot sun in front of Le Punisher, Susan said, 'Oh, stop sulking. What were you going to do? Take the bloody car on the plane with you?'

'It's the *principle* of the thing!' Julie said, stomping along, utilising the last argument of the doomed. 'You didn't even try and haggle! With the car that's over a hundred grand!'

'You know something, Julie Wickham?' Susan said,

putting her sunglasses on. 'You're the most tight-fisted millionaire I ever met.'

'God,' Julie said, stopping for a second. 'I am, aren't I?' She let it wash over her. She really was a millionaire. They both burst out laughing, holding each other's arm as they tottered off into the warm afternoon, both feeling the sunshine on their faces and the tingling rush of the champagne in their veins.

Had they not been so caught up in the moment, in the joy of being alive and, momentarily, one step ahead and of having successfully completed what they feared would be a difficult negotiation, they might have noticed the beige Mercedes saloon parked across the street from the nightclub.

They might have noticed the four men inside it.

Might even have noticed the one in the passenger seat, hefting the camera with the telephoto lens above the dashboard, pressing the button and snapping off several high-quality frames of them before they disappeared round the corner and back towards the hotel.

FIFTY-FOUR

Sitting on the stone steps of Cannes police station, a pleasant building on the avenue Michel Jourdan, just a little way back from the Croisette, Wesley turned as he heard a heavy door slamming and Boscombe was striding down towards him. You would never have called the sergeant's natural demeanour 'cheerful', or even 'pleasant', but this was something else. He looked as though, well, if you'd put an automatic weapon in his paws right now you'd have had a sizeable massacre on your hands. As he drew closer Wesley could see he was sporting two iridescent black eyes, one cut on his cheek, and an earlobe doing a good impression of a piece of broccoli. There was something else a little off too. That was it – he was wearing a pair of black uniform slacks that were at least three sizes too big for him. They flapped around his ankles like flares, obscuring his shoes completely. He hitched them up like a skirt as he drew closer and it took everything in Wesley's power to keep the grin off his face. He went for as neutral and respectful as he could manage. 'You OK, Sarge?'

'Am I OK?'

The last few hours had been a blur of phone calls and emails from Wilson, Wilson's superior, Chief Superintendent Tanner, and even, in the end, the Foreign Office. Once they'd got hold of the fellow at the Carlton who'd wandered off with Boscombe's ID things had got straightened out fast enough. It'd taken a while to get there though. Wesley's right ear was still ringing. The noise Wilson had made . . . Wesley had heard the man angry before, livid even, but this had been off the charts. At one point he'd just been making animal barking noises.

'Am I fucking OK, Wesley?'

'Easy, Sarge . . .' Wesley said.

'Those bastards worked me over!' Passing office workers turned to look.

'Come on,' Wesley said. 'Motor's down here.'

'Gave me a proper fucking hiding!' Boscombe hissed. 'Look at my fucking face, Wesley!'

'Well, fair's fair, Sarge. They did think you were a nonce. Remember that time we got that bloke in who –'

'Fair's fair?!'

'I'm just saying.'

'Fair's fucking fair?!' I swear to God, Wesley, when I get my hands on these women . . .'

'Yeah, you might want to watch it with that after . . .'

Boscombe glared at him.

'Joke. Come on, we'll get you a cup of tea or something. I've got a lead.'

'Lead?'

'Yeah, we traced a call from their penthouse to this number in Marseilles. I think –'

'Penthouse?' Boscombe had stopped walking and balled his fists up.

'Yeah, at the Carlton. Christ, you should have seen the size of it. The view from their terrace was –'

'Oh yeah – THEY HAD A NICE VIEW FROM THE TERRACE OF THEIR FUCKING PENTHOUSE WHILE I WAS GETTING BATTERED IN A FRENCH FUCKING NICK, DID THEY?!'

'Keep it down, Sarge. Don't want any more trouble now, do we? Here we go . . .' Wesley clicked the remote, opening the teeny Citroën. Boscombe stalked around towards the passenger seat, his flares flapping. Wesley couldn't help himself. 'What happened to your trousers?'

'I fell,' Boscombe muttered. 'Ripped them. They lent me some.'

'Oh, right.'

Wesley knew of course. He'd got a bit chatty with one of the arresting officers while he'd been waiting for the paperwork to get all sorted out. Nice fella, he spoke really good English and genuinely seemed sorry about the misunderstanding and all that. But the mess, he'd said. *Merde!*

They'd had to hose Boscombe down in the courtyard where they kept the dogs. The guy had even enquired after Boscombe's health and diet. He seemed genuinely concerned that a human being could produce the kind of effluent that Boscombe had pumped into his underpants. Oh man, wait till the guys back at Wroxham station heard about this one. Wesley was already curious about the welter of new nicknames that would be forming very soon.

FIFTY-FIVE

Susan was packing. They'd bought themselves a few nice bits and pieces in Cannes, mostly warm-weather stuff. They'd dropped the passport photos into the club. Everything seemed to be in hand and Susan allowed herself the luxury of fantasising that they might be about to get away with it, with all of it. Vanessa was lying on the bed across from her, her gaze flickering between Susan and the TV – some old Hollywood film in black and white. Julie had popped out to get them something to eat. Ethel and Jill were next door.

'Susan?'

'Mmm?'

'Can't I come with you guys?'

'Oh, Vanessa love, no. I'm sorry. It's just too dangerous. What if we get caught? What's going to happen to you then? After all that stuff back in Cannes you might be charged with being an accomplice.'

'Accomplice?'

'You know, with helping us.'

'But, I . . .'

'Besides, you're only fifteen! You need to be back at school. You don't want to be running away to South America with a bunch of old ladies!'

'You're more fun than any of my friends . . .' Vanessa pouted.

'Oh, love, that's nice to hear. But really, you can't come with us. It's impossible. You need to get home to your dad.'

'He's never there. He probably hasn't noticed I'm gone.'

'Don't be silly. I'm sure he loves you very much.'

Susan kept folding and packing, trying to think of a way to change the subject. Julie was getting too close to the girl – that was the truth. Susan understood why, but it . . .

Then, as though reading her mind, Vanessa piped up again. 'Susan?'

'Mmm?'

'Why does Julie care about me so much?'

'Eh? How do you mean?'

'She, back in Cannes, when I went off, she was so upset. She –'

'She's just a nice person. A good soul. That's all.'

Vanessa stared at Susan. Her dark brown eyes – piercing and intelligent.

Susan sighed and dropped the blouse she was folding. 'Look,' she said, coming round and sitting on the edge of the bed facing Vanessa. 'You can't tell her I told you this. It's something that happened a long time ago. Something she never, ever talks about. Promise?'

Vanessa sat up and pulled her knees up under her chin. 'I promise.'

'Well, when she was, ooh, not much older than you are now really, she had a baby. A little girl. It . . . she was born prematurely and only lived for a few days. It was something to do with her heart,' Susan said, surprised at how easily it was all coming out, this thing she hadn't spoken of in so long. 'Congenital heart defect. The kind of thing they'd have fixed now, but this was back in the seventies.'

'Oh, Julie . . .' Vanessa said.

'I sometimes think she thinks about her every day, you know. She'd have been over forty by now, Julie's daughter. With kids of her own . . . Well. Who knows? Anyway, there were some other complications with the birth and Julie had to have an operation shortly after that. A hysterectomy. So she couldn't ever, you know? She ran pretty wild when she was younger. I think she sees a lot of herself in you. As well as the daughter thing, so . . .'

'It's so sad,' Vanessa said, tears not far from her eyes.

Suddenly they heard the sound of footsteps in the hallway, then the scratching of a key in the lock. Vanessa wiped her eyes, Susan stood up and tucked that last blouse onto the top of her open suitcase as the door swung open and Julie came in, carrying four pizza boxes stacked on top of each other and a plastic bag bulging with Cokes and beers.

'And that's how you pack lightly!' Susan said to Vanessa, patting the top of her case.

'Here we go!' Julie was saying. 'Plain Margherita for Jill, big spicy one with extra chillies and jalapeños for Ethel – honestly, I don't know why she doesn't just hold a lighter under her bum – a Fiorentina for me and Susan to share and one double pepperoni with extra cheese for madam here. I don't know how you keep that complexion of yours, Vanessa,

I really don't. Honestly, all this sugar and cheese . . .' She set the pizzas down on the chest of drawers and handed Vanessa a Coke. 'Here you go . . .' She noticed Vanessa's damp cheeks. 'Hey! What's happened? What's wrong?'

'Just . . .' Vanessa gestured at the TV. 'Sad movie.'

'Ooh,' Julie said, joining her on the bed. 'Bunch up then!'

Susan smiled as she and Vanessa exchanged a glance. *I'd want you on my poker team, Vanessa*, Susan thought to herself as she watched the two of them snuggle up on the bed, munching pizza.

FIFTY-SIX

Alexei Tamalov moved briskly through the warren of rooms above Le Punisher – the ramshackle office complex he ran his many diverse businesses from.

Nodding a hello here and there he strolled on down the narrow hallway, glancing through a doorway into the phone room, where two of his employees – armed only with unlisted phone lines and an unlimited supply of coffee – worked the markets: buying and selling in the cracks of currency between various Eastern European countries. Across the hall from that was his import/export business, selling mostly automobiles and automatic weapons to China and the former Soviet Union. There was his main office with its bank of CCTV cameras covering the whole of the nightclub below, as well as the various other offices in the building (as anyone who ran a largely cash-based business knew, the system was prone to 'leakage') and, tucked away at the end, there was a room Tamalov liked to think of as 'Special Projects'.

This was reserved for the occasional jobs that came his way, that lay outside his daily business, and which required the drafting in of independent contractors. Like Franco, the Italian forger he had installed there to take care of this passport business.

Tamalov was still amazed that the two old women had agreed so quickly to his astronomical price. Still, as his grandfather Sergei used to say back in Minsk, 'A fool and his money were lucky to ever meet.' God knows what this pair were running from but it was a nice, quick score. He already had a buyer willing to go to fifty thousand for their Porsche and he was paying Franco ten thousand plus expenses for twenty-four hours of intensive labour: close to a hundred grand net profit for a couple of phone calls. If these hags had known anything about the forging business they could have got the job done for a fraction of the price. Ah, but as in so many of his lines of work, if people knew the business he'd be out of business.

'Franco? *Entrée?*' Tamalov shouted through the door as he knocked on it, extending this courtesy in case the forger was at a delicate stage of his work. Franco could be temperamental, but Tamalov had done the English ladies a favour here: the Italian was good. He took great pride in his work. Some fake passports you saw, it was like a child had been given some glue and scissors.

'*Si,*' Franco said from inside.

Tamalov stepped into the softly lit room: two desks facing each other, Franco the forger had all his stuff spread out on one. There were the transparent sheets

of paper used to cover the photo page on British passports, a pile of bought or stolen passports, scalpels, a
top-of-the-range laser printer and the three strips of
photos supplied to them that afternoon by Susan and
Julie. Benny was sitting at the desk opposite Franco,
frowning into the football pages of an English tabloid.
Benny was one of the bouncers from downstairs, a slab
of Algerian muscle who Tamalov sometimes used on
collection jobs.

'How's it coming?' Tamalov asked. They generally
conversed in French, though Tamalov's Italian was coming
along.

Franco yawned and ran his hands through his thinning
hair. 'These new bar codes are a bitch . . .'

'By tonight though, yes?'

'You shouldn't make promises you can't keep, Alexei.'

Tamalov thought for a moment. Sometimes the carrot
was better than the stick with employees. He could add an
extra thousand to the fee obviously, but there was one thing
the man liked even better than money. He was Italian after
all . . .

'Come on, Franco,' Tamalov said, slapping him on the
back. 'Get them done by tonight and come hang out in
the VIP lounge downstairs with me. There are a couple
of girls I know coming in later. Seventeen years old. Still
at school . . .'

Franco grinned. 'We'll be done,' he said. '*Pronto.*'

Tamalov laughed. So did Benny, looking up from his
tabloid. 'Ha. Eh, Benny? These Italians and women. Worse
than a Russian even,' Tamalov said. Then something caught

his eye on the front page of Benny's tabloid. Two faces he recognised.

He reached for the newspaper.

'Hey,' Benny said.

FIFTY-SEVEN

Boscombe and Wesley were experiencing what was becoming a very familiar situation: they were sitting waiting in a French police station. This one, in Marseilles, was significantly warmer than any of the previous ones had been. A ceiling fan whirred feebly and uselessly somewhere above their heads as they stared at yet another tableau of French crime posters: rabies, pickpockets, car theft. They had been there nearly an hour and Wesley knew without glancing to his right that the vein in Boscombe's right temple would be starting to throb. Indeed Boscombe's entire face was now an iridescent patchwork of bruises and cuts and he was taking shallow, irritated breaths through his flaring nostrils. Wesley tried for some levity. 'Still, probably pissing down back home, eh, Sarge?'

'Pissing down? Fucking pissing about more like. What the fuck is taking them so long?' He nodded towards the door where Lieutenant Halles, the Marseilles detective liaising with them, had disappeared some forty-five minutes ago. 'I mean, it's only some armed fucking rob—'

At this the door opened and the slender, linen-suited form of Halles appeared. 'Gentlemen, please . . .'

'About bloody time,' Boscombe hissed as they were ushered into a conference room.

There, already seated at the table, was an older man, in his fifties. He had a thick moustache, glasses and a sad, hangdog expression, the expression of someone who routinely saw the very worst that humanity had to offer. In front of him were a glass of water, a fountain pen, a notepad and a manila file about the thickness of the average telephone book. (Or, more appropriately given its contents, the thickness of a Russian novel.) Wesley sensed the man's gravitas right away. 'This is Inspector Dumas from Interpol,' Halles said as Boscombe and Wesley exchanged handshakes.

'Oh yeah?' Boscombe said, taking a seat across from Dumas. 'Interpol? Are we finally getting some real help on the case then?'

'Not exactly,' Dumas said, slipping the rubber band from around his file.

'Well, what's going on?' Boscombe said. 'We've been sat waiting out there for a bloody hour. Our suspects could be out of here by now and on their way to wherever. We need to get cracking, pal.'

Dumas took a sip of water and regarded this strange, angry Englishman. 'I'm afraid it's not that simple, Sergeant . . .'

He slid a photograph across the table to Boscombe.

FIFTY-EIGHT

Julie and Susan sat in the same booth at Le Punisher once again. A burly security guard had shown them in and then disappeared to fetch Tamalov. It was 6 p.m. and it was quiet as a church, as a mausoleum. No cleaners – the place was, well, not sparkling exactly, but you could see how, in a few hours, with the lights and strobes blazing, and the music pounding, it might resemble a drunk's idea of paradise. Julie thought it odd there was no bar staff around, getting things ready, then again, these days, clubs didn't really get going until midnight, did they?

'I checked the flights again,' said Susan, nervous, distracted. 'There's a 9 p.m. to London that Jill can just make and we can get the midnight to São Paulo.' They had run through their plan for smuggling the money several times now. It was the last big risk and had to go smoothly. It wasn't ideal, but what did they say? A good plan today is better than a perfect plan tomorrow and all that. Susan noticed after a moment that Julie hadn't said anything. 'She'll be OK, Julie, she's a smart kid.'

'Yeah, I know,' Julie said. 'Oh, here we go . . .'

Susan turned and followed Julie's gaze to see Tamalov striding across the big dance floor towards them, rubbing his hands together briskly, as was his manner. 'Ladies! How are we today?'

'Great, thank you,' said Julie. Susan smiled at him as she took an envelope from inside her jacket and slid it onto the table. 'It's all there,' she said. 'You can count it.'

Tamalov looked at the envelope but made no move to pick it up. 'Ah,' he said. 'I am afraid that the price has gone up a little . . .'

'Eh?' Susan said.

'What?' Julie said.

'How . . . how much?' Susan said.

At this Julie and Susan heard a metallic click and snap, the kind of noise both of them had only ever heard before in Hollywood movies. They turned round to see the bouncer who had shown them in and another, even larger, man standing there. They were both holding black snub-nosed machine guns, whose bolts had been the source of the click and snap.

'Everything,' Tamalov said, before adding, smiling, 'Mrs Fear.'

'No . . .' Julie said.

'Benny?' Tamalov said. 'We'll use the service entrance. Ladies – follow us to the basement please.'

FIFTY-NINE

Boscombe and Wesley were looking at a grainy black-and-white photo. It was taken at a distance, with a zoom lens, but it very clearly showed Susan Frobisher and Julie Wickham walking along wearing sunglasses. 'These are your bank robbers from England? Yes?'

'Yes they bloody are!' Boscombe said, grabbing the picture and staring hatefully at it.

'This was taken yesterday morning here in Marseilles.'

'Yesterday?' Boscombe said. 'Eh? Why the fu— Why haven't you arrested them yet?'

'As I say, it is not that simple.'

'Not simple? Listen, I —'

Dumas slid another grainy, telephoto lens photograph onto the table. It showed a white-haired man with a silver beard and a heavy gold chain around his neck. He was laughing at something off camera, a mobile phone pressed to his ear. 'Do you know who this man is?'

Boscombe and Wesley shook their heads.

'This,' Dumas said, taking his glasses off and polishing them with his tie, 'is Alexei Tamalov. Also known as Little Sergei, Dimitri Schenkmann and the Bear of Minsk. We've been after him for years. Gunrunning, drugs, credit and identity fraud, people trafficking, money laundering, you name it. But we've never been able to pin anything on him.'

'I don't see what this –' Boscombe began.

Dumas held a hand up. 'We have very good reason to believe your robbers are using this man to obtain false passports in order to leave the country. This might be our best chance to, what's your expression? Yes, to nail him.'

Dumas reached for his water glass and took another long, cool draught while Boscombe responded. 'Passport fraud? Bloody passport fraud? I'm talking about armed robbery here and you're going on about –'

'Sergeant Boscombe,' said Inspector Dumas of Interpol, 'do you know what the penalty for passport fraud is?'

'Ah . . .' Boscombe said. 'I think . . . well, you'd get a fine obviously and, depending on the circumstances,' he was totally free-forming now, 'maybe a –'

'Is it ten years?' Wesley said.

'Very good, Detective,' Dumas said.

Boscombe shot Wesley another hateful 'swot' look.

'Ten years in prison *for each offence*,' Dumas went on. 'If he's getting these ladies two or maybe three passports . . . twenty to thirty years in prison is hardly a parking ticket. It'd take this man off the streets for the rest of his criminal life.' He closed the file and stood up.

'So what are we going to do?' Boscombe said.

'*We* are going to watch and wait,' Dumas said, buttoning his suit jacket, 'until we catch him in the act. *You* may accompany us in an observational capacity but you are not to interfere with us at any point.'

'Is that right?' Boscombe bristled. 'Well, I'm afraid I'm going to have to speak to my superiors back home. I don't think they'll be at all happy about this.'

'Oh, I've already taken the liberty of informing them,' Dumas said, his hand on the doorknob now, Halles behind him, following him out. 'I spoke with a Chief Inspector Wilson? He feels it would be best if you . . . followed our lead on this.'

Boscombe snorted dismissively. 'Wilson said that?'

'Well, those weren't his exact words.'

'I bet they weren't,' Boscombe said.

'No, his exact words were "if that useless fat bastard gets in your way lock him up and throw away the key".'

The door closed behind the two Frenchmen.

There was silence as Boscombe's eyelid quivered and his vein throbbed.

'Old Wilson,' Wesley said. 'Always playing the joker, eh, Sarge?'

SIXTY

Jill lay on her single bed watching a game show in French. Ethel sat closer to the TV in her wheelchair, eating boiled sweets from a paper bag, mechanically unwrapping one after another and popping them into her mouth. Vanessa sat on the floor between them. After a few minutes Jill said, 'You don't worry about eating all that sugar, Ethel?'

Ethel looked at the sweet she was about to munch. 'No.'

'I mean, with your weight, type 2 diabetes, all that stuff . . .'

'Fuck no,' Ethel said.

'Really?' Jill said. 'Is there really any need to swear there? Couldn't you just say "no"?' Vanessa giggled. 'I mean,' Jill went on, 'look at the example you're setting for young Vanessa here.'

Ethel and Vanessa were exchanging an eyebrows-raised glance when there were three knocks at the door, a pause, then two more knocks: the code. Vanessa jumped up and went to open it. Just before she did Ethel said, 'Who is it?'

'It's us . . .' Julie said.

There was something in her voice, something defeated Ethel thought, but she said nothing as Vanessa slid the bolt back.

Julie stepped into the room, followed by Susan.

'What on earth's the matter with –' Ethel said as soon as she saw their faces. But her words stopped as the two huge Algerians stepped into the room behind them, followed, a moment later, by a short man with a silver beard.

'Who the fuck –' Ethel began, going to rise from her wheelchair. The lead Algerian whipped something out of his coat and Ethel felt the cold steel of a gun barrel pressed against her forehead.

'Sit down and shut up, old lady,' the man said. Jill stifled a scream as the short, bearded man closed the door behind him.

'Where is it?' Tamalov said.

Stifling a sob, Susan pointed to the wardrobe.

While the two gunmen trained their weapons on the girls Tamalov moved to the wardrobe and opened it. There, on the floor, covered by a few sweaters, was the grubby holdall. He knelt down, unzipped it, and whistled. 'How much?' he asked. No one said anything. Tamalov nodded to Benny. Benny pressed his gun against the crown of Vanessa's head.

'Just under four million pounds,' Susan said miserably.

Tamalov clicked his finger at the other heavy and, not without difficulty, he leaned down, grabbed a handle and swung the holdall up onto his shoulders. 'No!' Vanessa shouted. She launched herself at Tamalov, but Benny caught her a good backhanded slap, sending her tumbling onto one of the beds.

Jill was crying. Ethel stared straight at Tamalov.

'Please,' Julie said, fighting her own tears. 'Don't take all our money. We have nowhere to go.'

'Don't take it so bad,' Tamalov said. 'These things happen in business. You did well to get this far. Besides, I'm saving you a lot of headaches, ladies – you could never launder all of this anyway. Or you'd get caught trying to take it out of the country.'

'Why?' Susan said, standing quite close to Tamalov. 'Why are you doing this to us?'

Tamalov shrugged. 'Come on. You know the old Russian story. There was a frog sitting by the river. A scorpion came along and said, "Give me a ride to the other side." "But you'll sting me," said the frog. "I won't," said the scorpion, "I promise!" So the frog gave him a ride on his back. Just as they reached the other side the scorpion stung the frog. As the frog lay dying he said, "Why?" The scorpion said, "I'm a scorpion. It's in my nature."' He looked around the room at the crying, broken women. 'Hey, cheer up. We'll let you keep the car, eh? We are not total animals. *Au revoir*, ladies.'

SIXTY-ONE

Saturday night in Marseilles – a party town.

Boscombe and Wesley sat in the back. Dumas and one of his men were in the front. They had been opposite and down the road from Le Punisher for over two hours now. Outside, in the dark, the streets were beginning to come to life: young men in lurid shirts, girls in micro miniskirts and spiked heels tottering from bar to bar, music booming out from various doorways. The queue to get into Le Punisher was starting to snake along the block, the entrance to the nightclub guarded by two headset-wearing security men and a girl wielding a clipboard, deciding who was fashionable enough to cross the threshold. During the two hours they'd sat there, troubling news continued to come over the radio. The two English ladies had entered the night-club hours ago, around 6 p.m. They had yet to come out. (Of course. Although they were watching both the back and front entrances, it was impossible for Interpol to know that Tamalov's service entrance to the nighclub utilised part of the old warren of catacombs that ran under much of Marseilles. A door in his basement led to a tunnel that brought you out in an alleyway five hundred yards along the street. Tamalov had already been, gone and returned right under the noses of the surveillance team.)

'How long are we going to sit here?' Boscombe asked.

This guy, Dumas thought. He was like a child on a trip. *Are we there yet? Are we there yet?* 'I told you, Sergeant,' Dumas sighed. 'We can't just burst in there. We're going to wait until your ladies emerge with the documents and then we're going to arrest them and they will give us Tamalov.'

'In return for what?' Wesley asked, winding his window down. He was pretty sure that Boscombe, the animal, had been releasing a couple of stealth farts. He'd seen him shifting uncomfortably now and then, had caught the slight reek. At one point he thought he'd seen a frown cross Dumas's face in the front passenger seat.

'Well, we will have to cut a deal.'

'Oh yeah?' Boscombe said. 'Our collars get off with a slap on the wrist as long as they send your boy down? That's the deal, is it?'

'Collars?' Dumas said.

'Our arrests,' Wesley said.

'Alexei Tamalov is responsible for untold misery, gentlemen. He has had men killed. Your ladies are not exactly career criminals, are they? From everything I've read it seems to be a one-off crime with much in the way of mitigating circumstances. I am simply concerned with the greater good here.'

'Yeah, we'll see,' Boscombe said. He was sitting right behind Dumas, so he couldn't catch the slight smile playing across the man's face, but Wesley did. The cause of the smile was the fact that Dumas knew exactly why Boscombe was taking it so personally with these women. Earlier, at the station, one of the junior officers had shown Dumas a clip on YouTube: CCTV footage showing Boscombe screaming his head off while being dragged behind a minivan by his very balls.

Boscombe sighed and looked across the street, at people drinking at tables. Christ, he could murder a pint.

SIXTY-TWO

What would the collective noun for tears be? Ethel wondered. A meddle of tears? A dragoon of tears? A filibuster of tears? Whichever way, there was a festival of salty crying going on in room 38 of the lowly three-star Hotel Splendid right now.

Vanessa was weeping hard as she cradled Julie, who was making no sound, just big fat drops rolling down her cheeks. Susan was sitting with her head in her hands, rocking back and forth gently, interspersing her sobs with the words, 'Idiot, idiot . . . I'm such a bloody idiot.' Jill? Jill was something else. She was like fifteen old village ladies at a funeral: pacing back and forth, wailing, howling uncontrollably and occasionally uttering a piercing cry of 'Oh Jamie! JAMIE!' She was one notch off rending her garments. Even Ethel was dabbing at her eyes repeatedly.

Susan and Julie caught each other's numbed gaze now and then, neither of them quite able to categorise the panic, the terror sweeping over them. Or better to say 'the horror', for terror is the apprehension of the awful. They were beholding it. They were in the midst of it. They couldn't even pay the hotel bill.

What now? With no money and no life to return to? What now?

After it had all gone on for a few minutes, Ethel let out a deep sigh, blew her nose, and said, 'Oh, that's better. Right, so what are we going to do?'

Julie said, 'Eh?'

'We've had a good cry. Fine. What's our next move?' Ethel wheeled herself into the middle of the room.

'Move?' Susan said, having to raise her voice to be heard over Jill's wailing.

'Yeah,' Ethel said, then added, 'Jill? JILL? Shut up, love. That's enough.' Jill looked like she'd been slapped. She shut up. Vanessa sniffed and quietened down. The room was suddenly as silent as it had been loud.

'We don't have a move, Ethel. What move?' Julie wiped her face with the back of her hand. 'We can't go to the police. We can't go back home. We're finished.' Her lip started to quiver again.

Ethel took a long breath and shook her head as she considered her words very carefully before saying slowly and deliberately . . .

'You. Fucking. Bunch. Of. Pussies.'

Everyone looked at her.

She took a moment before continuing sarcastically, '*Boo-hoo. The bad men took our money, Ethel! What's going to happen to us now? We're finished, Ethel!* Are you telling me that this is it? *This* is our next move? FUCKING BALLS IS IT!'

She turned to Vanessa and, in a calm, conversational

aside, said, 'Vanessa, be a darling and run next door and fetch the bag that's under my bed, would you?' before turning back to the others.

'They're *gangsters*, Ethel!' Jill screeched.

'BALLS!' Ethel replied. 'BIG GIANT HAIRY BALLS! Gangsters?' She snorted so hard Susan feared the top of her head might explode. 'I was fighting fascists in the East End of London when these Russian cock-munchers were just a faint pulse in some Bolshevik rapist's pants. So who's for crying and who's for fighting? Eh? Because if you think I'm going to quietly wheel myself off to prison while these vodka-swilling . . .' Vanessa ran back in and slammed the heavy bag on the bed next to Ethel. '. . . borscht-munching, Trabant-driving, Cossack-dancing toerags tool about spending our hard-stolen cash then you're out of your bloody minds.' Ethel reached into the bag and pulled out Nails's sawn-off shotgun.

'But wha . . . what are we going to do?' Jill asked.

'Well, we know where he fucking lives, don't we?' Ethel said.

'But they know our faces, Ethel!' Julie said.

'They won't when I'm finished . . .'

Everyone turned.

Susan was standing by the dressing table. She had popped open the latches on her new make up-case. Susan had stopped crying. She was wearing a very different expression to the one she'd had a few moments ago. The eyes, the set of the jaw, she looked . . . she looked like Ethel. 'Ethel's right,' Susan said. 'Fuck this.'

Another voice piped up. 'Fuck this!'

They all looked at Jill, who even now was clamping a

hand over her own mouth, astonished at herself. Vanessa gasped as Ethel racked the slide on the shotgun, chambering a round. She looked up at the old watermarked ceiling and, in a voice that put concentric circles in the glasses of water on the chest of drawers, that shook the very plasterwork, screamed to the heavens: *'I'M COMING HOME, MA!'*

SIXTY-THREE

'JUST 'CAUSE SHE DANCE THE GO-GO, IT DON'T MAKE HER A HO, NO!'

Wyclef Jean blared from the walls of speakers, the dance floor starting to come to life now. Tamalov sniffed – the cocaine sharpening his sexual appetite even as it shrivelled his penis – as he surveyed the action from his perch in the VIP booth and found life to be good. *Nearly six million in euros.* He could take the rest of the year off. Hell, he could take the next decade off. Robbing robbers: the perfect crime. The VIP area was a small room with half a dozen big plush couches, roped off from the rest of the club by velvet ropes spanning an entrance through which the VIPs could survey the action on the floor, the ropes guarded tonight by Benny, who allowed only the closest friends or the choicest girls to pass. Benny was grinning from ear to ear – the thousand-euro bonus wad stuffed in his hip pocket, a thank-you for his help earlier. Spread the wealth, Tamalov believed.

The *CRACK* of another champagne cork caused him to turn and grin. Franco and Rolf and Harry, celebrating their good fortune, already with a few girls hanging off them, already doing blow right there on the table.

Tamalov, full of joy, full of magnanimousness, wanted to do something for Franco. It'd been worth handing Benny that thousand just to see the way his dark face lit up. Franco's finished passports had been masterpieces, not that they'd been needed in the end of course, but they might yet be resold with the photographs changed. They were safely tucked in the vault at home, along with the English money. Good old sterling: usually so solid. That was it – he'd come good on his word and find Franco a real peach tonight. A young honey to party with, to dance the go-go with them. He loved bringing young girls back to the house, the way they strode around his pool in their bikinis or their underwear, coltish, unsteady on their heels, their sexual characteristics sometimes freakishly pronounced, the breasts, butts and boxes almost too much for their undeveloped frames to handle. They all acted so cocksure and confident, as though this was the life they were used to at sixteen or seventeen, strutting around millionaires' homes full of coke and liquor. But, the best part, the most fun, was how, now and then, you'd see fear and uncertainty flickering in their faces, the sense of being truly out of their depth. Life was *good*.

SIXTY-FOUR

Yes, Susan had worked hard with make-up before, performing many reversals of age and sex that had proved undeniably convincing to the good people of Wroxham. There had been the hours transforming Mr Collins the butcher into a convincing alehouse hostess when they'd been short-handed for *The Taming of the Shrew*. There'd been the summer when she'd made Mr Wintergreen the convincing recipient of the love of Deborah Foster in *South Pacific*. Their ages had been sixty-one and twenty-three respectively. Or the time illness had forced her to transform Justin Bates (the understudy), nineteen at the time, into a passable Richard III.

But here and now, in the midnight hour in this cheap French flophouse, it could well be argued that she had accomplished her greatest work. If the reaction of her tiny audience of two was anything to go by anyway . . .

When Vanessa stepped through the doorway from the bathroom Jill's hand had gone to her throat and she'd sighed. 'Oh, Vanessa darling, you look absolutely beautiful.'

Vanessa wore a red wrap dress they'd bought her as a treat in Diane von Furstenberg in Cannes. Her hair had been cut into a sharp bob and her make-up brought out her lips and cheekbones making her look easily twenty-one years old.

Ethel contented herself with a more straightforward response: she nodded in approval and said, 'They'll be eating chips out of your knickers, love.' This was not entirely true. As Vanessa twirled for the ladies and the tightness of the dress across her rump was displayed, it became apparent that she wasn't (indeed that she couldn't be) wearing any knickers.

'Oh dear,' Jill cut in. 'Isn't that a bit on the raunchy side?'

'You look gorgeous, Vanessa,' Susan said, admiring her own work.

'Right,' Ethel barked, putting the handgun she'd been cleaning in her lap, clapping her hands together, 'we've had Beauty. Let's have the Beast!'

A muffled 'Piss off, Ethel' came through the thin wall to the bathroom, there was some shuffling and cursing, and then the door burst open and true silence descended upon the room.

Julie was backlit by the stronger light from the bathroom. She was striking a self-conscious pose in the door frame, pouting a little. The first thing that was apparent was the degree to which she'd kept her figure over the years. Generally, more recently, it had been hidden away in sweats or in the sexless uniform of the care home. Here it was encased in a tight black velvet dress, another purchase on the Cannes shopping spree. Susan had hitched the hemline up another three inches, displaying more of Julie's legs than had been seen for many years. But it was the hair and make-up that really did it, that really made Jill gasp and Ethel say, 'Holy. Fucking. Shit.' For Julie seemed to have halved in age in the last hour. Her hair had grown in volume and was spilling down her neck and into her cleavage. There were no discernible lines on her face, her eyes looked clear and unwrinkled, the eyes of a woman of twenty-eight or twenty-nine.

'*Merde*, Julie,' Vanessa whispered, looking at the apparition beside her.

'Hang on, hang on . . .' Susan said as she fumbled for the dimmer switch on the wall beside her. She dialled it down reducing the level of light in the room until it was closer to what you'd expect to find in a nightclub. The two of them looked like sisters. Definitely older and younger sister, but still.

'What do we think?' Julie said, cocking a hip, throwing an arm around Vanessa's shoulder.

'Well,' Susan sighed, taking in the amount of leg and cleavage on display, wondering for the first time if she'd slightly overdone it, 'if we don't get the money back we could make a fortune on the game.'

SIXTY-FIVE

By God the Englishman's snoring was intolerable, Dumas thought as Boscombe's bandsaw whine cut through the unmarked police car. He looked at his wristwatch again – just after midnight. He clicked on his radio and said softly, 'Rear unit, anything to report?'

'No,' came back the tired response.

Wesley yawned and shifted over in his seat, trying to distance himself from his boss. 'How long are we going to wait?' he asked in a stage whisper.

Dumas shrugged. 'This shithole is open until 4 a.m.,' he said. 'So as long as it takes, I am afraid.' He too was whispering and Wesley realised that they were both trying not to wake Boscombe, his snoring being preferable to his sarky comments and underhand farting.

Great, Wesley thought. *Another four hours of this*. He'd always imagined that being on a stakeout with Interpol would be a lot more exciting than this. Still, it could be worse, he reflected, gazing across the street at the queue shuffling closer to the velvet ropes outside Le Punisher. He could still be young enough to be putting himself through all *that* in the name of a good time.

Had Wesley looked closer, had he, say, walked across the street and up and down the queue, looking intently into the eyes of the hopefuls trying to gain entry to the club, he might have recognised at least one of the faces on display . . .

Julie's heart was thumping as she and Vanessa approached the rope. She'd just seen two couples in a row turned away. Granted one of them had contained a very drunk girl and the other a boy whose outfit said building site more than anything else, but still, they'd all been considerably younger than her. She felt Vanessa give her hand an encouraging squeeze as the group in front of them walked through into the hallowed portal of Le Punisher and the velvet rope fell back down and now it was their turn to step forward.

She heard Vanessa saying something casual in French as she went to crest the rope, acting as though it was her God-given right to be inside. It seemed to be working too, the rope was lifting and Julie, trying not to make eye contact, was simply following in straight behind her. But then, no, the rope was coming back down, in front of Julie, cutting her off from Vanessa, and the girl with the clipboard was looking her up and down. *Oh shit*, Julie thought. The girl was saying something to her in French. Julie reached for the words, trying to frame a response, but Vanessa was already in there, saying the words '*Stella McCartney, Stella McCartney*', and suddenly, magically, the girl was nodding, smiling, and the rope was floating back up and Julie too was on the inside.

'What was she saying?' Julie asked as they floated down the hallway, towards the booth at the end where you paid the entrance fee.

'She wanted to know where your dress was from!' Vanessa said, laughing.

'Christ,' Julie said, 'my heart's going like a fucking rabbit. Here . . .' She slipped Vanessa a hundred-euro note – one of the last hundred-euro notes they had – to pay their admission while she started thumbing a text with her free hand.

SIXTY-SIX

'FRIGGING IN THE RIGGIN, *THERE WAS FUCK ALL ELSE TO DO!'*

Ethel's idea of passing the time on stakeout involved rugby songs. Lots of rugby songs. Or rather, a handful of the same rugby songs endlessly and lustily repeated. She had just finished a charming ditty about a banker's daughter who opened her drawers for cash and was now on her second (possibly third, Susan reflected) rendition of something about a vessel called the *Good Ship Venus*. They had only been there half an hour. Jill, in the back, had long since put her headphones on, trying to drown out the onslaught with some Debussy.

Susan's phone beeped and she looked at Julie's text: *We're in*. She showed it to Ethel who nodded, drew breath, and went straight back into singing *'THE FIGUREHEAD WAS A WHORE IN BED AND THE MAST WAS A BIG BENT PENIS! FRIGGIN IN RIGG—'* '

'OK, Ethel! Please! I can't think straight,' Susan snapped.

Ethel shut up instantly, the world's filthiest jukebox unplugged. 'What's there to think about?' Ethel said.

'Well, what's going on in there for a start . . .' She nodded down the dark side street they were parked on, towards the main road and Le Punisher.

'That's not thinking, that's worrying.'

'Eh?'

'You can't affect anything that happens in there now,' Ethel said, popping a mint in her mouth. 'So you're not really thinking, are you? You're just worrying. Grant me the serenity to accept stuff and the balls to fuck up that which I'm not having and all that malarkey, Susan darling.'

'Have you ever thought about doing a self-help book, Ethel? Anyway – what about afterwards? Supposing, and it's a big suppose, all this comes off tonight and we get our money back. Do you really think this plan to get it all out of the country will work?'

'It's got to work better than the alternative, sweetie,' Ethel said.

'Which is?'

'Stay here and get arrested or killed.'

Susan sighed. 'You really do have a remarkably simple way of looking at everything, don't you?'

'Key to a long life, don't you know,' Ethel said. 'Forget all that rubbish about fats and sugars. Don't sweat the small stuff. Anyway, your old mucker Terry was right about South America, that'll be a doddle. They don't give a shit. I mean, they don't put your hand baggage through a scanner when you land in a country, do they? The real hurdle is going to be getting it out of France . . .'

Well, Susan thought, *it'll be a bloody miracle if we even get that far.*

SIXTY-SEVEN

Julie didn't know the song — it seemed to be just one huge, thumping bass note while the words *'around the world, around the world'* were endlessly repeated — but she was surprised at how easily, after two double vodkas, it all came back to her. She was moving her hips in a circular motion, her hands flapping gaily above her head, like many of them on the packed dance floor were doing. Vanessa was something else — a group of men kept an edgy semi-circle near her and she was batting off an advance roughly every thirty seconds. Julie had had two rough whispers in her ear herself.

They had worked their way across the floor, close to where a set of steps led up towards a velvet rope guarded by a bouncer and, Christ, yes, now they were close Julie could see through the smoke and sweat and strafing lasers that it was the very bouncer who had pulled a gun on them — the one who had come to the hotel — and, behind him, past the rope, perched on the edge of a plush sofa and talking animatedly to someone, she saw the shock of white hair. Tamalov.

She turned her back, facing Vanessa now, and wiggled her bottom in the direction of the VIP room.

Benny, in his turn, was scanning the crowd, when his eyes moved up off the (admittedly decent) arse of an old woman (certainly well into her thirties) in a short black dress and onto the face of the girl in the red dress she was dancing with.

Holy Christ.

Jackpot.

Benny took a couple of steps down the stairs to the edge of the dance floor and beckoned to the girl through the crowd. Vanessa saw him making the 'come here' gesture and danced her way towards him. Julie watched the guy shouting in her ear, Vanessa nodding, then shrugging. She went to turn away but the bouncer took her gently by the wrist and, smiling, shouted something else to her. Vanessa nodded and danced back to Julie.

'He wants me to go into the VIP area.'

'OK . . .'

'But just me.'

Dancing, smiling, Julie said, 'Can you handle it?'

'Of course. Don't worry, Julie.'

'I'll be watching, at the bar. OK?'

Vanessa nodded, pecked her quickly on the cheek, and writhed back through the crowd towards the waiting bouncer, giving Julie a sheepish grin before she tottered up the steps towards the dark, roped-off booth, her long legs wobbling on heels as she ascended.

Suddenly Julie wanted another drink very badly indeed.

Probably the mother, Benny thought as he lifted the rope for Vanessa and watched Julie disappear away through the heaving dancers. Nothing surprised him any more. He had a tiny twinge of conscience but that evaporated as soon as he pictured the boss's response to what he was bringing in. If he'd brought an old boiler like that other one in here, he'd be out of a job. Letting your own daughter go off with . . . Jesus Christ, what some people were capable of. Pimping your own flesh and blood. Still, being charitable, I suppose the woman knew this was a way for her kid to meet rich men, to move in better circles and all that. Still, if Benny ever had a daughter, she wouldn't be hanging out in places like this. Anyway, he knew he'd done good as he guided his trembling prize into the middle of the lounge and saw Tamalov's face lighting up as he slapped Franco on the back and reached for the champagne bottle. With luck another thick wad of notes would soon be getting tucked into his pocket.

The way of the world . . .

SIXTY-EIGHT

Jesus Christ, Sarge, Wesley thought.

Farting *in* his sleep now. Dumas wound down his window and looked at Halles, rolling his eyes in the driver's seat. 'This subhuman animal,' Halles said in thick French.

'How's that?' Wesley asked.

'Ah, I was just thinking of getting some coffee. Would you like some?' Halles said, looking at his watch. It was almost three o'clock in the morning and there was a tolerably short queue at the coffee and burger stand just along the street. In an hour or so, when the club closed, it would be mobbed.

'Don't suppose there's any chance of a tea, is there?'

Halles just looked at Wesley.

'Coffee would be fine, lovely.'

'You know what,' Dumas said, 'I'll come with you. Get some air . . .' As he stretched and reached for his door handle he turned to Wesley in the back seat. Boscombe was splayed out beside him, dead to the world, snoring lightly.

'Sorry — he's had a rough couple of days,' Wesley said. 'I don't think he got much sleep back in Cannes.'

Dumas nodded. 'Just, ah . . . sit tight please. We'll be back in a minute.'

'Sure.'

Wesley watched the two Frenchmen walk off towards the glowing neon, knowing they were talking about them. He gently flicked the V-sign behind the safety of the driver's chair and yawned.

SIXTY-NINE

Julie badly wanted another vodka, but two was definitely the limit if she wanted to keep sharp. So she sipped her mineral water and kept her gaze focused on the long mirror that ran above the bar. In it she could see across the dance floor behind her and just make out the raised entrance to the VIP area. She checked her watch. Nearly an hour she'd been in there.

'Madame?' A voice next to her said. Julie turned to see a man was speaking to her. He was tanned, leathery in fact, wearing a fluorescent-green T-shirt, and what very much appeared to be brown leather trousers. He was gesturing towards the bar, asking what she would like to drink. It was as though Julie's drinking with him was already agreed to, a foregone, piffling detail, and the only real question was *what* she would be drinking rather than if. To be honest it was a bold, forthright tactic that a less distracted Julie might well have had some time for. If, of course, the tactician had not been wearing brown leather trousers.

'No thank you,' she said, not taking her eyes off the mirror.

The guy persisted, tapping a sheaf of euros on the bar.

'*Non*,' Julie said, shaking her head.

The guy started ordering for her, pastis or something, gesturing to the waitress to bring two glasses to him and the bottle. Christ. And now here was Vanessa coming across the dance floor towards her. Julie turned as she passed a few feet away through the crush, her eyes, her entire face, saying 'follow me'.

'*Voilà!*'

Julie turned back to see she was being handed a glass of murky-grey, aniseed-scented goop. She took it, downed it in one, smacked the glass on the bar, said '*Au Revoir*', swivelled on her heel and followed Vanessa towards the toilets. 'Hey!' the guy shouted after her.

Once inside they both went down to the far end of the mirror and started fixing up their faces. 'How are we doing?' Julie asked in a side whisper.

'He's asked me back to his house for a party. Me and a couple of other girls in there.'

'I bet he has . . .'

'But this is good, no?'

'Yes, love. It's just . . . the dirty old bastard.' Julie sighed and started running her wrists under a cold-water tap.

'He's having his car brought round in a minute,' Vanessa went on.

'Right.' Julie started texting. 'What's he been talking about?'

'Oh, you know: his yacht, his cars, his houses, how big his dick is. Typical man stuff.' Vanessa made a face. She was all right this girl, Julie thought. She was all right.

SEVENTY

Boscombe was now in the deep REM stage of sleep you entered just before waking: Wesley could see his eyeballs flickering, almost vibrating under the eyelids, as the sergeant floated and glimmered through some Boscombe paradise, some green Arcadia of meat pies and criminals in striped tops, masks and swag bags being collared by good lads. Wesley could feel his own eyelids growing heavy too. He looked up the street: Dumas and Halles were deep in the coffee queue talking to another man, one of the backup team covering the rear of the building. He should probably get out there and join them. Get some air. Wake up a bit.

Wesley glanced over towards the entrance of the night-club, almost directly behind the coffee stand and hidden from the Frenchmen's view, and saw an open-topped Bentley whispering to the kerb and a valet-parker jumping out.

Several things happened at once.

Tamalov came briskly down the steps of Le Punisher, followed by a few girls and one swarthy, heavyset man.

The radio burst into life – an excited French voice jabbering away.

A red Porsche 4x4 slunk round the corner about a hundred yards behind the Bentley.

At the wheel, driving, it was . . . the widow! And the wheelchair woman, Ethel Merriman, was beside her.

'BLOODY HELL!' Wesley yelled. 'IT'S THEM!'

'Eh? Eh? Eh?' Boscombe said, blinking and jabbering and clutching around him as he jolted awake, like a mad, broken robot trying to reboot itself.

'OVER THERE! IT'S . . . HERE . . .' Wesley was trying to reach into the front of the motor, trying for either the horn or the radio, but it was like a bad dream: he couldn't quite reach the radio mike and he couldn't find the horn on this fucking French car. He couldn't open the door either: anti-criminal child locks in the back. He started shouting at Halles and Dumas, trying to get the window down, still trying to open the door.

Boscombe – crazed, half awake – looked blearily across the road. He saw a Bentley convertible peel off from the kerb just as an attractive prostitute in a tight black dress came running down the steps of the nightclub and threw herself into the back of a huge red Porsche.

Susan Frobisher was driving the Porsche.

Boscombe lost his own mind.

'FUCKING BOLLOCKS!' he barked as the Porsche took off down the street after the Bentley. Boscombe *hurled* himself into the front, into the driver's seat, while Wesley was still fumbling with the lock.

'Sarge! No!' Wesley shouted. 'The Interpol guys!'

'You snooze you lose, Wesley!' Boscombe snapped, seemingly unaware of the irony freely capering about here as he fired the engine and crunched the car into gear, causing Dumas and Halles to drop their coffees and start running towards them as Boscombe peeled off, flooring it, screeching round in a massive U-turn to follow the Porsche. Wesley scrabbled with his seat belt and rammed it home.

Boscombe slewed the powerful car across the wide boulevard – horns screeching, traffic braking around them – and accelerated hard.

Straight into the oncoming traffic.

'ON THE RIGHT, SARGE! ON THE RIGHT!'

In his post-sleep delirium Boscombe was convinced they were back in merry England. It was a fantasy he maintained for approximately three seconds – until Wesley started screaming as the scorching headlights of a monstrous truck bore down directly at them. Boscombe jerked the wheel hard to the right and the car hit the kerb at fifty miles an hour.

Time and space folded in on themselves. Wesley was aware that they had left the ground, that the tyres were no longer in contact with anything, and, for the second time in a week, courtesy of his boss, the detective constable entered the strange, slow-motion, underwater world of the car crash.

Boscombe was screaming too as an enormous plate-glass window loomed terrifyingly huge in his vision. He was dimly aware of the soft blue of a Mercedes sign before his hands left the wheel – useless now anyway – to cover his face.

There was the colossal smashing of glass as they went

through the window, then the crump of the landing, of metal on metal, and Wesley was being thrown forward, feeling his collarbone crack against the seat belt retaining him.

Boscombe was wearing no seat belt. Had it not been for the slowing effect of first the kerb and then the glass of the window – taking them down from fifty miles an hour as they left the road to just under thirty on final impact – he would surely have died. As it was he simply smashed his face off the windscreen very, very hard, knocking himself unconscious in the process. (Eyewitnesses would later describe how surreal the whole scene had been. The police car had screeched into the road, performed an enormous U-turn, gratuitously accelerated hard into the oncoming traffic, then swerved off the road and crashed through the window of the Mercedes showroom, coming to rest upon a brand-new SLK costing eighty thousand euros. All of this had taken just over ten seconds. It was all captured on CCTV and, under the heading 'COP FAIL', would soon be gathering twenty thousand YouTube hits a day.)

Several hundred yards away Dumas watched in unmitigated horror.

In the back of the Porsche half a mile ahead of all this carnage Julie had heard only a faint crash in the distance behind them. Then she'd warned Susan not to get too close to the Bentley in case they were spotted.

Wesley cried out in pain as he wriggled free of his seat belt in the smoking ruin of the car, deafening alarms all around him. He leaned forward and started slapping Boscombe, who lolled unconscious in the driver's seat. '*Sarge! Sarge!*'

'Mmff, rrnnghh,' Boscombe said.

'Are you all right?'

'Groo. Mmrghh.'

'Can you hear me?'

'Arrnnn, shrrppp. Unnfff . . .'

Wesley lifted his head up by the hair and saw that Boscombe had lost pretty much all of his front teeth. His nose looked like it had simply been reversed into his skull. All of this was immediately apparent; it would only be later, in the hospital, that they would discover Boscombe had also bitten off a quarter of his tongue and fractured two vertebrae.

It would be later too, at around 6 a.m. BST, that Sergeant Tarrant, just finishing up on the night shift, would make what would prove to be one of the defining mistakes of his career when he picked up a ringing phone on his way out of the station. He'd listened with growing disbelief. Then he'd gone to the cupboard in the kitchen and taken out the bottle of Famous Grouse the duty officers kept there for emergencies. He'd poured himself a treble and then made the call.

Drowsily, his wife fast asleep beside him, Chief Inspector Wilson had picked up. He'd listened. Tarrant's explanation seemed to take a very long time and during it Wilson uttered not a single word until the very end when he simply said, 'I see. Thank you, Tarrant.' Then he'd hung up.

Wilson placed the cordless phone back on its stand and sat on the edge of the bed. It was then that he felt the strange, not entirely unpleasant, tingling. Something not unlike a mild electrical current running through his left arm.

SEVENTY-ONE

Music oozed softly from the wall-mounted speakers out
by the pool, some ambient Ibiza crap Tamalov had got one
of the DJs at the club to put together for him. Tamalov
liked heavy rock — Iron Maiden, now that was a fucking
band — but when you had the ladies back it had to be either
ambient or disco.

Tamalov took a long draught of champagne and inhaled
the night air, the smell of pine from the forest and the sea
far below. (Well, he would have smelt all this had his nostrils
not been chock-full of very fine cocaine, more lines of
which Benny was now shaping on the glass dining table
beneath the covered patio that ran along the rear wall of
the 7,000-square-foot house. He was talking to two of the
girls they'd brought back from Le Punisher. Skanks of
course. Benny always got the skanks. Although, it had to
be said, at Tamalov's house, even the skanks were well worth
having . . .) He'd bought the place from an arms-dealer
friend back in the nineties, when he'd first started making

some real money. The arms dealer had bought it from a drug dealer in the eighties, who had bought it from a pornographer in the seventies who had owned the house since the death of the original owner in the sixties – an American bootlegger who'd built the place back in the thirties.

All of these men had made various improvements in terms of facilities, security and so on, and Tamalov had added a few of his own. It was, he liked to think, a pleasure compound.

Two more girls sat on the loungers by the pool talking. They were laughing, high as kites. The real prize, the real peach, sat talking to Franco. Or rather, Franco was talking to Vanessa, or, even more accurately, talking *at* Vanessa, for the Italian's conversation was now just a mad free-flowing jabber of cocaine-addled rubbish. By God she was young! That skin! Maybe seventeen at the most . . .

Mmm. Tamalov faced a difficult moral question here. He'd already kind of promised Vanessa to Franco, as a favour for services rendered. Now that Tamalov looked at this girl, in her red dress, with her long legs and bobbed brown hair, he found that he wanted her very badly indeed. What to do? Assert authority, move in on her, and just cope with Franco's upset as part of the deal? Or hang back, content himself with one of the skanks and let Franco have his fun? No, that was it. There was a way to solve all of this and avoid any unpleasantness.

He'd have Benny slip some sleepers into Franco's drink: drug him unconscious then he'd fuck the girl. Happy solution found, Tamalov walked around the pool to rejoin the party, raising his glass to everyone.

'Look at that fucking idiot,' Julie hissed.

They were in the woods bordering the property, the three of them dressed in black, with their balaclavas worn on top of their heads, like little hats. 'Ohh, God,' Ethel moaned. 'Just . . . just give me a minute.' She slumped down onto the pine needles, her back against a tree, sweat pouring down her face and caught her breath. It was the furthest Julie had ever seen Ethel walk – a good five hundred yards from where Jill sat waiting in the car, through thick woodland. They'd followed the Bentley for forty minutes, up into the hills winding along the coast, high above Marseilles, taking care to stay at a good distance. There was some rusty barbed wire just ahead of them – which Julie had already snipped with the pliers – and then it was a straight downhill run of about a hundred yards to the brightly lit poolside, where, even now, Julie could see Vanessa shaking her head as the swarthy bouncer offered her a plate of something and a rolled note. *Good girl*.

'What now?' Susan whispered.

'We've got to get down there . . .' Julie replied.

Julie and Susan were clutching two pistols from Nails's collection, the Browning automatic and the huge Webley revolver respectively. Behind them Ethel was holding the sawn-off shotgun. All three weapons were, for the first time in many years, loaded with live ammunition, the actual loading done – with what appeared to Susan to be terrifying deftness – by Ethel in the car on the way up.

'We can't just run down there,' Julie said. 'We need a diversion or something . . .'

'A diversion?' Susan said. Her heart was thumping. Her mouth bone dry.

'She's right,' Ethel said from behind them. 'Our front's

too exposed. Hundred-yard dash with no defilade. Suicide. Somme. Ypres.' She was rummaging in Nails's bag while she talked.

'So what are we going to do?' Susan asked.

'I wonder if this is the seven or the four?' Ethel said.

'Eh?' Julie said, not taking her eyes off Vanessa down by the pool.

'Only one way to find out . . .'

'What are you talking about, Ethel?'

'*Fire in the hole!*' Ethel hissed. Julie and Susan both turned in time to see Ethel launching something over their heads – her right arm extended full back, like a shot-putter – and then throwing herself on top of them, pressing them down into the warm earth.

'OK,' Tamalov said, standing with his back to the pool and letting his robe fall to the ground, 'let's get this party started, ladies . . .'

There was a distinct 'PLOP' behind him as something splashed into the water. He turned round and peered down into it, as did Benny and the two girls with him, both of them already down to their underwear. There was a grey shape, about the size of two tennis balls, sinking to the bottom.

Neither Susan nor Julie had understood Ethel's question about four and seven seconds.

It referred to the fuse length in the Mk II Mills bomb, the hand grenade that was standard issue to the British Army from 1915 until the early 1980s. The reason the weapon enjoyed such a long service span was its durability and reliability: it was a simple design that had rarely been bettered. Indeed one of the few improvements that had been made to the device occurred in 1940, when it was finally decided that the seven-second fuse that had been fitted up until then was, in fact, too long. It gave the enemy a chance to evade the grenade's blast or, even worse, throw the bugger back. So, in 1940, the fuse was shortened to four seconds. As the date stamp on the bottom of this particular Mills bomb had long worn off Ethel had no way of knowing the fuse length. Nails had bought three of them off a villain called Ian McKay in the snug of the Crazy Rat in Bethnal Green on August bank holiday weekend 1964. A fiver each they'd been. (A *lot* of money back then.) One had been used (unsuccessfully) to try and blow the door off a safe later that very year, one had been lost sometime in the 1970s and the sole survivor of the trio now sat at the bottom of Alexei Tamalov's pool.

Ian McKay had bought a box of twelve from an old soldier who'd snatched them from the armoury at Aldershot just prior to being demobbed in 1945. The grenades were part of a consignment that had left the Mills Munition Factory in Birmingham just before the outbreak of World War II, in the summer of 1939.

So the answer to Ethel's question was seven.

Seven seconds.

A second and a half between Ethel pulling the pin and throwing, two seconds in the air, another two and a half seconds for it to sink the three metres to the bottom of the deep end of the pool and one second for Tamalov to frown into the water and say, 'What was tha—' before –

KAA-BOOOOMMMMMMMM!

Of course, due to the increased density of the conducting agent, the force of an explosion is greatly magnified underwater – the grenade erupted, sending a plume of water and shrapnel over a hundred feet into the air. Tamalov was knocked flat on his back, his ears ringing like cathedral bells. Benny and the two girls, the closest ones to the explosion, were all sent flying thirty feet across the patio – all knocked unconscious.

Vanessa was screaming. Franco was stumbling around, his ears ringing, soaked head to foot, a mirror-full of drenched cocaine in his hands. He dropped the mirror and was reaching inside his jacket for his gun when he heard the sound of a pump-action shotgun being viciously racked and felt something very hard being pressed into the small of his back and the words 'Drop that fucking thing or I'll turn your fucking kidneys into pâté'. Franco understood the tone, if not the exact sentiment. He dropped his Beretta onto the deck and turned to see a very out of breath old lady, her face obscured by a balaclava with the word 'FUCK' scrawled across the forehead staring him down. He started to laugh at the demented sight but Ethel drove the butt of the gun straight into his face, breaking his nose, and Franco went down, hot tears spurting from his eyes.

'Julie!' Vanessa cried, recognising her before she even tore her balaclava off, as she scooped her up into her arms and hugged her.

Tamalov was struggling up into a sitting position by the pool when he felt a foot going into his chest, driving him back down. He looked up at the figure standing over him, its face obscured by a black balaclava that had the word 'FEAR' printed across the forehead in crude Tippex. It was pointing a very large handgun right at him.

'You're dead, all dead . . .' Tamalov was trying to say,

his attempts at speech hampered by the fact that he could not hear his own voice, only the numbing ringing in his ears.

He looked up – beyond astonishment – as Susan ripped her own balaclava off, revealing her red, sweating face, catching her breath as she said, with as much brightness as she could muster under the circumstances, 'Hello, Mr Tamalov. It's us, the Frogs!'

SEVENTY-TWO

Dumas wandered through the Mercedes showroom in shock, his feet crunching on acres of broken glass. It looked like a bomb had gone off: the blue neon Mercedes logo cracked, blinking and hanging by a wire, smoke and petrol fumes filling the air, his wrecked police car sitting atop the ruin of the SLK, looking like it was trying to mount it. The whole scene was lit by the soft strobing of the red and blue lights of the other police cars and the ambulance that had arrived, and soundtracked by the murmuring and gasps of the large crowd of clubbers that had gathered at the hastily erected 'DO NOT CROSS' line his men had erected. He turned to Wesley and tried to speak but found that words would not come. Wesley was strongly reminded of the perpetual expression of Chief Inspector Wilson.

'Looks worse than it is,' Wesley offered hopefully. 'Lick of paint . . .'

In the background, something caught Dumas's eye — a prostrate form on a stretcher being rolled towards the

waiting ambulance. They had, of course, lost both Tamalov
and the old English ladies in all the chaos.

'Bit of MDF . . .' Wesley went on.

Dumas started towards the stretcher. '*Pardon*,' he was
saying to the paramedics wheeling it. '*Pardon . . .*'

The two guys looked up from the prostate, gurgling form
of Boscombe, towards Dumas, and realised what he was
begging them for. '*Non! Non!*' the lead medic yelled,
shielding Boscombe as Halles came in from behind and
grabbed Dumas by the shoulders, holding him back. His
request for one clean punch at Boscombe's face being denied
he settled for kicking a large section of plastic bumper (it
had been torn off his police car as it mounted the kerb)
across the street and screaming 'FUCK!'

A uniformed gendarme came running under the police
tape and started whispering urgently to Dumas and Halles,
the three of them forming a huddle. Wesley shuffled closer.
He caught the words '*explosif*' and 'Tamalov' before Dumas
was clapping his hands together and shouting to his men,
several of whom started running towards their cars. Wesley
ran towards the ambulance where Boscombe was now being
loaded in, a thick surgical brace already clamped around
his neck, tight straps binding him to the stretcher as it was
hauled upright, his arms folded across his chest. 'Sarge?'
Wesley said. It was not unlike talking to the villain Hannibal
Lecter, lashed to his mad trolley.

'Urfff?' Boscombe said woozily. He had already been shot
up with painkillers.

'I'm just gonna go with these guys. I'll catch up with
you later.'

'Arroogghh!'

'Yeah, I think it's your teeth . . .'

'Eeef?' Boscombe said through his wrecked bombsite of dentistry. But Wesley was already off and running towards one of the French police cars revving its engine by the glass-strewn kerb.

SEVENTY-THREE

'*You think you can torture me? You stupid old bitches!*' Tamalov screamed. '*I have been tortured by the head of the KGB!*'

'Oh, this is *hopeless*,' Susan said, flopping down into an armchair.

They were in the living room. It was the size of a tennis court. Franco, Benny and the club girls were all in a corner, lashed up with duct tape. Tamalov was dripping wet and duct-taped to a chair in the middle of the room, shivering in his boxer shorts, surrounded by Julie, Susan and Ethel, who was now happily back in her wheelchair, Jill having fetched it from the car. Vanessa and Jill sat together on one corner of a long L-shaped sofa. Jill had her fists in her ears because they had just spent fifteen minutes repeatedly asking Tamalov where their money and passports were and repeatedly getting 'fuck yourself', 'fuck your mothers' and, more simply, 'fuck you' in response. In fairness, Julie thought, their attempts at 'torture' had been fairly lame: a couple of mild slaps in the face and some variants on the 'tell us or else' line of questioning. It had hardly been Olivier in *Marathon Man*.

'Look, just . . . just BLOODY TELL US!' Susan yelled.

Tamalov laughed.

'Right,' Ethel said, wheeling towards him. She put the barrel of her shotgun to his forehead. 'Where's our money?'

'Ethel!' Susan said.

'What? You think you can shoot a man in the head with that?' Tamalov said. 'Have you any idea what would happen, old woman? My brains on the ceiling, the walls, your faces? You think you could do that?'

Ethel's finger tightened on the trigger.

'Come on,' Tamalov said. 'Shoot! Hag!'

'Ethel!' Julie cried now too.

'Oh FUCK IT!' Ethel said, letting the gun drop. Of course she wasn't about to shoot the bugger in cold blood at point-blank range. She punched him very hard in the face, however. 'Ha!' he cried.

This was proving tricky, far trickier than they'd imagined.

'Oh, he'll never tell us!' wailed Jill. Again.

'Do shut up, Jill,' Julie said.

'The police will be here soon . . .' Vanessa said.

'She's not wrong,' Ethel said. 'Someone must have heard that grenade.'

'RIGHT!' Susan said, standing up. 'I'VE HAD JUST ABOUT ENOUGH OF THIS! Jill, Julie, help me drag him into the kitchen. Ethel, Vanessa, watch them.' She indicated Franco, Benny and the girls. 'Bring the boys in when I tell you.'

With a crash and a bump the three of them dragged the chair with Tamalov on it into the kitchen, the heavy doors closing behind them. Tamalov cursed them all the way in a blend of Russian and English: 'you stupid fucking bitches . . . useless daughters of whores . . . your cocksucking mothers are . . .'

'Oh really!' Jill said.

'Yeah, can we mute this please?' Susan said.

'Certainly,' Julie said. She flattened a strip of duct tape across Tamalov's mouth, reducing him to muttered 'Ummmmfs'.

'Right,' Susan said, looking around the vast marble-and-chrome space. She opened the enormous fridge and saw a whole chicken on the shelf. 'Good, I'm also going to need a bottle of ketchup, some red food dye, two plums, a glass of water, some TCP and a very sharp knife.'

'Oh, come on,' Jill said. 'What are you going to do with that lot? He's been tortured by the head of the KGB.'

'Yes, well,' Susan said, fishing a pair of rubber gloves out from under the sink, 'I used to be head of make-up and special effects for Wroxham Amateur Dramatic Society.' She snapped a glove on and looked down at Tamalov.

SEVENTY-FOUR

Susan worked incredibly fast, up to her elbows in the mixing bowl. The Tamalov household was very well stocked: he had everything except for the plums, but she'd made do with two peaches. She imagined the stones were a little large for true authenticity, but they'd probably get away with it. *You can create illusions of reality — make people think they've seen things they really haven't seen . . .*

'Julie,' Susan said, not looking up from the mixing bowl, into which she was now dipping a piece of chicken skin, 'get his boxer shorts off.'

'Uh?' Julie said.

'Quickly!'

'Uh?' Julie and Tamalov both said now.

Julie did so while Tamalov struggled and cursed.

Julie ripped them down to the floor. 'Oh,' she said, 'is it that cold?'

Tamalov grunted some muffled obscenities.

'Right,' Susan said through gritted teeth as she leaned

down and started slathering the mixture all over Tamlov's groin, splashing some of it on the floor, on his chest. 'Get ready to shout for the others, Jill.'

'I don't underst—' Jill said.

Susan grabbed the bottle of TCP and a dishcloth. 'OK, Julie, you'll need to pull his thingy back.'

'Do what?' Julie said.

'You know . . .' Susan nodded at Tamalov's groin. 'His . . . foreskin.'

'Dear God!' Jill exclaimed.

'And, ah, why are we doing that?' Julie asked.

'Oh, for God's sake – just do it!' Susan hissed. She was pouring a very generous amount of TCP onto that dishcloth. Tamalov's eyes widened and he started trying to say stuff through the tape gag.

'Ah . . .' Julie said, finally getting it. She looked at Tamalov's tiny, uncircumcised penis with some revulsion and swallowed. 'OK,' she said. 'Hardback for the full Kojak . . .' Out the purple peanut popped.

'Right, here we go. This might sting a bit . . .' With one hand Susan *rammed* the TCP-soaked rag into the very eye, the most tender part of Tamalov's tender parts, as, with the other hand, she simultaneously *ripped* the duct tape off his mouth, taking a bit of his lip off too.

In the next room Vanessa and Ethel were looking out of the big picture window with its views into the darkness, the lights of Marseilles twinkling in the distance. They were just fancying that they could faintly hear sirens in the distance when . . .

The scream.

It was inhuman – something an animal might make at

the most extreme moment of duress, in the moment before death.

'COME QUICK!' Jill shouted from the kitchen, as Susan taped Tamalov's gag back in place. 'THEY'VE GONE MAD!'

'You two.' Ethel pointed the shotgun at the gagged Franco and Benny, whose heart rates had just fairly spiked if their faces were anything to go by. 'Move it.' Vanessa helped them to their feet, their legs still tied together, hopping and shuffling towards the kitchen door, Ethel's shooter at their backs. They were pushed through the kitchen door and their eyes widened at the appalling scene before them.

Tamalov writhed on the floor, screaming into his gag, shouting, kicking, tears streaming from his eyes. There was blood *everywhere*, but nowhere more than his groin: it was a horror show, an operating theatre.

Susan stood beside him, panting, covered in viscera, with a huge kitchen knife in her trembling right hand and something red, wet and unspeakable in her left.

'Wh . . . what . . .' Vanessa gasped, her hands going to her mouth. 'What have you done to him?'

Susan threw a wad of gore onto the white-tiled floor in front of the two henchmen – a gout of bloody skin and a couple of ruined orbs – as she cried 'WE CUT HIS BLOODY BALLS OFF!'

Ethel said, 'Jesus. Fucking. Christ.'

Franco fainted.

Benny started screaming.

Vanessa started dry-heaving.

'YOU!' Julie said, pointing at Benny. 'You're next!'

Tamalov was going berserk, his face fluorescent with the

effort of trying to shout through his gag as Benny collapsed to his knees and started gibbering into his own gag. Julie ripped it off and it all came out very fast:

'Nonononopleasedownstairsingaragethereispanelin floorevcrythingthereIshowyoupleasenonoIbegyouplease!'

Tamalov moaned and started banging his head off the floor.

'OK, garage. Panel in the floor,' Susan said. 'Is there a back way out of here?'

Tamalov was trying to scream something through his gag. Benny hesitated. Susan held the tip of the knife to his balls. 'At the back of the garage! A tunnel! It runs five hundred metres! There is car at the end! Please, don't hurt me.' Benny was crying now.

Susan couldn't resist it. She slipped Tamalov's gag off for just a second. 'YOU IDIOT! YOU FUCKING FOOL!'

She slapped it back on.

'Great,' said Julie. 'Let's go.'

SEVENTY-FIVE

Jabber coming over the radio as they drove very fast through the dark hills, the first rays of dawn appearing in the sky to the east. Wesley was wedged in the middle of the back seat between two uniformed gendarmes, Dumas was in the passenger seat with another plain-clothes officer driving beside him. Dumas and the two gendarmes were doing something Wesley had only ever seen happening in cop movies: they were loading guns. Dumas was slotting fat brass cartridges into a nickel-plated snub-nosed revolver while the guys on either side of Wesley were checking the loads in their magazines before ramming them back into the butts of their sleek black automatics and pulling back the slide thingies. They made exactly the kind of noises as they made in the films, a metallic 'clack', except it was much, much louder in real life.

'How long?' Dumas said, snapping his pistol shut.

'Seven or eight minutes,' the driver said, glancing at the satnav's ETA and taking a bit off to allow for their speed.

'Remember, no shooting except on my order, OK?' Dumas said. The gendarmes nodded, grim yet excited.

Holy shit, Wesley thought as they skidded round a bend at ninety kilometres an hour, heading up into the mountains, *the Sarge would have loved all of this . . .*

SEVENTY-SIX

They were in a basement vault, raking the walls with torch beams. Julie's first thought was that it was not totally unlike the room where they found the late Barry Frobisher: hardcore pornographic videos lined the walls for a start. But there was more, much more. A huge cache of automatic weapons, a pile of forged passports of many different nationalities, a block of what she assumed was cocaine the size of a car battery, and there, smack in the middle of the room on a trestle table, was their holdall. Susan unzipped it. The money looked to be untouched. Nestling right on top, all burgundy and beautiful and proud, were three British passports: one each for her, Julie and Ethel. She passed one to Julie. They were nicely aged, with crenellations in the covers, little tears here and there, ruffled pages. You honestly couldn't tell the difference between these and the real thing. They examined the photographs. Remarkable. *Exactly* what they'd asked for. Masterpieces really – especially Ethel's.

'Back in business,' Julie said.

'No time for that,' Susan said. 'Come on. Let's get this over with . . .'

Back up the stepladder, back through the hatch, lugging the holdall between them, and into the strip-lit garage. They'd already found the well-hidden door to the secret passage. They could hear the sirens clearly now, closing in. Ethel and Jill were already saying their goodbyes. Just the five women, here in the garage. Susan grabbed Vanessa and gave her a tight squeeze. 'You take care of yourself, darling. Just remember what we told you to say and stick to your story.'

Susan stood back and Julie moved in. She embraced Vanessa and whispered something in her ear, something the others couldn't hear, while pressing something into her palm. Julie stood back, tears in her eyes.

'OK?' Julie said.

'*Oui*,' Vanessa nodded, fighting tears too, those sirens right on top of the place now.

'Right, guys, time to choose: the tunnel or the bum-palace.' This was Ethel, obviously.

'Goodbye, Julie.'

'Bye, Vanessa, sorry about this . . .' Julie said, peeling a strip of duct tape off.

SEVENTY-SEVEN

Dumas led the way down the long white hallway, revolver out, armed officers crouching behind him, watching his clenched left fist for a signal, Wesley right at the back, fervently wishing he had a gun, having, in fact, to stop himself shaping his hand into a childish pistol.

Dumas stopped, flattening his back against the thick stone wall, just before the wall arrived at an archway that led into another room. He could hear the crunching of the other officers' boots on the gravel outside as they went round the house, seeking other entry points at the back, on the side. (They'd long had a schematic of the place.) 'Alexei?' he shouted. 'Alexei Tamalov? I have a search warrant for these premises. Any attempts to stop us will be met by force.'

Nothing.

Dumas repeated the statement in Russian and then in English.

Still nothing.

And then, softly, came the sound of something breaking inside, something falling over. Dumas swallowed, cocked his gun and nodded to the officers behind him. He swung out into the archway, assuming a firing stance, both hands on the checkered wooden grip of the weapon.

He saw Tamalov, Benny, Franco and a couple of girls, all tied and gagged on the floor at the far end of the huge lounge. Tamalov was trying to crawl towards a doorway and had knocked a lamp off a table. He appeared to be covered in . . .

'Get a medic!' Dumas shouted behind him, coming into the room, motioning to the uniforms to fan out and check the rest of the place. Tamalov looked up at him, utterly miserable. 'Are you OK?' Dumas reached for the gag and slipped it off.

'IT'S KETCHUP! FUCK YOU!'

'SIR! THROUGH HERE!'

Dumas looked up. Another plain-clothes officer was standing in a doorway, pointing down a corridor, a corridor that led, Tamalov knew, to his garage. He realised that, from where he was laid out, Benny's face was tantalisingly close. He lashed out with his tethered feet and managed to kick the bouncer in the chin. 'That's enough of that,' Dumas said, pulling Tamalov a few feet away and signalling for his men to guard him as he headed towards the doorway.

Inside the garage three more men stood around an open hatch in the floor, shining torches down into it. A bound, crying girl – she was very young, very beautiful – was being attended by a female officer. She was saying in French 'I thought they were going to kill us!'

One of Dumas's lead officers, Fabio, heaved himself up

through the open hatch and said 'Boss . . .' as he handed Dumas a torch. Dumas shone it down into the basement room – *oh my.* 'There's more,' Fabio said, wiping sweat from his brow.

'How much more?'

'We'll need to bring the truck round,' Fabio said.

Dumas smiled as, behind him, Wesley crossed the room to where Vanessa was accepting sips of water from the kind French policewoman. He knelt down.

'Did you see them?' Wesley asked.

'*Pardon?*' Vanessa said.

'The old ladies?' Wesley said. Vanessa and the policewoman both looked at him. 'You know, the . . . the *les grandes dames?*' They both continued to look at him.

'The old ladies!' Wesley said. '*LES DAMES GRANDES!*'

'*Pardon?*' Vanessa said again.

'Oh for fuck's sake!'

Vanessa started crying and buried her face in the bulletproof vest of the policewoman.

'*Les* –' Wesley prepared to do some charades.

'Officer Wesley?'

He turned to see Dumas behind him.

'Thank you, but I think you and your colleague Sergeant Boscombe have "helped" us quite enough for tonight. We can take it from here . . .'

SEVENTY-EIGHT

Nice airport, gleaming in the afternoon sunshine.

Julie and Susan could see it from the window of the Novotel bedroom, where they stood drinking coffee. Julie was wishing for something stronger, but they had to stay sharp. This was it – the final hurdle, the last roll of the dice, the Alamo, whatever you wanted to call it. If this worked they were free and clear. But it was, they both knew, a fairly big if. They would be looking for them and no mistake.

'Well, I'm ready,' a voice said behind them. They turned to see Jill in the bathroom doorway. She had her little wheelie suitcase behind her. She even had her new driving gloves on, bless her heart, and her bottom lip was trembling. Jill was nervous for many reasons.

She was nervous because she was about to drive the unfamiliar rental car parked outside. (Hiring the car on the Hertz lot at the airport had been a testing moment. Julie had been waiting just round the corner in the stolen BMW belonging to Tamalov, the one that had indeed been parked up at the end of the long tunnel beneath his house, keys in the ignition, intended for getaways exactly like the one they had been making. She'd told Jill that if there was anything funny when she tried to hire the car, any 'just wait here a moment' or 'I just need to make a phone call' stuff, she was to get the hell out of there. But no: her driving licence and credit card had both gone across the counter and come back with a smile. It was proof enough that no one was on to her, that the trail still stopped with Susan, Julie and Ethel.)

She was nervous because she had to drive all the way across France on her own, all the way to the ferry terminal at Le Havre, a ten-hour trip. (They'd thought about Bilbao – which was far closer, just a three-hour drive – but decided against it because it meant crossing the Spanish border and why push your luck?) She was going to break it up and find a nice hotel for the night somewhere around the halfway mark. She was aiming to make a crossing to Portsmouth around lunchtime tomorrow. With a bit of luck she'd be home by bedtime.

She was nervous for her friends – who still had some very testing hurdles in front of them.

But mostly Jill was nervous because she had thirty thousand pounds in cash in her wheelie suitcase. Six house bricks of fifty-pound notes: two hundred notes in each brick.

'Now remember, love,' Julie said, 'just put your case in the boot and drive right on. The chances of someone like you getting pulled over for a full search are zero . . .'

'But, if you do,' Susan said, 'what do you do?'

'I tell them a man asked me to take it for him and I act all stupid and senior and ditzy.'

'Shouldn't be too hard.' They turned to see Ethel wheeling in through the connecting door to the next room. Jill smiled and said, 'Fuck off, Ethel.'

A collective gasp and then they all fell about laughing before, just as quickly, there were tears in Jill's eyes as she embraced each of them in turn. 'Take care of yourselves. I suppose I'll find out one way or another what happens to you, won't I?'

'Well, yes,' Susan said. 'I'd keep an eye on the news.'

'We'll send you a postcard, once we're settled,' Julie said, with a confidence she did not entirely feel.

'OK then,' Jill said, taking a deep breath, dabbing her eyes with the back of her hand. 'I'll be off. I . . . I'll miss you all so much.'

'Bye, love,' Ethel said. 'Good luck.'

The door closed behind her and the three of them watched from the window as, a few moments later, Jill crossed the car park below them, got into the plain white Renault and drove off.

'How long have we got?' Julie said.

Ethel looked at the clock on the bedside table. 'Three hours? A little more?'

'We'd best get down to it then.' This was Susan. 'We're going to need every minute.' She opened the suitcase full of all the stuff she'd bought in Marseilles and then looked at their passport photos very carefully. Yes, this was going to be a challenge and no mistake. 'Right, Ethel,' she said, taking some scissors out. 'You first . . .'

SEVENTY-NINE

They were getting some looks all right, Wesley thought, checking the expressions of various folk they were passing: concern, horror, sympathy and, predictably, on some of the younger faces, amusement. He was pushing Boscombe along in the wheelchair given to them by Marseilles hospital, as a kind of parting gift from the good people of France. Boscombe's legs were both straight out in front of him, up on the footrests, both encased in plaster. Only one leg was actually broken, but he'd done something complicated to his pelvis and they didn't want any movement below the waist, so they'd pretty much immobilised both legs. It was the head that was the real talking point, however. His neck was still bound by the thick surgical brace, making it impossible for him to turn round, meaning they had to stop every few yards in order for Wesley to hear the latest demand for water, toilet or whatever. He also had one of those mad contraptions around his skull, one of those metal cage jobs that seemed to bolt into his actual dome. It turned out – as the surgeon had cheerfully explained in the early hours of this morning – that Boscombe had come very close to killing himself. The vertebrae in his neck were appallingly damaged and had had to be fully immobilised. (And what a palaver it had been getting through security – with all this metal.)

The face itself was a livid patchwork of bruising, ranging from the iridescence of petrol in water to the yellow of a parrot's plumage. Boscombe also seemed to be drooling constantly, with Wesley frequently having to stoop and wipe his chin clean. Perhaps this was a consequence of him having bitten about half an inch of his tongue off. Safe to say that all of this was not making the sergeant the ideal travelling companion. In fact here he was again, banging on the side of the wheelchair for Wesley to stop and listen to him. Never mind – they'd be home soon enough.

'Sarge?' Wesley said, putting the brake on and coming round to the front, crouching down.

'Ooooo . . .'

Wesley smiled and nodded encouragingly, as you would to a small child or a simpleton.

'Oooood.' A goodly stream of saliva flecked and bubbled from his lips.

'Ooood?' Wesley repeated.

'OOOOOOD!' Boscombe was pointing at his mouth.

'Ah! Food. Righto. Let's see what we can find. Over here looks OK . . .' He wheeled Boscombe into the cafe closest to them and together they gazed at rows of glass-encased sandwiches and tarts, pastries and croissants, fancies and toasties.

'Mmmm,' Wesley said, catching the look of crazed hunger

in Boscombe's eyes. 'I think it'd be safer if we just found you some soup, eh, Sarge?'

'Uuuuck.'

'Yeah, maybe some scrambled eggs. Doctor's orders and all that.'

'Uuuurrrr.'

'Come on . . .' Wesley looked up and checked the nearest departures board. There it was:

BA 243, Nice–London Gatwick.

The gate wasn't even up yet – plenty of time.

He wheeled Boscombe off through the busy airport.

EIGHTY

Mother and daughter approaching security, off on the next leg of this once-in-a-lifetime round-the-world trip: Miss and Mrs Saunders.

Miss Anna Saunders was very chic, her slim figure encased in a wrap dress, sunglasses on, a tote bag over her shoulder. Her perfect hair and make-up would, from a certain distance, have led you to believe that she was in her mid-forties.

The years, however, had not been quite so kind to her mother, Mrs Heather Saunders. She was a stout woman in her late sixties, maybe even early seventies, with a lined, aged face. Actually 'stout' would be the kindest way of putting it. She in fact looked to be in the region of 120 kilos and was already sweating quite heavily from the effort of getting here from the entrance.

'Boarding passes and passports please.'

Anna Saunders handed them over, removing her sunglasses and making direct eye contact with the girl examining them, the girl guarding the entrance to the actual security line, where the other passengers were doing their thing: removing shoes and belts, taking out laptops and so on. Anna laid a protective hand on her mother's shoulder, to let the girl know they were together and that she was in charge.

The only reaction from the girl was the slightly nicer smile afforded to passengers holding first-class tickets, as both these ladies did. (This also gave them a greatly increased cabin baggage allowance. Something both Miss and Mrs Saunders needed to make full use of.) '*Merci*. Have a nice flight.' The girl handed the tickets back.

'*Merci beaucoup*,' Susan said. 'Come along, Mother.'

'Coming,' Julie said, waddling after her, cursing inwardly and thinking, *Mother? I'm only six months older than you and don't you forget it, missy! Last time I toss a bloody coin with you, Susan Frobisher . . .* Christ, Julie wondered, was this what it was like to be obese? She had to be lugging an extra thirty kilos around the breasts, belly and bum, and her heart was pounding like mad as they joined the queue and Susan swung their bags up onto the conveyor belt. *Remind me to stay thin*, Julie thought.

Further along in the terminal Dr Thomas McKenzie approached security slowly in his wheelchair. McKenzie was overweight too, though stylishly dressed in a baggy linen suit and panama hat. He fanned his bearded face with the back of his boarding pass before handing it over to the assistant, who was saying, 'And have you packed your bags yourself, Dr McKenzie?'

'Ah did. Aye,' McKenzie spat gruffly. Ethel had decided that gruffness would be part of her character. She was a bit worried about the beard though, given the sweat pouring off her.

A hand landed on the shoulder of Dr Thomas McKenzie. 'Can you come this way please?'

'Eh? How come?' The security guard looked down at her oddly. Behind the guy, two queues along, Ethel could see Susan and Julie. They were almost through.

'We must X-ray your wheelchair.'

'Oh, right enough, son,' Ethel grunted. 'I'll just get up . . .'

'No need, we can do it with you sitting in it.'

'Naw, son – I'm no having aw they X-rays fired intae me.'

'Pardon?'

'Fucks yer baws up, like.'

'Please, just remain seated and we can—'

'Yer no pumping aw that shite intae me.' Ethel didn't exactly do panic, but if they X-rayed her . . .

'Just step over here.'

Ethel was out of the wheelchair now and leaning against the walk-through scanner, panting heavily. 'Just, just give us a minute here . . .'

Another security person, a girl, was stepping towards her with one of the electric wand things that they ran over you. 'Sir, if I can just . . .'

'Ah'm sorry,' Ethel said, 'ah'm needing tae empty ma bag.'

'Your bag? It is on the belt, yes?'

'Naw. Ma bag. Ma colostomy bag.' Ethel made some gestures. The two security guards looked at each other.

'I shouldnae have hud that steak and eggs fur breakfast . . .' Ethel said.

The girl seemed to understand something and a hurried exchange took place in French. 'Please,' the man said. 'Just step through the scanner.' He wheeled her chair off to be X-rayed separately.

Four minutes later Dr McKenzie sat in his wheelchair in a remote aisle of the duty-free shop quietly conferring with Anna and Heather Saunders. 'Jesus,' Ethel said, 'I thought I'd had it then.'

'OK, it's OK. It's fine,' Susan said. 'Everything's OK.' She was pretending to leaf through a Fodor travel guide and they were speaking to each other out of the corners of their mouths.

'OK, phase two,' Julie said. 'How will we do this?'

'Toilets are over there.' Ethel nodded. 'I'll go in, I'll take two of the cases, you give it a minute and then follow me in with the other two.'

Julie nodded.

'Right, be careful,' Susan said. 'I'm just going to go down there and grab a coffee.' She looked up at the departures board: BA 117, Nice–Rio, gate 43.

Boarding was due to commence in thirty minutes.

EIGHTY-ONE

Soup and bloody mushed eggs – this was it. This was his diet for the next few weeks. Boscombe stared hatefully at his plate. Even the eggs hurt to swallow. He glanced at the two newspapers on the table – a local one and a copy of the *Sun*. They had made the cover of the local paper: a photograph of the wrecked Mercedes showroom and an accompanying article. Page 4 of the *Sun* had the same picture plus a smaller one of him inserted in the corner (a still taken from his Sky News interview a week ago) and the caption 'SACRE LES BOYS IN BLEU! BRIT BLUNDER COPS!' Fucking . . . journalists.

'All right, Sarge?' He looked up, Wesley looked sated after his huge feast of croissants and coffee. 'I'm just going to run over to duty-free and grab a few presents for the kids. You'll be all right here for a minute, eh? Here, let me just . . .' He pushed Boscombe's wheelchair a little closer into the table for him.

Boscombe nodded. 'Mmmmf, Uhhnnn.'

'And I, ah . . .' Wesley hesitated. 'I spoke to Chief Inspector Wilson there. It's . . . not great. Anyway. Back in a minute.'

Wesley strolled off and Boscombe went back to reading the papers. Yes, there really was no other way to put it: what a total, absolute bloody shambles.

As Boscombe turned to the football results, five hundred yards away Ethel and Julie emerged from the toilets. To the casual passer-by it looked like a fat, bearded, wheelchair-bound man in a linen suit being helped by a lady in her sixties whose dress was a little too big for her. The eagle-eyed observer would have noticed that Dr McKenzie and Mrs Heather Saunders had both lost quite a bit of weight in the last few minutes. They each had two wheelie suitcases of cabin baggage proportions – perfectly admissible for first-class passengers. Each bag was packed with just under a million pounds, the money that had just been taped to the bodies of Julie and Ethel.

They found Susan in the little coffee shop near the gate.

'How did we do?'

'All sorted,' Julie said, patting the nearest case.

'Right,' Ethel said, 'I'm gonna go and load up on sweets for the flight. Back in a tick.'

'Careful, Ethel,' they chorused as she rolled off in search of boiled treats.

A hundred grand a week or whatever that loser's on and he still can't put the ball in the bloody net? Boscombe turned the page. *Oh, here was another one. Bloody Premiership these days.*

Mint humbugs? Or rhubarb and custards? Toffees? Or maybe some of these mental-looking French sweets? *The agony of choice*, Ethel thought.

If they're getting paid all that money the least they can do is score the odd bastard goal. Boscombe looked up and across the concourse, towards the shop opposite. There was a fat old guy in a wheelchair, looking at sweets. *Christ, what a loser. Do I look like that?* And how long would he have to be in this bloody thing? Trying to get an answer out of those French doctors . . .

Why not get the lot? Ethel smiled. She was, after all, a millionaire now.

Boscombe looked again, closer this time at the actual wheelchair.

His heart stopped beating as his eyes settled on something. A sticker.

'WHERE'S THE BEEF?'

Jesus. Jesus Christ.

Just at that moment Ethel sensed someone looking at her and she looked up towards the restaurant across the way.

Their eyes locked.

All the pain, all the humiliation and exhaustion of the last week exploded within Boscombe. Ethel grinned wickedly.

Both wheelchairs took off at exactly the same time.

Ethel was wheeling herself very fast in the direction of Susan and Julie.

Boscombe, much more inexperienced at propelling himself in a wheelchair, smashed into the table, then the chairs behind him, before finally getting out of the place. He saw two gendarmes chatting near a water fountain and wheeled up to them.

'EEENNNN! ARRRGGHHH!' Boscombe said.

The two policemen looked at him.

'URRRR! G-FUUUCC!' Boscombe was gesticulating, pointing in the direction Ethel was headed.

'*Pardon, monsieur?*'

'GNNAAAAAAAAAAAAAAAA!' Boscombe was now turning a lurid purple, sweat pouring down his face and a thick broth of saliva bubbling from his lips, desperation flying from him.

The gendarmes looked at each other. 'Ah!' one of them said, the penny finally dropping. He took hold of the handles of the wheelchair and started pushing Boscombe across the tiled floor. 'RRRRNNN!' Boscombe said, pointing at the fleeing Ethel. 'FFFRRRR!'

'*Voilà!*' The gendarme said, stopping.

Boscombe looked up at the door in front of him.

The disabled toilets.

With a string of unintelligible obscenities flying over his shoulder Boscombe frantically started wheeling himself after Ethel. The gendarme watched him go, puzzled, as his colleague walked up saying, 'Huh?'

'*Les handicapés mental.*'

'Ah.'

Julie and Susan were both watching the monitor that was saying 'BA 117, NOW BOARDING'; the words 'Where the hell is Ethel?' were actually forming on both their lips when Ethel went rocketing past their table, doing a good ten miles an hour on a slight downhill curve. 'GET ON THE PLANE!' Ethel shouted as she passed, coffee cups rattling in their saucers in her wake.

'Eh?' Susan said.

'What the fu . . .?' Julie said.

They just had time to start gathering their things as another blur of human, chrome and tyres went hurtling by.

'Was that . . .?' Julie said.

'The plane,' Susan said. 'Let's get to the bloody plane.'

Wesley walked back into the coffee shop, laden with teddy bears and chocolate, to see the table empty and Boscombe gone. Maybe popped to the loo. He checked the monitor. Still not boarding.

He signalled to the waiter for another coffee.

She had maybe a hundred yards on him, Boscombe reckoned. Thank God his arms were the one part of him still working. He was getting the hang of it now too, pushing the metal rims of the wheels hard forward and then letting them roll, then pushing again. He seemed to have reached a slight downhill slope now, speeding up.

Ethel glanced over her shoulder, she could see the demented form of Boscombe — mummified legs, caged head – coming after her, gaining. Evasive action, she decided.

'Hey!' someone shouted as people leapt out of her way.

Boscombe watched, astonished, as she made a hard left into some kind of gift shop.

Ethel came rattling along a big wide aisle, shouting 'MOVE IT!' at dithering shoppers, and glanced over her shoulder again as Boscombe came cornering fast into the shop after her. With amazing dexterity Ethel reached out and grabbed a chunky bottle of Chanel No. 5 off a shelf. She slowed a little, letting Boscombe get within thirty feet of her – he was wheeling like mad, his eyes fixed on the 'I BRAKE FOR NO ONE' sign – before she launched the bottle over her shoulder. The scream from behind her told her she'd found her target, the perfume bottle smacking very hard off Boscombe's forehead. But still he kept coming as Ethel exploded out of the other side of the shop and headed full pelt for an automated walkway.

Deftly, unseen by Boscombe, preoccupied as he was by blood pouring into his eyes from the fresh gash in his forehead, Ethel pegged her passport and boarding card into a bin.

This was a suicide mission now.

Julie and Susan were *running*, heading for the gate, pulling two heavy, cash-stuffed wheelie cases apiece, as the tannoy announced 'Final call for BA Flight 117 to Rio . . .'

Ethel hit the walkway hard, its extra few miles an hour adding speed to her churning wheeling as Boscombe came barrelling out of the gift shop behind her, his wheelchair tilting crazily, almost capsizing, as he shouted and swore, realising that his path was blocked by an enormous French family. 'MMMMMFFFF! URRRR!' he roared, screeching left, missing them by inches. He saw Ethel rocketing away on the walkway, everything looking hopeless until he spotted the golf buggy veering in front of him – the kind of vehicle airports use to take the very old or the very important to their destinations – and, with an extra thrust of the wrist, he caught it up, grabbing hold of the rear bumper, the vehicle pulling him along even faster, the driver oblivious to his piggybacking passenger.

Ethel pummelled along the moving walkway, shouting '*ALLES ALLES! VAMOS! SCHNELL!*' and 'GET OUT THE FUCKING WAY!' People were leaping aside, jumping off.

Julie and Susan reached the gate to find that there was still a queue at economy boarding, but it was all clear in the business and first-class line. The (gorgeous) young steward smiled as he held out his hand for their boarding passes. But then, just as the machine was reading their bar codes, the green light coming on, pronouncing them to be good, the phone at his elbow started ringing. 'Hello?' he said. He listened, looking at Susan and Julie, then beyond them to the other queue. 'Mmmm. *Oui. Oui.*' He put the phone down. '*Mesdames*, please, wait here a moment.' He walked off towards two colleagues who were conferring over a clipboard nearby.

'Should we just make a run for it?' Julie said out of the corner of her mouth.

Ethel came tearing off the automated walkway just as Boscombe let go of the golf buggy and, for a split second, he could almost touch her hair, flying behind her in a mad frizz of grey as Ethel wheeled for her very life, catching another downhill now, both of them really speeding up as, ahead, Ethel saw two escalators, both going down. She thundered towards the right-hand one and, in a display of skill that would surely have put her in the top-five wheelchair drivers worldwide, smashed her brakes on the moment she hit the metal, stopping on a dime, the escalator taking her gradually down. Looking back up as she disappeared Ethel saw two things. Firstly, the scrum of gendarmes and security guards running towards her in the distance, finally alerted to the wheelchair version of the Le Mans rally happening within their airport, and secondly – Boscombe.

It would be fair to say that only being used to driving a wheelchair for a few hours – as opposed to over a decade – Boscombe lacked the skills possessed by Ethel. Roughly twenty seconds after she hit the right-hand down escalator Boscombe hit the left-hand one. But he didn't brake – he went smashing, barrelling and bouncing down at full speed, his body being thrown up off the chair with each impact on every step. Ethel could hear his muffled screams. *This was a very bad idea* – was what went through Boscombe's mind.

They stood there, too scared to run, the few remaining economy-class passengers now boarding, the airline crew in a huddle, talking in a low murmur a few yards away.

'Ethel,' Julie whispered. 'What the hell's happened to Ethel?'

Susan looked back the way they had come, over Julie's shoulder, and saw two gendarmes approaching with a third man between them, in a suit and tie, an airport official of some sort, with a laminated pass dangling around his neck. *Fucking men*, Susan found herself thinking.

She felt her grip tightening on her two wheelie cases, as she whispered to Julie, 'Don't turn round, darling.'

'What is it?'

'Whatever happens, the last few days, I've had the best time I've ever . . .'

'Hey, hey, don't cry . . .' Julie said, reaching for her.

'Oh well,' Susan said, almost about to offer her wrists up in a 'throw on the cuffs' gesture as the officious-looking trio approached . . . and then walked straight past them and up to the last few economy passengers. 'Excuse me, madams?' they said to two ladies.

'Yes?' an English voice said.

'Step this way please . . .'

Julie and Susan both watched as the women were led

off towards a doorway nearby. The two women did, it had to be said, bear a fair resemblance to Susan and Julie before Susan's intensive hair and make-up session this morning. Suddenly another voice piped up behind them, 'Miss and Mrs Saunders? Please, we can board you now. I'm very sorry for the delay.'

'What was all that about?' Julie asked.

'Oh, nothing to worry about. Please, this way . . .'

And with that they were led off towards the magical kingdom in the very nose of the plane.

'I love first class . . .' Julie whispered.

'No one messes with you . . .' Susan replied.

He couldn't find the brake. He couldn't even begin to touch the wheels – they would have flayed the skin from his hands. As Boscombe thundered down towards Ethel their eyes met horribly again. Ethel glanced ahead – the end of the track and there, about thirty feet ahead of that, a huge ornamental fountain. She came off the escalator just as Boscombe came rocketing past her, gripping onto his wheelchair as though it were a crazed, unbroken horse, his face a mask of blood and pain.

Ethel solved his braking problem for him. She took her grabbing stick and thrust it into the spokes of his right-hand wheel.

If a movie director could have filmed the scene it would have been Sam Peckinpah: Boscombe flailing through thin air in slow motion, screaming soundlessly, onlookers gawping, jaws a-dangle, the sparkling water of the fountain rushing up to meet him and then, the huge splash as he hit the surface, drenching a family eating ice cream nearby.

Ethel braked to a skidding, screeching stop just before

she hit the wall of the fountain. She had a few moments to savour the sight of the spluttering, floating Boscombe before she heard the clomping of running boots very close behind her. She turned and saw that she was surrounded by some fifteen men, a mixture of police and airport security, many of them with their guns drawn and pointed at her, the men in their turn sizing up this strange, bearded old gentleman in the baggy suit and the panama hat. Ethel produced her hip flask, tore off her beard and, still in character, asked the mob:

'Would any of you boys care fur a wee dram now?'

EIGHTY-TWO

They couldn't believe their luck would hold even as they sat there in the soft blue-tinted light of first class, their hearts pumping hard in their chests as they graciously accepted champagne and extravagant menus. Even after the doors closed (fifteen minutes late, following a ruckus when the two English ladies were finally allowed to board, both of them muttering and complaining) and the plane began taxiing out towards the runway not twenty seconds went by without either Julie or Susan craning their neck round, expecting to see a huddle of police and stewards coming for them. Even as the 747 lumbered into the sky and the tilting sun shot light through every porthole in turn, they were still expecting the captain to come over the speakers saying something like 'Ladies and gentlemen, due to security reasons we will now be returning to Nice airport . . .' It was only when they levelled in the sky, and they could see the Mediterranean Sea far beneath them, and the 'Fasten seat belts' sign went off with a bright 'ping', and the steward was almost instantly at their elbow with fresh flutes of champagne, that they finally turned and looked at each other. Susan raised her glass.

'To Ethel.'

'Ethel,' Julie said.

There were certainly still things to worry about and Susan started to enumerate them. There was the close to four million pounds in cash in the compartment above them that they were hoping to just breeze through customs in Brazil with. If that happened then they had to find somewhere to live. They also had to find a way to keep their money safe and to have access to it. They had to –

'Susan?' Julie said.

'Mmmm?'

'Let's just get drunk, eh?'

Susan stopped mid-sentence and looked at her friend, sitting there, still in old person's make-up and flowing kaftan. Forty-five years she'd known Julie Wickham and even now, in that get-up designed to age her by a decade, she still looked twenty-one. 'Yeah,' Susan said. 'Let's get drunk. Do you think we can get another one of these?'

'I think we can do whatever the hell we want . . .'

Julie found the button on her handset, the little stickman holding a drink on his tray, and pressed it as the great plane banked, the Bay of Biscay coming up ahead of them now, tiny boats dotting the water far below as they headed west, into the sun, towards whatever was going to happen to them.

EPILOGUE

THREE YEARS LATER

Our camera sweeps down on a cold Sunday morning in January, in Wroxham, Dorset, where it finds eight-year-old Jamie Cummings running around the back of the scrum on the school rugby pitch, his arms extended to receive a pass, his mother Linda and his grandmother Jill cheering from the touchline. His operation in Chicago had been an astounding success. Linda had cried with joy when Jill told her she'd had a lovely time in Wales with her old friends and that one of them was now very rich and had agreed to give her the thirty grand still needed for Jamie's operation, no strings attached. Linda hadn't even asked any questions. Jill asks forgiveness every Sunday in church for her part in the wickedness and for Ethel, Julie and Susan to be forgiven their sins too.

Panning across town, through pelting sleet and wind, we come to the tired signage and near-empty grandstands of

Wroxham Rovers FC, who are at home to nearby Didford United, both teams playing to a very healthy turnout of 128 fans.

We pull focus on the wet, tired, lined face of Constable Hugh Boscombe, who walks the touchline in full uniform. The ball skids through the mud quite close to him but Boscombe is oblivious. For he is dreaming of half-time, of the two meat pies and the styrofoam cup of Bovril he will consume over by the snack van, where he will endure the weekly jests and taunts of the locals, to many of whom he is still known as Lewis Hamilton after that little driving mishap in Marseilles a few years back. Later, after the match is over, he will return to the station to sign off his shift, where he will have to endure the ritual humiliation of shuffling by the glass wall of the office of Detective Sergeant Alan Wesley. Their overlapping promotion and demotion were the final sadistic acts of Chief Inspector Wilson prior to his retirement.

Moving north, but not too far north, to the village of Tillington, the camera drifts into the town funeral parlour and surveys the few mourners at the sparsely attended service for the late underworld figure Nails Savage, who has just died at the age of ninety-two, having recently served eighteen months of a three-year sentence for aiding and abetting. Shortly after his release, Nails found a mysterious package in his post.

There was no letter or covering note. The box simply contained 100,000 pounds sterling, tightly banded in wads of fifties. It was postmarked through a routing service in Panama.

Nails used a good chunk of this money to fund one last

sunshine cruise of his own: a five-star trip to Bangkok, where he picked up the sole occupant of the front pew at today's sad occasion – and the ultimate cause of his death – his 22-year-old widow Sun-May. Sun-May is still haunted by her late husband's last expression on this earth, spoken as he ejaculated gratefully inside her, a fraction of a second before his heart exploded, the sighing elegy of 'Oof – you fucking wrong-coloured beauty . . .'

The lens refocusing now as it whirrs through cloud and over seas, heading due east, over the Channel to Paris, into a lecture theatre of the university, to where an attentive first-year student on the Business Administration course makes notes in the front row. Vanessa Honfleur is known by her peers as one of the hardest working in her year. The reason for this is simple – Vanessa can't quite believe she is here. She thought attending university was a dream that happened to other people. True, she'd had a wild few months after she'd come into the money, but the words Julie had whispered in her ear in the garage of that huge house on the outskirts of Marseilles had always come back to haunt her: 'Under my bed. Don't waste it . . .'

She still tingles when she remembers the moment the following day, after the police had released her, when she went back to the hotel, the room key Julie had stuffed into her palm hot in her clenched fist, the moment when she opened the door, got down on her hands and knees and looked under the bed to find a carrier bag with over 100,000 British pounds in it, nearly 140,000 in euros. Enough for her to rent a small apartment while she finished school, enough to get her here. She thinks of Julie often, this woman who changed her life, and hopes she's doing well.

If she could only have followed the camera as it leaves the lecture theatre to rocket south and west, crossing the Atlantic Ocean in a blur of light before swooping down out of the sky just outside the coastal town of Vitoria, in the Espirito Santo province of Brazil, just over five hundred kilometres north of Rio.

The camera moves along the streets of one of the town's affluent north-western suburbs, finally drifting over the well-kept hedges of the 1.5 million-dollar home belonging to the two retired English businesswomen known locally as Ruth and Helen. Lucas the gardener is trimming back the lemon tree that overhangs the wall of the kitchen while inside Amanda the cook is grilling some chicken for lunch. She knows the ladies of the house will want wine with their meal and has already iced a bottle of very good white burgundy.

Lucas, Amanda and Fernanda the maid – who is busily making beds down the hall – are all treated very well by their employers, paid above the local rates and tipped heavily on their birthdays and holidays, the same employers who can now be heard laughing loudly out by the pool . . .

The pool is large and tiled in aquamarine, with a frothing jacuzzi at one end. Ruth Steele is floating on a lounger in the late-morning sun, a Diet Coke nestling between her thighs, while Helen Davies, less of a sun-worshipper, is on a lounger in the shade of a parasol, reading the two-day-old copy of the *Daily Mail* which contains the article that just caused their laughter: a faintly hysterical piece on the 'Arctic' January cold snap that continues to grip the United Kingdom.

Three years ago, when Ruth and Helen were still known respectively as Julie Wickham and Susan Frobisher, they strolled through the first-class fast track at Rio immigration with just under four million pounds in their hand baggage. No one gave them a second glance.

They encountered a few problems thereafter of course. Buying a property in cash was never going to be straightforward. They took a suite at the Carlton in Rio for a few weeks and did some digging . . .

This being Brazil and Julie being Julie they soon found someone who could put them in touch with a realtor who – for a not inconsiderable fee of course – was able to put them together with the kind of seller for whom a cash deal presented not a problem but an opportunity, resulting in the splendid five-bedroom, four-bathroom villa with pool and half an acre of gardens now presided over by Lucas, Amanda and Fernanda. Over drinks to celebrate the deal their vendor quietly introduced them to a banker who was also sympathetic to their situation and who – again for a reasonable fee – assisted them in opening the account where the just-over-two million US dollars they had left after the house purchase and sundry expenses (including a new Mercedes SLK apiece) is now parked at a rate of 5 per cent, earning them around 100,000 dollars a year in interest which they split as a salary.

Their needs are simple. They eat, drink, swim and sightsee. They play cards and backgammon out under their lemon and orange trees. They are popular members of the small ex-pat community and routinely entertain guests and visit with others. No one ever doubts their story that they were partners in a very successful chain of hair salons back on the south-east coast of England who sold up at exactly the right time.

They wake every day in their respective bedrooms, each with a balcony giving onto the pool and gardens, grinning with joy at the life they've made for themselves. So far, every morning has been Saturday morning, Christmas, the first day of the school holidays. And now, as Amanda heads out through the large kitchen to tell them lunch is ready, we leave them, the camera craning up and away, heading due north, over the grey Atlantic for a long, long way before whipping left, heading west and inland over the glittering billion-dollar battlements of Manhattan.

Onto the island itself at the lower end, Wall Street, then zipping uptown on this chilly afternoon, the camera rocketing along 6th Avenue as though strapped to the bumper of one of the hurrying taxis. Arriving in Midtown, at Rockefeller Plaza and the studios of NBC television, where it zooms down many hallways before coming through the open door of a dressing room and an American voice saying—

'How we doing in there?'

The voice is coming from Trisha, the second assistant director on a programme called *America Today!* and it is directed towards the occupant of the make-up chair, facing a huge mirror surrounded by light bulbs: Mrs Ethel Merriman.

'All good, darling,' Ethel replies, 'but I could do with having this fella freshened up . . .' She is holding out an empty champagne glass which had, until a moment ago, contained a nice, strong Mimosa.

'No problem!' Trisha trills, taking the glass.

Ethel burps happily and says, 'Excuse me, love!' to the nice giggling gay lad touching up her forehead.

Ethel isn't nervous – it's her second time on the show. The first time was just over a year ago, upon the US hardback publication of her memoir *I BRAKE FOR NO ONE!* (the cover featured Ethel in her wheelchair giving the finger to the camera). Back then the book was simply a hot UK title with the curio value of having been written by a very elderly woman just out of prison. Since then, as everyone knows, the 'frank, funny, upbeat tale' of Ethel's involvement in one of Britain's biggest bank robberies and of her extraordinary life leading up to that moment has become a publishing phenomenon. It has been translated into thirty-seven languages with worldwide sales of over five million copies. The film, TV and documentary rights have all been sold for enormous sums with Helen Mirren slated to play Ethel.

All of this has made Ethel a millionaire several times over as she enters her nineties.

Her trial had been something. She had been charged with armed robbery, assaulting a police officer, illegal possession of firearms, obtaining a false passport, criminal damage, GBH and obstructing the course of justice. When the judge looked up to see how these charges were being received he saw that Ethel was eating a sheet of paper with a biro shoved up each nostril. She answered all questions in song and twice attempted to strip naked in court. It took the jury just fifteen minutes to find her guilty and another three minutes to accept her plea for diminished responsibility on the grounds of insanity. With time spent on remand taken into account Ethel served seven months in a low-level psychiatric institute, which was the time it took her to write *IBFNO*, as all her team now referred to it in emails.

'OK, then. Here we go!' an underling says, handing Ethel the fresh Mimosa. 'Are we good? Shall we drink and roll?'

'Lead on, Macduff . . .' Ethel replies cheerily.

Off they roll, down the corridor towards the set, where Ethel can already hear the laughter and applause of the audience, waiting to welcome her.

John Niven

Kill Your Friends

Meet Steven Stelfox.

It's London 1997: New Labour is sweeping into power and Britpop is at its zenith. A&R man Stelfox is slashing and burning his way through the music industry, fuelled by greed and inhuman quantities of cocaine, searching for the next hit record amid a relentless orgy of self-gratification.

But as the hits dry up and the industry begins to change, Stelfox must take the notion of cut-throat business practices to murderous new levels in a desperate attempt to salvage his career.

JOHN NIVEN

The Amateurs

GARY is a sweet and decent man. Only two things would improve his life – having children with his gorgeous wife Pauline, and a lower golf handicap. Both are unlikely.

PAULINE is wondering how she ended up living in an ugly little house, driving a second-hand car and making a living dressing up as Tinkerbell. She is planning to leave Gary for a self-made carpet millionaire.

FINDLAY, the Carpet King of Scotland, wants to trade in his obese wife for a younger model. But if he goes for a divorce she'll take him to the cleaners. If only there was some way she could be made to disappear ...

LEE, Gary's luckless brother, has botched one too many drug deals. Local crime overlord Ranta Campbell gives him one more job – one last chance to get it right. Lee's done some bad things – but murder?

When Gary gets smashed on the head by a golf ball and miraculously develops an absolutely perfect swing, everyone finds their fates rest on the final day of the Open Championship.

'Gripping, sexy, violent and outrageous'
MIRROR

'Screamingly funny'
SCOTSMAN

John Niven

The Second Coming

SENT FROM HEAVEN ... RAISING HELL

God takes a look at the Earth around the time of the Renaissance and everything looks pretty good – so he takes a holiday. In Heaven-time this is just a week's fishing trip, but on Earth several hundred years go by. When God returns, he finds all hell has broken loose: world wars, holocausts, famine, capitalism and 'fucking Christians everywhere'. There's only one thing for it. They're sending the kid back.

JC, reborn, is a struggling musician in New York City, trying to teach the one true commandment: Be Nice! His best chance to win hearts and minds is to enter *American Pop Star*. But the number one show in America is the unholy creation of a record executive who's more than a match for the Son of God ... Steven Stelfox.

'Confrontational, blasphemous ... and bloody funny'
INDEPENDENT ON SUNDAY

'Believe me, this book is going to cause one almighty stink ... Niven provides hilarious, perceptive entertainment ... Only the truly ignorant will take offence. But then they usually do'
HENRY SUTTON, DAILY MIRROR

'Jesus battles oppression, hypocrisy and the satanic forces of Simon Cowell – sorry, "Steven Stelfox" ... funny and smart'
INDEPENDENT

ALSO BY JOHN NIVEN

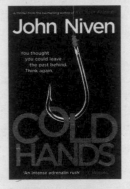